Sons of the Pioneers

John Givens

• • • • • • • • • • • • •

Sons
of the
Pioneers

• • • • • • • • • • • • •

Harcourt Brace Jovanovich
New York and London

Printed in the United States of America

Library of Congress Cataloging in Publication Data

Givens, John.
Sons of the pioneers.

I. Title.
PZ3.G4519So [PS3557.I85] 813'.5'4 77-73052
ISBN 0-15-183775-9
ISBN 0-15-683815-X pbk.

First edition

B C D E

Part One

· · · · · · · · · · ·

Floyd Cloudfinger

Old man Todd drags himself to his feet, his left arm frozen from the stroke he had last year. "Here's to you," he says to his pal. "Here's to health and another productive seventy years."

"Very kind of you, Mr. Todd, very kind," Donnard says and drains his glass.

"What are your thoughts on this auspicious day? What have your years on the street taught you?"

"Never give a sucker an even break."

"Yes, well yes, Mr. Donnard, there would be a certain amount of cynicism."

"I was there the day they shot Big Jim and saw how the bloody bath water seeped through the ceiling, staining it into the shape of a map of America. And I was there the day Big Jim's boy gunned down the man that ordered the contract on him. And I stood in that alley beside the boy and watched the body blink. And I was the one that told the boy that if he didn't pull that trigger a second time then and there, he'd have it hanging over him."

"But the boy couldn't do it," says Todd.

"The boy couldn't do it. He stood there holding the

pistol pointed between the guy's eyes and the hammer cocked back and nobody in the alley but me and him and the mark, but he couldn't do it."

"What'd you tell him?"

"That he'd have it hanging over him, hanging over him."

"Well yes," says Todd, then raises his glass again. "But here's to health! I hope you live forever!"

"I very nearly have. Or at least some mornings it feels that way. Cold rainy mornings, the icy air."

"Pain in the lower back," says Todd. "I suffer from it too."

"And in the elbows and knees, pain in the bending."

"Fingers, wrists."

"Feet!"

"Feet! Very definitely feet, frosty mornings and stiff shoes, odd how you don't notice it until you're old."

"In the joints, it's the problem of stiffness."

They stop and look at each other. "Did you ever think you'd get so old?"

"I thought I'd be killed," says Donnard. "Remember how we used to say we'd likely get rubbed out before we were thirty?"

"And then for forty we said it, and then fifty."

"I don't remember saying it about sixty?"

"Sixty-five, we said it for sixty-five, I believe."

"That's a fact. We said it for sixty-five."

They sit quietly for a minute, staring at the glittering row of whiskey bottles lined up behind the bar. The front door swings open and somebody steps in out of a rainy afternoon, but they don't bother to look around.

"It's a shame the boy didn't pull that trigger."

"Stiffness," says Todd turning to his pal, his good eye

squinted up. "Stiffness in the joints and . . ." He stops, delaying it, making sure Donnard knows what's next. "And . . ."

Donnard has to grin. The same joke always comes up sooner or later.

"A lack of stiffness in the joint!"

"Heh! Heh! Haw!" cackles Donnard. "That's a fact now!" Then *haawk!* he roots up and rolls out a bundle of spit that's always rattling around in the back of his throat.

"There used to be spittoons," he says, and hangs it off, lets it slide into the sawdust spread on the barroom floor. "Don't know where a body's supposed to spit anymore. . . ."

A ratty old lady down at the other end of the bar shakes the rain off her shoulders. "Whiskey!" she shouts. "Dying of thirst waiting here, god damn it!"

"Dying," says Donnard and Todd says, "lack of stiffness in the joint!" to make him laugh again. He says how that stiffness business always tickles him.

It's a typical late afternoon in the Rolling Ring Bar. The clientele is mostly made up of solitary seniors using the bad weather as an excuse for tying one on a little earlier than usual. Donnard and Todd sit quietly in the dark rear corner of the bar, holding themselves aloof from the general rout as much as possible. They used to stay back there because it gave them a clear line of fire at the front door, but that doesn't much matter anymore. They're just a couple of old retired hit men following sentimental habits.

A group of tourists is arranged around one of the card tables, drinking beer and going through their guidebooks. They're tired now, and so not as obnoxious as when they are fresh, but Donnard and Todd are still careful to ignore them.

"If only Harold could've pulled that trigger . . ."

"But he didn't," says Donnard, looking in his glass.

The bar will begin to fill up in an hour or so. Some of the old-time ramblers will start sauntering in, thumbs hooked in fancy-tooled belts. They'll stop just inside the door and case the joint with a hard eye as if they thought there was still a chance they could get bushwhacked. That kind of dramatics will make Donnard and Todd feel a little livelier. There might be a fistfight later, or maybe even a shoot-out, and if a tourist occasionally picks up his camera and moves right into the middle of everything to get a good picture, well, there just isn't much they can do about that. Fortunately, most of the tour groups are jaded by the time they work their way down to the Rolling Ring.

The place itself still looks pretty good. The barkeep is an ex-pug with a flair for polishing glasses. There is a rinky-tink piano with a guy who can play it and smoke a cigar at the same time. All the furniture is old, and heavy, and made in the U.S. of A., particularly the hardwood staircase that leads up to the second floor rooms where the ladies will be lounging about, cracking their knuckles, getting loosened up for the pleasures of the evening.

"Another round, Mr. Donnard?"

"Don't mind if I do, Mr. Todd."

"A bunch of hooey," somebody says walking back toward the toilet. Donnard waits until he's past.

"He shot him in the alley behind the old Vogue Theater. He was hiding in back of some crates and he stepped out and drilled him. He was holding pretty well but he had to wait too long. He saw him come in down at the other end of the alley, but the guy was cagey, he must've figured something was up so he came in slow."

"But at least he shot him."

"He shot him and it knocked him down and the mug lay on his back staring up at the sky, blinking. I said shoot him again but Harold just stood there looking down at him. I said, "You shot him once, shoot him again, nobody's looking." The boy just stood there staring at him with his father's old Colt .44 in his hand hanging down, still smoking."

"At least he shot him once."

"He shot him once but he didn't kill him."

"The boy was pretty young."

"Fourteen. He was fourteen."

"He did do it though."

"He did it but it wasn't enough. 'That's the man that ordered the contract on your father,' I said. 'Ten years we've been waiting and now all you got to do is pull the trigger again and we're square.' The boy just kept looking at him, watching him blink. If he'd've pulled that trigger, all this wouldn't've happened. We'd still be getting some respect around here."

"That's a fact," says Todd, nodding his head so vigorously his dewlaps tremble. "You can't let something like that go. You got to stay with your traditions."

"Hell," says the bartender, "like I always say, the guy could've bled to death lying there by himself. It was just bad luck that he didn't."

"Luck isn't the issue. He stood there looking at him and then he walked away. It wasn't so much getting him dead. I could've bumped him off myself. It was the principle of the thing. The guy killed his father; he should've wanted to do it."

The bartender shrugs. He's heard the story a thousand times. Whenever Donnard gets a little drunk and sentimental he starts reminiscing about that afternoon fifteen years ago. A couple of roughnecks come in and sit at the other end of the bar, so the bartender moves down to take care of them.

"Well," he says, going, "what the hell anyway, it's all over."

"It isn't over," says Donnard. "It's just waiting."

Then an Indian comes in. He's about as mean looking an Indian as anybody in the room has ever seen. He stoops a little as he comes through the door, shambles up to the bar and sits down quietly. The tourists nudge each other awake and start gathering their camera gear together.

"It isn't over," Donnard says a little louder now, yelling at the bartender. "It isn't. The boy stepped out and shot him, dropped him cleanly at thirty yards. He wasn't scared or anything. No luck involved, no sir. Pure skill was what it was, and good coaching. If there was luck, it was bad, and what was bad about it was the blinking. The boy stood there looking down at him and a little trickle of blood was coming out of the back of the guy's head although you couldn't see the wound. The guy was lying flat on his back and his eyes were blinking, looking up at the sky, and the boy was watching his face and it was that blinking that got him. "Shoot him," I said, but the boy couldn't do it. He didn't have the necessary meanness."

"That's a fact," says Todd. "And he still doesn't."

"Well, we stood there in that alley that day and the guy was on his back blinking and the boy was standing there and I said shoot him but the boy didn't say no. He just stood there looking down at the guy's face and . . ."

"Shut up."

"Huh?"

"Shut up," says the Indian again. "Shut up."

"What?"

The Indian puts down his beer glass and looks at Donnard. The tourists are at the other end of the bar, blazing away with their cameras. "Oh boy, oh boy," one says, "a fight!" The Indian doesn't pay any attention to them.

"Perhaps you don't know who I am," says Donnard.

"Shut up."

"You ever heard of the Baine Gang?"

"Shut up."

Donnard sits back and looks at him. He's got his six-shooter tucked under his arm and if the Indian makes a play, he'll give him a taste of hot lead.

"There used to be lakes full of fish," the Indian says in a low voice, not exactly looking at Donnard anymore. "There used to be trout streams and p-ponds full of p-p-perch. It's all gone now, all p-p-p-poisoned! And do you know why?"

Donnard just looks at him, surprised.

"P-p-progress!" the Indian sneers. "Fucking p-progress!"

A salvo of flashcubes goes off in the Indian's face and he stands up and stalks down the length of the barroom.

"Everything's gone!" he shouts. "Bears slaughtered, b-b-buffalo smashed, driven from the grasslands!"

The guys sitting at the bar start not looking at him pretty carefully. Nobody wants to get involved. It's going to be the bartender's problem, let him handle it.

"P-p-p-progress!"

It's raining harder outside, vertical gray lines splashing against the wet street. A couple of guys stare out the window, likely thinking how nice it would be to be out there. A fry cook who works in some dump down the block makes the mistake of glancing up at the Indian as he stalks past. He stops and glares at him.

"You p-p-paved the best grazing lands, turned them into p-parking lots. You know why?"

"People have to park?" the fry cook guesses miserably.

"B-b-b-because you hate nature!"

"Oh."

"You believe in creeps like Zane G-g-g-g-grey!"

"Oh," the fry cook says in a small voice, trying to indicate that he thinks the conversation is over.

"Motherfucker!" shouts the Indian. "Who's Zane Grey?"

A dog wakes up and growls but his owner kicks him. "For christsakes don't get him mad."

There's an old-timer sitting down at that end of the bar with his walrus mustache fluffed up full of beer foam. He's too scared to wipe it. He knows the Indian's standing right behind him; he can smell the pemmican on his breath. Nobody sitting at the bar knows anybody else. Each guy is a stranger with these interesting thumbs he's never noticed before, figures now's a good time to get busy studying them.

"One of you trespassing cocksuckers is going to tell me who Zane G-g-grey is!"

Nobody says anything.

"You b-b-build b-bowling alleys on the sacred b-burial grounds. You don't respect nothing but money and b-b-big tits."

The dog starts growling again and the Indian spins around, drops into a crouch. "Who said that? Who's laughing?" He pulls a big tomahawk out of his trenchcoat. The dog's owner hunches up his shoulders apologetically, looks accusingly dogward to let the Indian know who's guilty. The pallid fry cook peeks over his shoulder, lets out a little groan.

"You think it's funny?"

The Indian waves the tomahawk over his head, then *wham!* sinks it two inches into the bar, a finger's width away from the fry cook's pale hand.

"Who's Zane Grey?" he demands in a low voice, his eyes mean and yellowed like a bowl of milk somebody shit in.

"A writer?" the fry cook whispers.

"What kind of writer?"

The tomahawk shrieks as it's wrenched free from the wood.

"Books," says the fry cook in a very small voice, "about horses?"

Ka-wham! The tomahawk slams into the wood again.

"Horses?" the Indian says. "Only horses?"

"And, uh . . ."

The Indian is towering over him, the glinting steel blade of the tomahawk cocked above his head. He's poised, waiting, an evil grin on his mug and his rumpled trenchcoat hanging from his shoulders like wrinkled gabardine wings.

"Hell of an Indian," says a tourist in a quiet, awed voice, "as good as in the movies. Too bad my brother Melvin isn't here, he's crazy about action and adventure."

The fry cook must obviously figure he's going to get hit. His eyes are squeezed shut and his face is sweaty; likely his days of slinging grease are coming to an end. Donnard and Todd watch with rheumy eyes. They aren't interested in getting involved, although they aren't scared, either. They have enough residual professional curiosity to enjoy watching the Indian work. The tourists are all out of their seats now, peering through the view-finders on their cameras. Their thumbs hover over their shutter buttons, ready for the photograph of a lifetime.

Nobody moves. The fry cook's lips begin to feel toward the word he has every reason to believe may be his last. The room is electric with tension, all eyes on the Indian.

Click! A tourist cracks first, inadvertently squeezing his shutter. "Damn!" he says and quickly cocks his rewind lever, relieved to see that the tomahawk is still poised above the fry cook's scruffy head.

". . . cowboys."

Nothing happens. The fry cook gets ready to feel that heavy blade crashing into his skull, except it doesn't. He opens one eye and sees the Indian in the mirror, still standing over him holding that hatchet, but with a slightly puzzled expression.

"Say it again, g-g-g-god damn!"

The fry cook says "cowboys" again, and the tourists slowly begin to lower their cameras, obviously disappointed. The Indian glares at the group lined along the bar, then turns on his heel and stomps out of the barroom, muttering how it isn't fair. . . .

"Who was that guy?" says Todd, and the bartender tells him his name's Cloudfinger. It seems he's been in once before, looking for his sister. He got mad that time too and tried to pick a fight with some tourists so the boss threw him out. She's very particular when it comes to having outsiders intimidate the customers, even if they are only tourists.

"Well yeah," says Todd. "You don't want something like that getting down to where it's public property. It'd be bad for business. Any idea where that fellow lives?"

"Try under the Third Street Bridge."
"Much obliged."

Spring rain bundles down into the Inner City, lashing heavily into the narrow alleys and splashing up cones of water from pools formed by the broken asphalt. Every now and then somebody dashes from one doorway to another, holding something over his head and laughing like he thought the rain might hurt.

The figure of the big Indian trudges down one of the narrow alleys, the collar of his trenchcoat flipped up and his hands buried in his pockets. He's been in the Inner City for a week now, and it's still the only part of the metropolitan area he knows. He's seen the slender glass towers of the new Civic Center from a distance, but he's never bothered to go there; it's too far to walk and there's not much public transportation.

He passes the lighted doors of bars and bordellos, some of the latter slightly disguised as massage parlors, although nobody really cares anymore. The Inner City has been pretty well insulated from the suburbs. The Indian ignores the occasional groups of white faces trapped behind steamy plates of glass, the sleepy-eyed whores who gaze at his passage with the blank disregard of well-fed fish, briefly freed from the hustle by the bad weather but already getting bored.

"You're going down, Floyd Cloudfinger," the Indian says to himself. "You're going down to tear her out of the heart of the city. You're getting you your sister back."

He turns a corner and there's a wino settling in a doorway for the afternoon. He's got a couple of cardboard boxes to protect him from the damp and a full fifth of muscatel. He's humming happily as he forms the boxes into a seat, making himself as comfortable as possible. The Indian stops and stares at him.

The wino sees Cloudfinger and looks a little worried.

"I killed a man once who drank that same g-g-grape."

"Today?" asks the wino, not understanding.

"B-b-b-before," says the Indian. "When I was in the desert. I g-got b-b-b-busted."

The wino hands over his bottle regretfully and Floyd takes it but doesn't leave, just keeps staring at him.

"Aw," says the wino, "it's hard to find dry cardboard this late in the day."

Floyd doesn't say anything so the wino has to decide.

"You killed somebody?"

"When I was a kid. Years ago. I p-paid my time. I did twelve years."

"You get any time off for good behavior?"

"I didn't do no fucking g-g-good b-behavior."

The wino figures it must be just about time for him to be going. He tugs his hat down over his eyes and shuffles off into the rain, likely heading for a dry place under one of the bridges. Floyd sits in the doorway and unscrews the cap on the wine bottle.

"You're getting your sister back."

He tilts the bottle up and takes a deep pull, then wipes his mouth on his sleeve.

"Sweet wine," he says. "I don't guess there's any harm in drinking before you go get your sister back."

He takes another long drink and wipes his mouth again. He never stutters when he's talking to himself; his voice always sounds out clear and strong, the way he thinks it ought to all the time.

"Getting your sister back after all these years. Isn't that fine."

There are people passing along the alley now. The rain has lightened into nothing more than a drizzle. It's only about four-thirty, but a lot of the bars and restaurants have their neon signs turned on because of the premature darkness. The complicated patterns of tubes spell out words or pictures that burn behind hazy nimbuses of moisture, indistinct and mysterious.

Floyd Cloudfinger stands up. He's a little unsteady but that doesn't bother him because he feels good again. There are a couple of inches of wine left in the bottom of the bottle; he figures he'll save that to drink on the way. He's going to go get his sister. He sticks the bottle in his coat pocket, making sure that the cap's screwed on tightly. He checks his tomahawk and it's tucked safely inside his trenchcoat where it can't get wet.

"Protect the blade against rust," he says aloud and a couple of people glance at him as they pass by, but nobody pays much attention.

He starts off awkwardly down an alley that ought to lead him out onto the riverbank. The main entertainment quarters of the Inner City are lined along both banks of the Duck River, and although Floyd doesn't have any plan for finding his sister, he seems to feel that this area must be the best place to search. He shuffles slowly down the alley, people pushing past him on both sides. His shoes are soaked and the leather is swollen out and squishy but he doesn't seem to mind, or even seem to notice anything's wrong.

He walks as far as the Third Street Bridge, and when he gets there he stops and stares moodily into the water, wishing he had some more wine. The bridge is crowded with people and in some places the flow has almost stopped. He looks at the bottle again but it's empty now, so he drops it into the river and watches it bob away.

There's a girl in a red vinyl raincoat looking at him. She's a cute little blonde with a saucy smile, but Floyd's never seen her before. He leans over the wooden bridge railing and gazes down into the dark river. "Oh Great Spirit," he whispers, "Oh Father of the Long Waters, of the Waving Fields of Grain . . . ," then stops, knowing he's blown the invocation. He seems to remember some Indian saying something like that in a movie, but the river in question was the Big Muddy, so the prayer probably wouldn't work for a punk little river like the Duck. Floyd believes there must be some way to get in touch and he strokes his hand against the curved railing, feeling the weathered grain of the wood and trying to use that to plug him into the prayer he can't seem to find in words.

He continues on up toward the middle of the bridge, mixed in with the people shoving past him on both sides, the metal tips of their umbrellas brushing against his shoulders. The girl in the raincoat is following him. She's standing a few yards away pretending to be interested in the lights reflected in the water, her silvery blonde hair shining in the rain like shreds of wet plastic.

Somebody in front of Floyd slips and there's a moment of panic before the crowd divides into two streams and surges past. At the eastern edge of the bridge is a stone staircase that leads down to the riverbank. Floyd looks for the girl in the raincoat but doesn't see her in the mob. There is a gathering place for hoboes and ragpickers under the bridge. They've made a permanent camp there, a place to sort through the rubbish they collect, to find things that might be repaired and possibly sold. They build a small fire out of driftwood salvaged from the river and keep a communal pot of soup simmering. They've fed the Indian even though they're afraid of him. They recognize that he's an outcast too, and so don't question his silence. When he shows up, they give him a coffee can full of soup and he sits far back in the blackness up under the bridge where they can't see him. When the slurping stops, they wait a few minutes until they figure he's had a chance to leave, then send somebody for the empty can. This is not a popular job, since the Indian sleeps there sometimes, and on those occasions whoever goes to fetch the can has a good chance of getting kicked. They have a few folks who have been prematurely released from mental hospitals and they like to send them on the theory that since they're already traumatized, being attacked by a gigantic Indian can be seen as just another typical element of their day.

Floyd sees the girl again. She's working her way along the inside of the bridge, still looking for him. He ducks back into the shadows and when she tentatively starts down the stairs, his arm hooks out and snags her by the ankle.

The hoboes can hear her yell, but they know better than to involve themselves in the Indian's business. It gets quiet, so a couple of the braver guys work their way up the side of the embankment, expecting to find a body with its throat cut. They're disappointed though; Floyd and the girl are just standing there talking to each other. The

Indian is hard to make out, lost against the concrete support pillar, no more than a huge gloomy shape in the shadows. His face is obscured but he seems to be listening to what the girl is saying. She's obviously not trying to escape. They can see her eyes glinting under the bridge lights like wet coins. She laughs and tosses her head. She throws out poses like a movie star, shaking glittering sprays of raindrops from the folds of her shiny red coat.

The girl takes his arm and they start back up the stone steps. The two hoboes squatting in the shadows watch them leave, silently sucking their tongues.

"Hell," says one finally. "How's that Indian do that?"

"Beats me. Who's that pussy, anyway?"

"That's Little Eva. She's about as exotic a dancer as there's ever been in this town."

"You seen her?"

"Not so much in real life as in the poster pictures they got stuck up in front of the club. They glue little sequins right on the photographs covering up where the good parts are, but a fellow can see those live with his very own eyes if he's got the money to pay his way through the door."

"Yeah?"

"Over at that club they call The Fumbling Hen. But you know they got those photographs in the marquee case behind a piece of glass and I heard if the sun hits it just right, why that glue will melt!"

"Is that a fact? Well, well . . . "

"It's the trick of timing. Being there on a hot day before the manager notices and comes out with his tube of glue."

"But how come they care so much about covering up the good parts?"

"Sound business sense. They don't want the tourists getting a look at it for free. People in the trade call the spangles curiosity prickers. It's where the money is."

"Well, well . . . "

"Tourist money's what keeps the Inner City going."

"Well, well, curiosity prickers is it . . . ?"

"Business is business."

"Hah!" says Little Eva, stripping off her pants. "I didn't *have* to come with you, you know. Half the dudes in the Inner City'd pay fifty bucks to get into me."

She's thrown her clothes all over the room. Floyd looks at her and wonders what in hell he's doing here.

"What'd you've done if I hadn't come?"

He tells her he would've slit her throat and she just laughs. "Sure you would, Sluggo, sure you would. Listen, you know who my guy is? You ever heard of Laughing Harold? You know what he'd do to you if you hurt me? Huh?"

Floyd just looks at her.

She shrugs; it's a joke to her, an hour's entertainment, something to fill up the dull slot before the Inner City really gets in motion. The Indian told her he was looking for his lost sister, who the hell cares about his sister? She's never done it with an Indian before is all, how come he has to go and get psychological on her? He's lying on the bed still half-dressed, looking at his picture book. She goes over and sits beside him. "Which one do you like best, huh, Sluggo?"

Floyd doesn't say anything, just turns the page.

"What's the picture? A banyan tree? Are there only pictures of trees? What's a banyan tree? 'A member of the mulberry family, it has branches that send out shoots which grow down to the soil and root to form secondary trunks.' Well fuck me, how 'bout that! It doesn't *look* much like a mulberry, does it?"

Floyd turns the page. There's a picture of a eucalyptus and they read about its rigid leaves and umbellate flowers. There's even something about its useful gums and resins.

"That's a pretty good one, you like that one? That one turn you on?"

She slides her hand down and forces it into the crotch of his jeans. "Heck! Not yet."

He doesn't say anything but just turns another page, so she sighs and settles back but then gets restless again right away. "Hey, why don't you try a conifer? You know, an evergreen, something with cones."

Then it's later and Cloudfinger's sitting on the window sill watching it rain and Little Eva's jumping up and down, bouncing on the bed, breasts jouncing to the exaggerated *sprong! sprong!* of a broken spring.

"You ever do time in the slammer? My boyfriend never did, he's Laughing Harold like I said. He's a real high roller. People call him Laughing Harold 'cause he's so happy."

She leaps off the bed and stands with her hands on her hips, trickles of sweat running down, sliding across her pink belly. She turns and slumps into the nearest chair across from the bed.

"Actually, he's sort of half my boyfriend and half my guardian. He takes care of me. After the divorce neither of my parents wanted custody of me so I sort of ran away. They were going to put me in this home. I used to be a drum majorette, though, head majorette for the marching band."

She jumps up and runs over, leans on the bed.

"So you think I'm too young, huh? I'm almost seventeen, and look a lot older. Other people have sisters too, you know, you don't have to get so psychological about everything." She brushes back strands of golden hair stuck to her forehead and asks him if he thinks sex is dirty. She tells him that some people like to pretend that it's dirty sometimes because that makes it more fun.

"Do you ever do it with animals? You said you lived out on this farm with a bunch of sheep, you ever make it with a sheep? I tried to do it with a weimaraner once but it didn't work out. The dog didn't get turned on to me either. I was younger then though, only fifteen, and some men paid me to do it, members of some kind of weirdos' photography club. They got real nervous, dropping lenses and tripping over tripods, it was a scream. Everybody was interested in me except this dumb dog, all *he* wanted to do was fetch this disgusting old tennis ball he'd been slobbering on for about a hundred years. My girl friend said that kind of thing is really degenerate but actually it's just boring. Those guys got the dog so upset he pissed all over one of their camera bags, but I didn't care, I got my dough, that's all I wanted. I don't think I'll ever try doing it with an animal again though. They're just different from us, you know? We always said the only one that would be able to do it with a dog would be Stinky Lorraine 'cause the dog wouldn't feel any inferiority complexes with her. She shaves her eyebrows instead of plucking them; when the hair starts growing back, it looks really weird. She doesn't use a deodorant either, and after gym she never takes a bath, that's why we call her Stinky Lorraine. What do you think about the new vaginal sprays? Seems kind of stupid but I guess it's just like toothpaste, you know? What do you think?"

Floyd just looks at her.

"Say, what do you want to talk about, anyway?" She hops over to the bathroom and then stops in the doorway and coyly asks him if *that* would turn him on, watching her tinkle. She giggles again and skips inside, slamming the door behind her.

Cloudfinger's sister was sixteen when she disappeared. He remembers her as standing silently, her faded dresses hanging from her bony shoulders, flowing down with the same elongated stillness as the coarse tresses of her straight black hair, deadening as the falling of flat rain on a windless afternoon.

She loved fabrics; he remembers how her fingers would run along the tightly woven textures of wool blankets in the co-op store, tracing the bold geometric patterns. She wanted to become a weaver but they were poor so she had to take in laundry and by the time she got finished with one day's load she was too tired to do anything but lean over the stove and eat her dinner of cold pinto beans and tortillas and then collapse onto the cornshuck pallet in the lean-to.

Sometimes he'd be left playing by himself in the dust in front of their cabin and would suddenly feel her eyes on him and look up and find her standing on the rotted front porch or under the cottonwood trees, the deep brown hollows of her eyes and cheeks glazed by darker shadows. Even as a kid he instinctively knew that something bad was going to happen and that someday he was going to have to try to do something about it.

Little Eva's teeth flash, "I'm back!" Her tongue flicks out and tastes the air. "It's me," she giggles, pretending she was gone a long time. "Did you miss me?" She starts telling him what it was like marching in front of the band.

She was the star, and wore her hair longer then. She had a gold lamé costume cut high on her hips like a leotard and wore ballet slippers instead of those clunky boots the other little girls had to wear.

She sits cross-legged and tugs on the Indian's blunt fingertips, touching them against the red teeth marks left by the elastic band of her underpants. Her curly yellow hair and nervous eyes trill summers spent on groomed suburban lawns, the land as the successful fathers divided it into its most basic forms: the fenced rectangle of the tennis court or rolling velvet oval of putting green, and always the requisite cube of purified turquoise swimming pool water that reflected on its flickering surface a cloudless sky burned empty by the sun.

"I'll never see my parents again, Laughing Harold will take care of me. Sometimes I miss my friends though."

She fits the Indian's index finger up inside her, sags herself and sighs her eyes closed. She slides back into those summers spent with her little pals lined up beside her, a row of childish bodies tucked into tiny bikinis and basted with tanning oil, lying silently with continuing sunbursts exploding behind their eyelids while their various fathers ringed them solemnly, sat stiff-faced behind black lenses, elastic bathing suits singing with the strain of erections smothered under bundled-up beach towels.

Sweet Little Eva grinds on the Indian's finger using moves she's learned from the movies, catches her beat and strains against the cords of her orgasm, then sinks back into herself, relaxed again and sweaty with her lips wet and her eyes glazed softly, but comes back to it, twists around, sits up and fakes a pout. "What's the matter, don't you like me? Don't I turn you on?" She shifts her shoulders so her long breasts sway, she wants her Indian, then bounces up and stumbles jumping off the other end of the wet bed. She poses with one arm flung up toward the stained ceiling and the other elbow canted out, hand on pink hip. She gives him a moment, giggles, and starts humming: "Tra-la, tra-la, tra-la-la-la!" She begins to show him her old baton routine, marching in place in the middle of the sleazy hotel room, frowning at a part she can't quite get right and starting again: two, three, four—one! two, three, kicking head-high on the beat, forehead still beaded with licks of sweat as she's dancing for more than just the Indian since the glitter ringing in her eyes isn't simply the bells of money anymore but the steeper angle of the dextroamphetamine crystals she took in the bathroom that is finally beginning to work its way into her bloodstream.

The Indian feels himself expanding, enlarging to fill the room as mountain canyon echoes start hammering into his ears, somehow hooked to a pain dragging up out of his stomach, the fear driving him up off the bed while Little Eva's heart pumps slugs of ruby blood beneath the heavy beat of her long breasts, beneath the pale breastbone that the skinner has to sever quickly on the first axial cut, cracking through the ligaments and peeling back the ribs in time to expose the last spasmodic shudders of the dying jewel. . . .

"Hey asshole Cloudfinger," yelled Billy Twodogs, hiding behind the baseball backstop. "I hear your sister got a job working as a hooker in the city! Haw haw!" then stopped laughing and took off running, screaming for help at the look on Floyd's face as he came after him, knowing he couldn't run far enough.

Then it's later and Cloudfinger's in the bathroom throwing up, hacking hot wine down the porcelain throat of the toilet bowl.

"What's wrong, huh? You sick? Hey, I'm sorry, you know? Really, I didn't know, I thought you wanted to make it, really, I'm sorry, what do you want anyway?"

But Floyd's a child again and his old man just back from the war is standing in the doorway, a black shadow outlined by the setting sun's deep reds and absurd purples. His father's arms are gone, blown away in Belgium, nothing left but paddles, flapping like an angry penguin, bellowing: "Why won't somebody light my fucking cigarette!" And then dishes are jumping off the table and Floyd has pissed his pants and is crouched down among the shards, hiding under the table and his mother's voice is up there out of sight asking him, what's he afraid of? And then her hands are darting under and blowing down on him like dark birds.

And then his sister has taken him down the road to where the big white horse of Grandfather Eagle-who-stopped-talking is and is asking him if he wants to give it some grass and he does, so he's feeding the horse and she's telling him how his father's going to live with them and he has to try to understand about what happened to him and Floyd doesn't actually understand what she's talking about but the sound of her voice makes him feel better.

"Listen," says Little Eva, "I don't know but I better go, okay? Okay if I go?" She's hurrying, grabbing her clothes and putting them on, can't find one shoe, throws herself under the bed looking for it, "Okay if I go? Okay? The door's locked and I can't find the key. You still in there? You coming out? Huh?"

Todd is on the phone talking to Laughing Harold. "There's this Indian," he says, "we might be able to use him. He looks pretty tough."

"Tell him how big the Indian is," Donnard says.

Todd listens for a minute then hangs up.

"What'd he say?"

"He said that was fine."

"He didn't care?"

"He didn't seem to care very much, as a matter of fact."

"What was he doing?"

"I think he was in bed with a lady."

"What makes you think that?"

"Giggling."

A group comes in and their tour guide gets them settled at a couple of corner tables. This is the Evening Adventures Incorporated tour and they have a standing arrangement with the Rolling Ring. The tour guide comes up to the bar with a pay voucher and a list of drink orders. He glances down at Donnard and Todd, then shrugs. "Not my fault, pop," he says, "I'm just trying to make a living." He helps a waitress carry a couple of trays of drinks over to his group.

"I wish I wasn't so god damn old," says Todd. "I'd crack that smart aleck."

"Rocky Hill didn't get old."

"Rocky Hill?"

"I don't suppose you remember Rocky Hill."

Todd's upper lip has a mustache of beer foam. "Good-looking young fellow," he says, "a real sharp dresser but dumb as the day is long."

"Face like a diseased potato, as a matter of fact," says Donnard, "but smart as a whip."

"You're thinking of Bugsy Cleaver."

"Rocky Hill."

"You're mistaken here."

"It was Rocky Hill. Bugsy Cleaver's the guy that shot him, back in '34, or was it '35?"

Todd looks at him. "Something of a memory problem here," he says. "Bugsy Cleaver got shot in 1932! He got it when the mob hit Slick Flagellong's gang! You're thinking of somebody else."

"I believe it was Bugsy Cleaver. Yes, a tall skinny guy that wanted to be a sports announcer but never amounted to anything more than a two-bit numbers runner. Rocky Hill was a torpedo and so Bugsy must've figured rubbing him out'd help him move up."

"You're thinking of Gus Williams."

"Huh?"

"Gus Williams."

"Never heard of him."

"Never heard of Gus Williams? You *are* getting old!"

A tourist sneaks up behind them, taps Donnard on the back and when he turns around, he gets a flashcube in the face.

"God damn!" he says, trying to blink away the momentary blindness.

"Easy," says the bartender, handing Donnard a free beer. "No trouble now."

"Gus Williams, huh?" says Donnard, still mad but resigned to the fact that he can't do anything about it. "He have some kind of nickname?"

"Gus Williams? Hell no, he's the guy who shot Philly Marbles."

"Hah!" says Donnard, the loose skin over his throat wobbling in excitement. "I got you now, that was Pete Thompson. We called him Petey-boy Thompson."

"Yer ass!"

"Good old Petey-boy Thompson! Hell of a card player, he was, except he had a weakness for trying to draw to an inside straight, it must've been the drama of the long-shot."

"Hell," says Todd, "you got it all wrong." He's shaking his head trying to appear confident but he knows the advantage is shifting away from him. Donnard starts sucking his dentures down from his gums and popping them, a sure sign that he's zeroing in for the kill.

Just about then Maude strolls in, stops and cocks out a hip. "How're you doing, boys?"

She must be the oldest professional woman in the Inner City. She looks a little like a Mae West with all the juices drained out of her, ninety pounds of harridan draped in layers of lace and jewelry, her face all slick and snazzy with make-up. She knows just how wide she can stretch her smile before the pancake cracks and fault lines fan up her cheeks. For Maude, personal business has pretty much degenerated into an exercise in futility. Fortunately she worked her way into a solid managerial position and is even the secret owner of the Rolling Ring. She made enough money in her prime to retire but never even considered it. She says she likes the trappings and illusions of the life even if the actual banging part has shrunken to a trickle.

"Anybody here going to buy a lady a drink?"

Donnard springs for the price of a sherry. He'd like a little audience now that he's got Todd worried.

"Harold in yet?"

"He said later."

"He say anything about the dog race tonight?"

"No problem," says Donnard. "He said he'd stop by the dog barn on his way back."

"It's the Silver Wringer, right? I got a pile on him."

"That's the pooch."

Maude stands up to go over and sit with the tourists, maybe get a couple back after the tour.

"I hear Pigeye's fast."

"He's fast, but the boss is going to take care of him."

"Sure he is," she says with a careful smile. Todd gives her rear a little half-hearted squeeze as she walks by, but she can't feel it.

"Foam rubber ass," he mutters. "I *thought* it looked store-bought."

"Everything's breaking down," Donnard agrees.

"Women wearing rubber butts and the place clogged up with tourists every night."

"Say mister, you a real gangster?" Donnard says in a squeaky falsetto that he seems to think sounds like a tourist.

"Disgusting!"

"Big Jim wouldn't've put up with all this shit. He'd've handled it, you can bet."

"Poor Big Jim, we won't see the likes of him again."

"He was a giant of a man."

"I recollect the time Gus Williams paid Thick Pantery ten bucks for every .44 cartridge he could swallow. Big Jim was the only one that could stop it."

"I'd forgotten about that!" Donnard laughs. "I'd forgotten. But say, was that fellow's name Gus Williams?"

"That was it, all right; the same guy that shot Philly
Marbles."

"Huh? Wait a minute, wasn't that . . . ?"

"I believe he swallowed seven," Todd says. "With nothing more to help him than the occasional drink of water."

"It was Petey-boy Thompson, Petey-boy Thompson
shot . . . "

"Big Jim said it was the stupidest thing he ever heard of.
Gus Williams couldn't quit laughing. Imagine, he kept saying, imagine a guy dumb enough to try and swallow a
bullet!"

"But was that fellow's name Gus Williams? I sure don't
remember that."

"Yes yes, good old Gus Williams."

"I sure forgot that guy's name. . . ."

"Good old Gus. . . ."

"I could've sworn it was Pete Thompson. . . ."

"Yes sir, Gus Williams. . . ."

Donnard and Todd stand teetering on the riverbank near
the Third Street Bridge.

"Under there?"

"That's what he said."

"Darker'n hell under there."

"He said under the bridge."

"After you."

They go clambering down the stairs, leaning on each
other, not real crazy about all the shadows. Todd kicks a
tin can and it rolls down in front of them. They both
freeze. They're a little nervous about probing into dark

corners, getting ambushed being the gunsel's basic occupational hazard.

"Anybody home?"

They can hear the sound of water dripping somewhere. They move deeper under the bridge, picking their way cautiously until they see a fire with a couple of guys sitting by it.

"A moment of your time?" asks Donnard.

The hoboes don't look very busy, but they don't say anything either. Todd hands one of them two bits and he looks up and says, "Sure gents."

"An Indian, a large fellow, given to violent outbursts, the barkeeper at the Rolling Ring Bar said he could be found under this bridge."

"He ain't here now."

"Do you know when he'll be likely to return?"

The hobo just shrugs.

"I might know," another one says and holds out his hand.

"How much?"

"Half a dollar."

"Hell, for half a dollar I might know where he went," says the first one quickly. Donnard digs around in his pocket until he comes up with four bits.

"At the Buckingham Palace Hotel. He's got a pussy with him."

"Very kind of you," says Todd.

"I might know when he'll be back for a dime," the other hobo says hopefully, but it's too late, the two old gangsters have already started back up the river bank.

Floyd Cloudfinger's in motion, stalking through the blue

gloom of wet alleys, searching for Little Eva. He let her go but now he wants her back. The night sky is clearing above him, snarled in the silver fists of stars. He hears the broken *clack-clack-clack* of a gigantic mechanical crab left over from some undersea adventure movie and fastened to the rusty superstructure on the roof of a seafood restaurant, which might be nothing more than a movie set itself. Floyd stops to watch the steel legs' absurd gesticulation, beneath which one neon sign shines FISH and another EATS, the terminal *s* a little fluttery from the rictus of a dying tube. The Indian looks at the restaurant door, but there's no way to know if it's real or just some piece of junk, refurbished, then abandoned for the gawkers to believe in.

A swabby lurches by, his peacoat muffled up around his ears, hunched against the splatters dripping from the sodden eaves. Floyd looks in his face but there's nothing there, he's just another sucker.

Then Cloudfinger's on the river bank, again drawn to the dark Duck, the smooth waters that once soothed the loneliness of the heartland back before the fish were poisoned, before the leaves of the bordering willow trees contracted blight, blistered and shriveled into black crisps. The Indian's brogans are filled with rainwater again and the bottoms of his pants are soaked. It'd be nice to be someplace where there was coffee and something to eat, a blazing fire to sit around, shuck pillows and a quilt, somebody awake all night with a rifle in the doorway, and an old man telling stories about how it used to be. . . .

Evidently there weren't any promises made. Floyd knows that, even though he can't operate on it. He doesn't have any hopes, that's what he pays for peace, and this thing about his sister is just what he told himself he'd do once he got out of the slammer. He figures it always ends the same way, the trapped wagon train relieved by the hard-charging Seventh Cavalry shooting L.A. Indians so inept they have to have saddles under the blankets or they'd fall off their ponies. The cheering kids' throats open in the last moments of secret anonymity before the lights come on showing how shabby the theater is and forcing them to file out singly into the desert afternoon with nothing left but to tear at each other with dull knives.

All he's got is an angle on Little Eva. She's somewhere between him and the wasteland the Urban Renewal Program created beyond the edge of the Inner City. He figures she'll have to try to get past him sooner or later.

He hears a strange noise in the empty road beyond the alley so he jumps behind some crates but there's a rat in the shadows that runs up and starts nipping at his heels.

"Shoo!" he whispers. "Get outa here!"

The shuffling sound he heard in the road stops so Cloud-finger wants to be as quiet as possible. She must be waiting for him to make his move, but he can be patient, he learned how in the joint.

He remembers the dead wino at the train station when his father came home from the war. The steam was blowing from the locomotive and his father walked out of it, lurching from side to side, drunk in the morning with another man beside him helping him. Both were dressed in the khaki uniforms of the victorious army except the sleeves of his father's jacket were flat and empty, tucked neatly into the jacket pockets and secured by large safety pins. Then the boy Floyd was yelling and running to hide behind the station building except there was that dead wino with the flies walking on his face and then his mother caught him and dragged him back. . . .

The rat charges again and Cloudfinger isn't ready for it so he falls a little to the side, thumping against an empty barrel. He'd like to take a swing at the damn thing with his tomahawk but that'd make too much noise, and he probably couldn't hit it anyway. The rat darts back just out of reach, then challenges him, sitting up on its haunches and chattering, whiskers twitching in indignation.

Cloudfinger hunkers down and the rat creeps a little closer, then pauses, beating its bald tail angrily against the asphalt. Floyd's trying to hear any movement in the alley before he goes out but it's dead quiet down there. He offers the rat a piece of pemmican and it gets a little closer, sniffing suspiciously. It picks the piece up and takes a bite, just tasting the edge, then throws it down and spits out the bit in its mouth.

Floyd's mother held him in front of the two ex-soldiers. "He killed a hundred krauts, burned them alive in a building, and look what they done to him, the bastards." His father's friend was drunk too, his eyes small and red in the harsh morning light. "I ain't never been to any desert before," he said looking at Floyd's mother. "He told me to come. He's a hell of a soldier. That'd be his boy?"

"This is Floyd."

The man pulled a bottle of whiskey out of his pocket and took a swig, then held it up for Floyd's father, pressing the bottle against his lips and tilting it back, spilling the whiskey down both sides of his mouth in two drools that dribbled onto his soiled khaki coat. "Nice-looking boy, he'd be about six?"

"Four and a half. He's big for his age."

"He is that. Well, his daddy killed a hundred krauts, in a French farmhouse they made into a gasoline depot, over in France, with a flame thrower when they was all asleep at night. His daddy's one *hell* of a soldier."

Floyd's father didn't say anything, just kept staring at his mother, his eyes bloodshot and swollen, waiting for her to say something about it. . . .

He's just about to the corner when the rat hits him again. It comes out of another section of shadows, an enraged little ball of fur and teeth charging right up his pant leg like it wanted to rip into his guts. Floyd figures it has to be at least rabid and hops to the side with a yell, beating at it with his fist and whacking the thing off him finally but at the same moment stepping on a roller skate some damn kid left behind and falling flat on his ass.

He rolls over and can hear running footsteps retreating deeper into the alley. The rat's holding its ground though. It's scratching at the dirt and pebbles in the gutter with its front paws, getting ready to throw a load at the Indian.

The boy Floyd was crying because his sister was crying and they were all up in the middle of the night and his mother was standing backed against the door, clutching the front of her torn housedress over her breasts. She was panting like a wild mare in the hot darkness and his father was saying something terrible to his mother and moving sideways, awkward as a baby chicken with its oversized feet, but even Floyd knew that he was lining her up before trying to kick her again. . . .

Under the freeway overpass the Indian rests for a moment. There's junk everywhere, mostly empty beer cans blown down from the cars that used to use the freeway before this section was closed for repairs and never re-opened. Floyd feels pretty good about the way he's kept Little Eva moving. They're right out at the rim of the Inner City. Beyond them is the wide belt of desolation gouged by the Urban Renewal Program, a flat plain of dead earth stretching for miles. There's a rounded midden of rubble every two hundred yards or so, and the whole lunar surface is blank and silvery in the starlight.

"Hey you, g-g-g-girl!" Floyd yells. "You're out here somewhere; you're scared, you want to g-go home."

He listens but it's quiet, she doesn't answer. He hadn't thought she would. He'd like some good tough line like they say in movies when they're trapped, but he can't think of anything.

"That's no-man's land! Wild d-d-dogs out there! P-pets of the d-d-d-dead! They'll cut you d-down!"

Floyd starts moving laterally, figuring she'll remember where his voice came from and be watching for him from that direction. Just as he gets around the thick cement trunk of a freeway support pillar, he steps in a pile of plastic spoons that crackle like dry twigs. There's a pause and then a rush thirty yards behind him. He can hear her working her way down under the far end of the underpass and realizes he was wrong, she wasn't where he thought at all. Little Eva makes a break for it at the same time he jumps out running, but she's got too good a lead and is gone.

Floyd runs into the next alley over, trying to keep her cut off from the river bank. All the buildings in this area are deserted so he figures if he can keep her trapped in the labyrinth abutting the Urban Renewel desert he'll have a pretty good chance of keeping in touch with her. It's five or six blocks to the nearest big avenue and none of these little alleys go all the way. He comes to a dead end. Written

on the wall in flakey letters a foot high is an old sign:
BEWARE OF THE ROYAL RUBY VIPERS. Floyd takes a right then
a left, hoping he's still parallel with her. It's darker down
this alley and so narrow he could touch both walls with his
outstretched hands. There's a naked light globe burning
down at the other end with two children waiting under it,
dressed only in dirty white underpants and clear plastic
rainhats. Their skin glistens silvery in the rain light and
their eyes are big and so pale blue at first he thinks they
must be blind.

"You kids see a girl running, or walking fast?"

They just stare at him with those huge, moist eyes and
again he gets the feeling they're blind. Their skin is so
thin, so translucent, he can almost see the delicate blue network of veins. He thinks the one on the left might be a
girl, although they look so much alike it's hard to tell.
Their heads wobble loosely as if their necks were springs,
and they stand confronting him, calmly holding hands.

"She didn't come this way, huh?"

The larger one turns to the other and Floyd notices for
the first time that he must be holding some kind of stiff
gray fish hanging behind him. Floyd can see the dead fins
and tail sticking out, the same color and texture as the
child's leg, and a lot more substantial.

"You ain't the Ruby Vipers, are you?"

But they just stand there watching him and he feels a
shudder slide through his whole body, which means somebody must be stepping on where his grave will be. He's
stopped, his knees locked, and that alley behind those kids
seems a lot darker than it was before.

"How come you're here?" he asks them. "What d-d-do
you want?"

They both smile, beautiful transparent smiles that don't

have any warmth in them at all. Floyd's got his hand in his coat, feeling for the butt of his tomahawk. If one of them makes a move toward him, he's pretty sure he'll take a swing at it. There's about enough room on the side of the smaller one to get by, and Floyd knows he'd better be walking, and walking fast, because that tomahawk very likely might just glance off them, or worse, glide through them like it was cutting mist.

His father never taught him how to hunt. There was nothing to hunt where they lived anyway. He'd like to stalk Little Eva the way they do in the movies but there's no scent, and asphalt's a lousy place for footprints. All he's got is that she's likely as lost as he is, and accident ought to work in his favor.

But he hasn't heard anything from her for a long time; he might've lost her. She could've outrun him, or gotten past him farther up somewhere and so made it to the river bank. But she should be scared; she should be listening at every intersection and trying to be as quiet as possible, in which case she would still be moving parallel to him, half a block over. He figures he's got nothing to lose and so turns left at the next corner and starts walking faster, hoping to surprise her.

The buildings along here have been deserted for years, but some of the windows seem to be lighted and when he peers in one, he realizes that it's an abandoned textile mill, the kind of place his sister should have worked in. The awkward-looking machines are dusty and covered with generations of spiders' webs, but for some reason a couple of light bulbs are still burning in the back of the building.

Floyd turns the corner and Little Eva's prying at one of
the boards nailed over the door.

"Oh!" she says. "Was that you? Somebody was following
me. I was scared. I thought I recognized your voice, but I
wasn't sure. . . ."

She starts backing toward the open alley, still smiling
while Floyd moves with her.

"Listen, you're a little bit too rough, but I'm not really
mad, you know?"

Floyd springs into the middle of the open alley and she
freezes.

"What do you want?"

"You."

"Why? What'd I do to you?"

"Nothing."

"What do you want me for?"

"B-b-b-bargaining."

"Listen, my boyfriend Laughing Harold can help you.
He's the top attraction in the Inner City, and everybody
knows him. He can get you some kind of job or something.
You could get some money and still keep looking for your
sister. I don't know anything about her, honest I don't.
Well, I better be going. I have to dance tonight; I don't
want to be late. You're not mad, are you? I mean, I'm not
mad so if I'm not, I don't see why you should be, right?"

The Indian is still standing between her and the river.
She starts walking back toward one of the parallel alleys.
The Indian stays right behind her, waiting for her to try
to make a run for it.

"Oh. You're going this way too, huh? I thought you
were going that way. Well, we can walk along together.
Although I'm only going a little ways, in fact just as far

as the next street. I get lost down here easily. If you want
to see Laughing Harold about a job, you should go to the
Rolling Ring. Do you know where that is? Near the Third
Street Bridge. Actually, I'm not going this direction any
farther. I forgot, I have to stop at a girl friend's house, so
I'll see you around, okay? Go see Laughing Harold, he'll
help you, he helps everybody, okay?"

Floyd figures everything's angles. He knew she'd go down
a block then cut back toward the river and so was ready
for her. Now she's running and he's right behind her, but
she's fast, faster than he would have guessed, and she's
moving away from him, her bare white legs flashing in the
darkness.

It seems like he ought to be enjoying it, but it really
isn't any fun. Floyd doesn't deal with the fact directly, but
he's seen enough movies to know that he ought not to
win. . . .

"Show it to him."

"Where's it at?"

"In the haversack, fuckhead."

The man didn't let nobody talk to him like that, but
there was nothing he could do about it, you couldn't bust
a cripple, specially a double-amputee war hero.

He pulled something out of the sack and put it in front
of Floyd. It was wrapped up in a piece of dirty sheet and
tied with yellow twine.

"You, boy, open it."

"He don't want to," said Floyd's mother. "He's scared."

His father just started walking toward her with a tired
look on his face and she kept her eye on his right foot saying, "All right, all right, all right!"

"Open it, boy," said his father's friend.

"It's okay, honey," his mother said. "It's a toy he brought you from the war."

Floyd started pulling at the strings but he was too afraid, he couldn't get anything loose.

"You, Gloria, help your brother."

She got it open and it was a mechanical dog. Tied up in another smaller piece of sheet were a bunch of tiny green rubber balls.

"Turn the key, boy."

Floyd wound it up and the little metal dog started wagging its tail and then pretty soon out popped one of the green balls, right out of its round metal asshole.

"Put that ball in its mouth, boy. It eats its own shit. That's how it works; that's how you activate the chewing mechanism."

Floyd did it. He was starting to cry again. The dog's metal jaws went *crack-crack-crack* and the little green ball disappeared.

"The Germans made that dog. The boy that had it before you got a bayonet stuck in his guts."

"Over there in France," said his father's friend. . . .

Floyd watches her spring into the courtyard, a silver puppet dashing across the star-washed sands. She must be tired by now but she doesn't show it; her stride's still smooth. For the last half block he's known where she would have to end up because the alley dead-ends in front of the Thirty-Three Intervals Warehouse, one of the few places in the Inner City he knows well. He leans inside the gate resting and looks across the courtyard to the long dark building forty yards away.

An Indian had died here, shot down as he was trying to retrieve some totem belonging to his tribe. As a boy Floyd had heard about it and this building was one of the first places he came to see when he arrived in the Inner City.

Inside it smells like dust, and the kinds of dry mold that thrive on dead flowers. It's a single hall, lined on both sides with the huge, broken statues of discredited deities, ancient demons no longer of interest even as tourist attractions and so forgotten here, mixed together like a fractured history of the inability of the religious to agree on the forms of the divine. They're back to back, cheek to jowl, ass to elbow; some without heads, some without arms, some glaring horribly and some with the glassy lunatic smile of the saint. The Indian feels fine among them. He likes the chaos implied in their deformity, likes the sense that each, no matter how splendidly executed, is finally and totally proof of a failure. And he particularly likes them now that hidden somewhere among them crouches his prey, Little Eva.

Every fifty feet or so a small light bulb glows dustily amid the wooden webbing of the complicated rafter system. The hollow building ticks to the sound of water dripping somewhere down in the moist bowels at the far end. The Indian stalks her, poised for any sob, any panting, or even the too-contained silence of a held breath, sensed rather than heard. He sniffs the musty air of wood smoke, incense, and again dead flowers. He slides to the far side and begins working his way down among the dark gods, conscious of their glazed eyes and knobby wooden muscles, the multiple arms brandishing flaming swords or barbed ropes or throwing discuses, all the various symbols of their threats and promises, the rosary, the lotus, the noose. A lot of the statues still have name cards on them, labels left over from when the tourists used to come. The neat little tags explain the god's name and period and elevation in one hierarchy

or another, but the Indian doesn't have to read these, he's
met them all before, in dark alleys, in electrical storms, in
nightmares. . . .

He fits himself behind each throne, feeling into the naked
black corners, fingers tapping toward the expected touch
of live skin, the moist whiteness of the girl's body quivering
like a peeled doe. He works methodically around the base
of each statue, constantly listening for the flurry of motion
in any other section of the warehouse that will home him
to her again.

Cloudfinger came to the Inner City after he had a dream
about his sister. He saw her standing on the Third Street
Bridge, people gliding past her like fish while she stood
unmoving, gazing at him. Her face wasn't detailed, it was
there, but it was like his dream didn't look at it. She was
wearing a long, pale gray silk evening dress with a pattern
of lavender wisteria flowers curling around the bottom of
the skirt. Duck River sparkled green beneath the bright
orange bridge. It was afternoon and she was standing looking at Floyd waiting for something. Her hair was wound
into a roll on the back of her head, but clumsily fastened
with some hairpins and an ornamental comb. Wisps had
come down loose, floating around her pale face like an airy
frame of black threads. Her mouth was open as if she was
saying something, but the rules of the dream that kept her
face from forming kept the words soundless. They were
only words, without any meaning, and the only thing he
could know for certain was the green water sliding under
the old bridge. . . .

In the middle of the hall, dominating the seventeenth
interval, sits the biggest statue, the Demon King of Hell,
like a gigantic anthropomorphic beetle with ten arms and

eleven heads, surrounded by a halo of grimacing antlered angels and deformed birds. The god's central head stalk is split and parts of the faces of the heads on the left side are missing, leaving only the grain of raw wood, blackened with years of smoke. Cloudfinger strokes the cold stone flagging behind the huge god, his fingers sliding past moist pads of moss, then moves slowly around to the front. The offertory dish before the god is piled with withered flowers and on the center of this bed lie the desiccated inner organs of some small beast, bits of wrapping paper still stuck to them with dried blood. Cloudfinger looks up into the god's glittering banks of eyes, the tiny light bulbs overhead filling them with malevolent diamonds.

"You don't scare me," Floyd whispers, "but you used to, you used to, there were days when I couldn't get off my bed because I knew you were behind the door, any door." He gazes up into the broken faces, then spits on the god's immense knee, the little pellets of moisture beading up in the thick dust. "Not anymore, not me, not even at night in the dark, I'm past it. You just come back around any time you think you can take me, I'm always waiting."

Floyd continues down the row, searching behind the silent images. It's lighter at the other end of the hall and he looks that way every now and then, wondering why it's not as dark as the section he's in. Then he freezes. There are some people sitting down there, two rows of them lined up on benches next to some kind of kiosk illuminated with dirty brown light bulbs.

He slides back into the shadows and starts working his way down among the idols. As he gets closer he realizes that only one of the figures is human. The rest are wooden statues of angels, dressed in ragged old clothes. The angels have their heads bowed. Their eyes are turned down, like they were gazing in melancholy revery at something in their laps.

The old man sitting among them gets up and hobbles over to where Floyd is hiding. He's moving slowly and leaning on his cane, but advancing straight toward Floyd as if he could see in the dark. His face is mostly brown, but patches are dull white where the skin pigment has died, giving his head the mottled inconsistency of a hyena's skull.

"Hello, hello, hello! You don't have to be shy, young fellow, Mrs. Poppy is open."

Floyd steps out of the shadows, his hand resting on the butt of his tomahawk.

"We don't get many customers here, tourists don't come much anymore, but Mrs. Poppy is open, open for business."

Floyd follows him over to the benches. There's something weird about the angels. He figures it must be that he's never thought of one as sitting down. They're always flying or floating, or hovering like helicopters.

"Don't worry about the boys. Mrs. Poppy gets lonely when I have to be away at the river so we arranged them to keep her company."

Each is wearing a coat, fitted awkwardly over the bulges of its wings, and some even have hats on. They're evidently from a single set since they've been carved out of the same kind of wood, with more or less identical sexless faces.

"Mrs. Poppy's named them. This is Gabriel, and this one's Michael and this one's, uh, I forget some of the others. This one with the knothole in his cheek's named Bob."

He tells Floyd they dressed them up in old clothes to make them seem more like folks.

"Here's Mrs. Poppy, now don't be shy, young fellow. Look at the menu."

Stapled in front of the kiosk is a printed cardboard sign

with the word MENU and a list of a dozen or so entrées, each of which has been carefully crossed out leaving only the very bottom one, SOUP OF THE DAY.

"Soup? Young fellow, would you have some soup? Step up and tell Mrs. Poppy."

The kiosk looks empty but Floyd goes up to it. Sitting on a piece of rug down inside is the oldest woman he's ever seen. She must be over a hundred years old. She's completely bald and her face is so sunken and wrinkled that at first it's hard to make out much more than the place where the nose pokes out. Floyd gradually realizes that one eye is completely blind, nothing but a black slit, and that the other has some sort of pale blue cast in it.

"Don't be afraid of her, young fellow, she likes to know what the young people of today are doing."

Her mouth opens. *"Croak?"*

"Yes, Mrs. Poppy, a customer. Go ahead, order what you'd like."

"Do you have any soup?"

"Skroak?"

"Yes, Mrs. Poppy, this nice young man would like a bowl of soup."

One yellow claw pulls itself out of the black rags she's wound in and slowly rises past her face, pressing up toward the counter.

"Take the bowl of soup, young fellow."

Floyd looks again. There's nothing but the quivering yellow hand, its shiny brown fingernails hooked like talons.

"Take the soup."

Floyd pretends to take a bowl from her empty hand. He's careful not to touch her. He doesn't know how that would feel, but he's pretty sure he wouldn't like it.

"Be careful, don't spill it. It's nice and hot."

"*Droak.*"

"She says that'll be fifty cents."

Floyd doesn't know if he ought to pull out some real money or not.

"Here you are, Mrs. Poppy." The old man leans over the counter and hands her a bottle cap.

"*Grak.*" The hand clutches the bottle cap and slides back into the folds of her robe.

"There's a place there by Fred. He's the one in the topper."

Floyd looks behind him. It seems to be getting darker. The lights are still glowing but they have become weaker. The Indian sits heavily between two of the wooden angels. He looks down the row but the end is lost in gloom, and it appears to be much longer than it did before. He feels an odd need to stare into his lap like they are, to sit very quietly in the darkness and wait for the old man's voice to pull him back. . . .

Floyd is standing in a sun-filled alley again. He's found his father just like he did all the other times, slumped back among the garbage cans behind the Dew Drop Inn. Floyd is seeing the couple of empty bottles of T-bird, each with a straw sticking out of it, the kind they use in hospitals, the kind you can bend and not cut off the flow, good for a man that does a lot of drinking in gutters.

Then Floyd feels he has noticed the smell of piss and has guessed that a dog did it on the old man, except he can imagine somebody telling him no, the old man pissed on himself, and not knowing which it was makes him uneasy. Floyd has pushed his father with his foot and he's rolled over, his head lolled back and his filthy brown throat folded open like a dying lily.

Then Floyd's got the straight razor in his hand, unopened. He must be about ten and has been carrying one for about a year now. There wouldn't be anything to it, just another wino in an empty alley. Floyd remembers patches of puke on the old man's coat collar when he folded it back, the razor shaking in his hand like a dowsing rod leaping for water.

Then Floyd's mother is sitting in front of their cabin, watching the sun go down over the desert, waiting for something. . . .

"Paw, wake up! Wake up!" Floyd is back farther away but the boy Floyd is up close and he can feel the tears heating up behind his eyelids. Floyd knows the boy Floyd won't let them fall out, he knows that's part of the rules.

"Wake up, god damn you!" The boy has been told you ought never to open out your razor unless you were willing to use it, but his thumb keeps picking at the little steel blade flange sticking out from the end of the handle. Floyd knows he has to step in and stop the boy but he can't make himself move.

"Paw . . ."

Then the old man is behind him whispering in his ear.

"Soup, young fellow, a warm place to stay. I can tell you what it used to be like."

"No, I g-got . . . "

"Mrs. Poppy's fond of you. We know what you want."

Floyd looks at the angels falling away from him like reflections in a broken mirror.

"You don't know why they're looking in their laps? You can't guess what they're looking for?"

Floyd shakes his head in the darkness.

"They don't know if they're boy angels or girl angels. And do you know why?"

Floyd feels the old man's spittle lacing his cheek. He reaches one hand in front of his face but it closes on empty air. The only remaining illumination is in the kiosk where Mrs. Poppy's hand has appeared as if in echo to his own, crawling along the counter like a broken spider trying to escape.

"There's nothing there! Haw! They're neither!"

"I g-got to g-g-get . . . "

"She likes you, young fellow. Mrs. Poppy likes you, I can tell." He sticks his cane in Floyd's ribs. "She was a looker when she was in her prime, sweet and juicy as a ripe fruit, and spry! The things she could do to make a body laugh. All dried away now," he says, his voice sinking. "All dried up and blown away, tastes like ashes and's as gritty as sand. It's a shame she had to get so old, a shame. Say, can you see that?"

Mrs. Poppy's hand has clenched itself into a fist with one finger pointing crookedly at the ceiling. There's something black hanging in the darkness. Floyd can just barely make out the shape. It must be another of the angels, strung from a beam, the black rope knotted around his wooden neck.

"He tripped Mrs. Poppy years ago. We made an example of him for the others. Sometimes when the wind blows he rotates."

"I g-g-got to get b-back."

"That girl you were following went down into the basement. There's a trap door down at the other end of the hall. I'll show you later. But listen, that basement is nothing but a net of tunnels. She can't get out. You don't have to worry about her. You can go collect her whenever you want to, so don't try to rush off. Mrs. Poppy'd love for you to have some tea. Here," he says, holding something in front of Floyd's face. The Indian takes it. He can tell by the shape that it's a bottle cap.

"Over that way. See the little flicker of light? You can pay her for it yourself. She's very fond of you."

Part Two

• • • • • • • • • • •

Harold Baine, Alias Laughing Harold

Grease that electrode, Marky."

"Say what?"

"The Vaseline. Smear the end of that electrode with the Vaseline petroleum jelly."

"What for?" the boy says, staring at his uncle, his mouth sagging open.

"So it won't be such a surprise sliding in."

The greyhound strapped to the steel table starts whimpering when it feels Maldeflour shove the electrode up its anus.

"It knows," the boy laughs, "it can *feel* it!"

"It's happened to it before. Lots of times."

"It learns up real good, don't it?"

Maldeflour checks the moist straps binding the dog's legs to the table. He's a big fat guy with a ringworm problem so acute it'll probably kill him some day. His nephew asks him if he can turn the crank.

"You think you can do it?"

"I can do it. I'll toast his balls!"

"Okay boy, give him about thirty seconds."

Marky starts turning the crank on the generator and the

dog howls. Maldeflour stays right behind him to make sure he does it right. The boy smells rank. He pisses in his pants sometimes and that soaks into the eating sugar he keeps in his pockets, although he doesn't seem to mind when it gets a little crusted or the taste changes. The boy never washes, either, but that doesn't bother Maldeflour since he seldom troubles to take much in the way of baths himself.

"That'll be good enough, Marky."

"One more shot!"

"That there'll do, Marky."

"It moves him around some, don't it, Uncle?"

The dog is still shuddering as Maldeflour unfastens it. Drools of saliva are pooling down under its mouth and its eyes are staring out glazed and crazy.

"Feel here, Marky. Grab hold of this leg muscle."

"It's hard as iron!"

"Electricity's what does it, boy. It's a kind of those isometrics of exercise, except quicker. You make you a dog strong quick, Marky. A dog's legs want to be strong for the dog track world. One thing you got to watch out for, though."

"What's that, Uncle?" He's sucking on a handful of sugar. The top of his fist is cleaned pink where his tongue licks it.

"It can burst the heart if you aren't taking care."

"I'll take care."

"Too much electricity's bad for dogs."

"I'll pay attention."

"See that you do, boy. These here greyhounds dead aren't even fit eating."

They push the dog into a narrow wire cage. It twists around trying to lick its anus, still shaking.

Maldeflour wipes his hands on his filthy coveralls. "Two more dogs to go." He levers open a bottle of beer on the wire latch of a dog cage.

Then Laughing Harold's standing just inside the dog barn door, leaning casually against the door frame, his hat pulled down hiding his eyes. He's cleaning his fingernails with a little metal file. Maldeflour sees him and stops drinking. He straightens up and starts edging toward a beat-up old desk where he's got a pistol.

Laughing Harold asks him if he isn't forgetting something.

Maldeflour's still trying to slide over to the desk. Harold looks up briefly and says he doesn't believe he heard him. There's a little bandage on his throat where he cut himself shaving.

"I didn't say nothing."

"Who's that guy, Uncle?"

"Shut your hole."

"Your boy, Mal? Nice-looking kid. Looks a little like something you'd find living in an alley, but what the hell, boys will be boys. It is a boy, isn't it? Sure it is, sure it is, you can tell that by looking at it. What do you feed him, Mal?"

Laughing Harold slips the little file into a leather case and puts it back into his pocket. He touches his fingertips gently to his throat to make sure the bandage is still in place.

"You know, Mal, if I hear that desk drawer open, I'm going to have to drill you."

Maldeflour stops moving.

"Much as I'd hate to, of course," Harold says with a laugh.

"I don't owe you nothing! I don't want you to bother me no more. I got to mind my business."

"We've been pals for a long time."

"I don't need it no more. I'm legit."

Harold laughs again, then moves into the barn. Marky scoops out another fistful of sugar and starts sucking on it.

"It could be very simple," Harold says. "Pigeye loses the race like he's supposed to, like would happen under normal circumstances. Maybe he's getting old, maybe his legs don't have that good kick anymore, you know?"

"I don't know nothing."

"That's what my man Roy told me, that you'd become real stupid recently. He was afraid you might have an accident, you're getting so careless."

"I got friends, too."

"Is that right?" Harold starts circling in toward Maldeflour. There's a lot of dog shit on the floor and since Harold's wearing a good-looking pair of new two-tone wingtips, he's not being as careful of the fat man as he probably ought to. Just about when he has to pick his way through an unusually fertile section of the floor, Maldeflour sees his chance and suddenly lurches for the desk drawer. Harold jumps on him right away, banging the drawer shut on his hand.

"Hit him, Marky! Get behind!" The fat man yells but his boy just stands there watching, his lips crusted with sugar.

Harold spins Maldeflour away from the desk and throws him into a pile of stacked-up dog cages.

"I hate this kind of misunderstanding," Harold says,

straightening his coat and checking to make sure the carnation in his lapel wasn't crushed. A little trickle of blood has started seeping from the cut on his neck. "I'm surprised at you, a dumb move like that."

"Get out of my barn."

Harold pulls out his six-shooter. He's carrying his father's old Colt .44, not the most practical weapon on the market, but full of memories.

"Pigeye loses, like I said. I got five C notes on the Silver Wringer and I need the money."

He looks at Maldeflour for a minute, then hooks the pistol back under his arm and starts to walk out. He stops in front of the door and turns.

"Everything's getting a lot more complicated. I can sympathize with that. I don't mean for you to suffer. But try to see things from my position. I got a reputation to uphold. Try to put things in a historical context. If someone else's into you, just let me know, I can take care of him. Pigeye's got to lose. It's not just the money, it's pride, too. You fuck up and I'll be back. You can count on that. Call the cops if you want to, they cost more than I do and can't offer half the services."

"I ain't afraid of you."

"You should be, you should be. Sometimes I have to do things I don't much want to. Up until now we've been riding on luck, but that can't go on much longer, not the way the place is coming apart."

"You don't . . ."

"Look! We made a deal on this race. You got to live up to your side of it, understand?"

Maldeflour doesn't say anything so Harold turns and walks out the door. He knows the fat man would be more than willing to shoot him in the back, but he figures he'd hear the desk drawer open in time. He'll move faster once he gets in the alley.

"What's he want, Uncle Mal?"

"Shut your hole, Marky."

Roy is waiting for Laughing Harold on the corner. He's the lookout, skulking under a streetlight with a snap-brim fedora shading his heavy eyebrows. He's about as inconspicuous as a beer truck at a christening.

"I didn't see anything boss," he says, glad that Harold is back. When Harold became president of the Royal Ruby Vipers, he made Roy his warlord and they've been together ever since, with the exception of a brief tour Roy spent in the slammer.

"We going to walk back boss?"

"I don't guess there're any buses down here anymore."

"He going to fix that dog okay?"

"I hope so Roy, I certainly hope so."

They walk along in silence. This neighborhood is almost empty. About half the buildings are boarded up and abandoned, and most of the basic public services have been allowed to die out. Even the local rats look a little lean.

Roy drags his left leg when he walks. Some kid in a rival gang shattered his kneecap in a rumble years ago. Harold always felt bad about the fact that Roy got hurt, and tried to take care of him. There was a period of awkward late adolescence when they were too old to be in the Royal Ruby Vipers but not old enough to start to put the Baine Gang back together. Harold spent most of his time with his childhood sweetheart, Beatrice, but since the younger kids had gotten a corner on the numbers-running business and wouldn't let anybody over eighteen in, there wasn't much for Roy to do except stick up liquor stores.

He wasn't too bad at the liquor store work, except he had an unfortunate habit of picking up a fifth of ninety proof and heading down to the river bank for a celebration, a modus operandi that even the cops managed to figure out. Around that time Harold had himself plugged into the criminal justice system well enough to know who to pay to get the arresting officer to ignore the collar, but it didn't work once, and Roy fell for one to five. He was on the streets again after eighteen months, but he was bitter. It wasn't fun anymore, and spending all day watching TV in the joint hadn't done his leg any good, either.

"Hey mister, you a real gangster?"

"Get out of here, kid."

"No honest, are you?"

"Get the fuck out of here, kid."

"No, really, would you sign my tour book?"

"What'll we do, boss?"

"Walk faster, Roy."

"Cause I've seen TV gangsters on TV and . . ."

"He's still following us."

"Hey mister, wait up!"

"Ignore him, Roy."

"I could bust him?"

"Just more trouble."

"Hey mister . . . !"

They get back to the Rolling Ring but Harold doesn't go in right away. He decides to stand out in front and watch the people stroll by.

"Bring you a beer, boss?"

"Thanks Roy, later."

The rain has softened into a gentle mist and the bars have their lights on because of the premature twilight, getting the evening under way early. A lot of the daytime tourists are still hanging around, but they seem tired and could probably be easily intimidated. The first drunks are staggering in the streets, some arm in arm and singing, others perched alone on the edges of gutters, spaced like a random scattering of red-eyed scarecrows. There's a fight in progress half a block away, and it doesn't look like anybody is going to try to break it up. From a window above a broken-down bakery a woman wearing an orange wig is yelling about stolen milk, her voice cracking with the heavy energy of her fear, while below her boys roll old rubber tires toward a trash fire burning on the sidewalk.

Harold spots a group of nighthawks coming up the far side of the street and looks the other way, pretending not to notice. They're a recent development down here, cut-rate whores that operate in packs, trying to turn a dozen tricks a night, and not above a little assault with intent if the time is right and the lights are low.

One of them sees Harold and comes swaggering across the street on six-inch stiletto heels, her body advertised by a satin halter and a pair of cut-off jeans not quite as tight as a thin coat of cheap paint.

"Head for ten bucks, huh slick?"

"I'm busy."

"Do it right in front of your pals for twelve-fifty. Show everybody how you're a big man."

"I said I'm busy."

"You look like a local," says the whore, pouting up a kiss that's crooked from the lipstick-soaked sore on the corner of her mouth.

"He is," Roy says, coming back with a beer.

"Oh yeah? How about you, meat face?"

She dances an awkward shimmy in front of them, slinging her loose tits behind their shiny satin bags in a parody of seduction. They both ignore her so she turns and struts cackling back toward her pals, one of whom jerks up her skirt and starts banging the air at Harold and Roy, shouting, "Ten bucks! ten bucks! ten bucks!" her voice about as pleasant as a winter wind in a junkyard.

"Damn!" says Roy, "but I'd . . ."

"Yeah I know, but be cool, be calm, they'll go away."

The other nighthawks get into the act too, dancing and jabbering and making so much noise that even the woman above the bakery shuts up long enough to find out what's happening. Just about then the rubber tires on the trash fire catch and the acrid black smoke drives the nighthawks up the street.

"Dirty bitches with their goddamn . . ."

"Yeah, well Roy, what the hell," Harold mumbles, smiling vaguely at the wet nimbus around the streetlight on the corner.

"But *damn,* boss, they . . ."

"You know Roy, it's just because of the tourism, that's all. You know the old regular customers, the agents and salesmen and all, they wouldn't mess with anything like that. It's these tourists coming in out of the suburbs trying to deal with their paranoia by confronting it in the ghetto."

"Huh? Their who?"

"That they're afraid. That means the fact that they're afraid."

"Yeah, shit they should be. Those nighthawks are, are . . ."

At the far corner the women separate into two gangs, shrieking laughter and curses at each other in parting, their shrill cries punching above the street noises and their bare arms flashing off-white in the rain light like the bodies of fish being waved in the shadows of the market.

"Yeah, well Roy, they have a hard time. It's funny how something as simple as hooking could get so fouled up. I guess it's because where the money's getting to be, you know?"

"Well, yeah, boss, I mean, but not exactly . . . ?"

"Well, you got the basics of people buying the right to do things to each other. That's been from way back. And when things start coming apart it's in these basic kinds of businesses that the bad cracks first start to show up and . . ."

"Hah! Bad cracks! You said bad cracks and those . . ."

"Roy. This is serious."

"Yeah, shit boss, sure, fucking is . . ."

"No, but not just that, Roy. It's gotten so all the high prices are in pain now. A john'll pay double to do something he thinks the whore might not like."

"Yeah, people don't have . . ."

"But that's lousy, Roy, don't you see it? Something went wrong somewhere, too many crummy pleasures requiring somebody get hurt."

"Yeah, I guess so, boss."

"Hey mister . . . ?"

"It's that kid again!"

"Look kid, get out of here, okay? This is no place for . . ."

"No, really, can you sign my tour book? I got to get a gangster, see? I got a bookie already, here, see? And this fancy one is a prostitute, and these two messy ones are winos except I didn't need two but the one signed and then the other had to too and . . ."

"Okay, gimme the goddamn book and then get out of here, okay?"

"Thanks, mister. Laughing Harold, what is . . . is that a name? That don't seem like a regular name and . . . okay, okay I'm going, but say, you know an undercover cop? I get an undercover cop and . . ."

Harold slams the door in the kid's face and walks up to the bar, Roy following behind him, dragging his dead leg.

"You can't even lounge around anymore without some . . . ," he says, turning into the blinding pop of a flashcube.

"Damn."

"Boss, you . . ."

"I got to get in the back Roy before I . . ."

"Yeah, here this way, can you see okay?"

"Before I kill . . ."

The tables in the back of the Rolling Ring are usually reserved for the regular customers. The ceiling is lower back there because of the big staircase coming down from the second floor. The place is empty now except for Leroy, a good-looking dude in a gaudy pink suit.

"Say Harold man, how're you doing?"

"Say Leroy."

Harold sits down at the next table. He and Leroy play cards sometimes, but they aren't exactly pals. Leroy's a pimp, and Harold's enough of a snob to want to preserve a basic distinction, although Leroy pulls in more cash in one night than Harold makes all month.

"You got any directions on which pooch's happy tonight?"

"I wouldn't put any money on Pigeye."

"You think old bacon face hasn't got the ankles?"

"I think he might be a little on the sick side, as a matter of fact."

"Is that right? Well, I guess we can just about figure who that's leaving, can't we?"

"You tell me . . . Hey! Get out of here with that camera! You aren't supposed to be back here. Roy?"

"Okay boss, I got him."

"Put the gold on the Silver's how I read it," says Leroy, "the gold on the Silver."

Harold leans back in his chair until it's propped against the table behind him. He hangs a cigarette from the corner of his mouth and sits staring like he was reading something written on the far wall, although actually he's just near-sighted and too vain to wear glasses. His clothes look a little seedy, although they have the obvious flair of the flashy downtown style. His face is long and appropriately pale for someone who spends most of his life indoors, and his skin has that classic sallow tinge that's at its best in the subdued light of an Inner City bistro. He's grown a skimpy little mustache that tends to make his slightly unsavory appearance almost endearing.

"Hey boss, I got rid of him."

Harold pries open the aspirin bottle he keeps in his pocket.

"Could you get me a glass of water, Roy?"

"Sure, boss, you want another whiskey?"

Harold doesn't answer. He looks like a television announcer who finished what he had to say too quickly and so is trapped in the white light of the camera, nothing but a piece of tense meat waiting for the rescue of a network commercial.

"There isn't much pleasure in it anymore, Roy. Not much pleasure at all."

For Maude, at least, the night world is nothing but bad theater. The guts slid out that day thirty years ago when they planted Big Jim Baine. When he died, she said she just shriveled up inside. She said that her body might belong to her customers, but Big Jim was the only man that could touch her heart.

"Or whatever," Todd said, since all the touching Big Jim ever did with the ladies was a lot more carnal.

"That would be a damn long poke," Donnard agreed, "even for him."

Laughing Harold is willing to put up with Maude's jawing because she was like a mother to him, along with a dozen or so other whores who were beached when Big Jim died.

"We loved your father, Harold," they used to like to tell him, weeping their mascara into black streaks down their cheeks, "we really did!"

With Big Jim gone, the task of raising his boy fell to his associates. Laughing Harold never had a real home, so there didn't seem to be any reason why he shouldn't continue living on the second floor of the Rolling Ring Bar. At least there would always be plenty of people around to look after him.

In the late afternoon the boy would go from room to room while the ladies got ready for the night. His mouth stayed shut but his eyes were wide as he watched them paint themselves and pluck their eyebrows and unwind the pieces of tissue paper that they used to put a wave in their hair. They touched their breasts with powder puffs and speculated in soft laughing voices about the customers who would be coming. They sat around half-naked in their lacy bras and panties, and it seemed like each of them had a photograph of his dead father on the wall, draped in black crepe, sometimes even with the ruby eye of a votive candle burning in front of it, reminding the boy of Christmas, when a lot of the whores in the Inner City would make the trip to the Rolling Ring to give him presents.

Before work, one of the whores would always be detailed to tuck him in. Sometimes as she was helping him change into his pajamas, she'd fiddle with his little pecker and ask him what it was for.

"To do pee-pee."

"Is that all?"

He'd look at her puzzled and as often as not dive into the bed and hide his head under the pillows giggling. That meant it was time to get tickled and if the whore wasn't in a hurry she'd ripple his ribs good for him while he rolled around and squealed in delight.

"Is that *all* that you're going to do with it?"

He'd hide under the covers and start barking like a puppy.

"When you get big, aren't you going to use it for something else? Aren't you going to be giving the ladies their pleasure?"

"*Bark-bark-bark!*"

"You're a silly little doggy, aren't you? I'm going to cut it off!"

"No!" he'd squeal and dig deeper down into the bed. The whore would tug him out and finally get him squared away but he'd be so excited he couldn't sleep. He'd hold his penis cupped in his palm to calm himself until he became drowsy. Even as a baby he never sucked his thumb. Right from the beginning he soothed himself to sleep by gently pulling on his little pink prick.

"There's no respect anymore," says Maude, sitting at the bar and muttering at anyone within range. "Nobody cares about their product, no sense of responsibility." The bartender keeps just far enough away so she can't aim anything at him.

When Donnard remarked on the control she exercised over her smile, Todd pointed out that she never was much of a smiler anyway, things didn't seem to please her. She was always right on the edge of disappointment, just waiting for fate to kick her on in.

"That's a fact."

"She tried to follow Big Jim into his hole and we all figured it was because she was so grieved but actually it was more personal. Maude was an early feminist. She always said the world was unfair to women and when the man she considered to be more or less hers somehow got hit, she must've said, there, you see, that *proves* it! She always felt she had a good reason to be a sourpuss, but it was a stroke of sheer good luck to have it out where folks could see it like that."

"I don't reckon she ever even noticed that Big Jim didn't get much satisfaction out of that afternoon," said Donnard.

"We thought she got it out of some magazine, but I guess she always had it inside her. You could tell by the way she enjoyed feeling bad."

"That's a fact," Donnard said. "And I guess in the long run she come out better than anybody since she got a good amount of that feeling bad stirred up and spread around town where everyone could benefit from it."

Todd smiled, asked Donnard if he wouldn't have another shot of old Red Eye. Donnard allowed as how he would.

"Bartender!"

That day when Maude flung herself on Big Jim's coffin, they had to unpeel her. She tried to jump down into his grave and they had to hold her back. After they got him properly covered up with dirt, she started shrieking at the Snobble brothers, or rather what was left of them since Billy the Butcher was already dead and Orville had been blinded and Bandy was all taped together and hung from crutches and not looking real cheerful about the Snobble family's future. It was pretty obvious Donnard and Todd were just toying with them.

"Maude went after the Snobbles with her fingernails and a couple of the boys had to hold her back while we took Bandy and his brother and stuck them down in the basement," Todd said.

"Bandy yelling and crying all the way."

"He was, wasn't he; I'd forgotten about that. But how about another round?"

"Don't mind if I do."

Laughing Harold was four at the time. He stood there at the rim of the hole, dressed in a cute little black suit, his hand held by a whore he didn't know. He picked up a clod and threw it down in, *thunk* against the hollow-sounding oak box. No doubt he didn't know what was inside. People kept staring at him and that made him restless. He wasn't exactly afraid, but the whore that was minding him kept hugging him and weeping, calling him her poor little angel. He struggled and punched at her to get away because she was smothering him.

After the box was buried, Donnard and Todd stood behind him. He looked around but they didn't say anything. Donnard held up a package. Todd opened it and pulled out his father's six-shooter and showed it to him. Most of the hoods and whores had started getting into their long black cars for the ride back downtown but a few stopped to watch. The pistol hung above him glittering silvery in the bright morning sunlight and he must've thought he wanted it. It was so heavy he dropped it the first time but they picked it up and handed it to him again. It was a chrome-plated Colt .44 with pearl grips. Engraved along the barrel were the names of every woman Big Jim had ever slept with. The names were tiny and crowded together, like he never doubted he was going to need a lot of room.

"One thing though," said Todd, "was that the barrel was only about two-thirds filled. Big Jim was cut down in his prime."

"That's a fact," said Donnard.

When they gave it to him he was still too young and was mostly attracted by the sparkle of the thing. After he was older he used to read through the hundred-odd names, squinting, trying to make out the little letters, perhaps wondering which one of them might have been his mother.

He added only one name, all by itself—Beatrice.

"What'd she want?" Todd had said.

Donnard shook his head, finger-combed his wavy brown hair out of his eyes and fitted his hat back on. "Maude's a wild one."

"She wants one of the Snobbles?"

"Bandy, she wants Bandy, she says Bandy's the one that sold the boss."

"How come she thinks it was Bandy?"

"I don't know."

"You tell her it likely wasn't that simple?"

"Nobody's telling her nothing. She's whooping and bawling and hollering and running around the room trying to get out. They're keeping her locked up. They thought she'd get weepy drunk and go to sleep but all she did was get wild. They even tried to get some music on the radio."

"Music?"

"To soothe her down. It didn't work."

Todd looked at Donnard. "It isn't really fitting that she should be the one to do Bandy."

"Bandy's a two-bit punk."

"Yeah, but she's only a woman."

"You want me to go do them then?"

Todd kept looking at him. "If the Snobble boys are involved, it seems a shame to waste them. Once they're gone, there's not going to be much of a link leading back out to whoever ordered the contract on Big Jim. Let's hurt them a little, then talk to them one more time."

"They're pretty scared, they're likely to say anything."

"I know. That's the problem."

Big Jim had told the Snobble boys to stay downstairs and watch the door while he took a bath. Bandy wanted to get laid and saw his chance. He talked Billy the Butcher into waiting there alone while he and Orville went across the street for a quickie. That was the mistake. Billy Snobble was a cold-hearted killer but he was also the only guy dumb enough to let the torpedoes get through the door. Nobody liked him much. They called him the Butcher because he got ugly when he used his bowie knife. Maude still believed that Bandy set it up figuring the hit men would let Billy take a dive, but all Bandy was interested in was a piece of ass. It was just bad timing.

The torpedoes mumbled something and Billy said, "Huh?"

They mumbled again.

"Say what'd you say, I can't hear you?" Billy opened the door.

As soon as he realized what was going on, he went for his hog's leg, a regular old-style fast-draw competition, except he always wore this baggy zoot suit and the hammer of his Colt got hooked up on one of his belt loops and he was so excited he blew a hole right through the top of his foot.

Later on, Bandy said how it didn't seem fair that everybody should get punished for one guy's stupidity and Todd didn't even bother to remind him that he was the one who was supposed to be guarding the door.

Billy got his rod untangled but by that time they were on top of him and had already got the loop of piano wire twisted around his neck.

"Catch hold of his other arm," one said.

"Where's it at?" said another.

"I don't know, can't you find it?"

"It must be under him."

"Never mind then," the first guy said, and that must've been just about the last thing Billy the Butcher heard in this world.

Big Jim didn't have much longer. He probably caught the sounds of guys' boots running up the stairs, a couple of wrong doors kicked in, likely a screaming whore or two, and then the bathroom door smashed open and two guys standing there grinning with tommy guns.

It was narrow in the bathroom so they had to stand shoulder to shoulder and one of them griped about how he kept getting burned by the hot shell casings flipping out of his partner's gun. "They ought to modify these damn things," he said later. "They ought to design them so they throw the empties forward, the same direction as the bullets are going."

"How d'you think you can do it?"

"You could weld you a flange on here at the exit port, get you a good piece of brass and that'll solve her. You get them empties going out forward, the innocent bystanders wouldn't have anything to worry about."

The guy had little white blisters all over the top of his hand. He said it didn't hurt at the time but it hurt later. They shot two pans each to make a lasting impression.

"It was damn comical the way a bunch of the bullets got to ricocheting around together inside that old iron bathtub, like they was chasing each other around, groups of them, the whanging sound like a sort of crazy jitter music. Except we didn't notice that the bloody bathwater was leaking out all over our feet ruining our shoes."

"Yeah."

"We ought to get extra money to afford new shoes."

"Yeah."

After the funeral, Donnard and Todd got drunk. They figured they'd get mean and go bust somebody. They said they'd go up to the other part of town and just start in on some sucker walking down the street. They thought they'd be able to get mad.

But the whiskey didn't seem to catch hold. They said

they felt like two empty zoot suits hung on coat racks carved out of turds.

"I don't guess we'll see anybody like the boss again."

"No telling how the boy'll turn out, him spending all his time peeping on the whores."

"That's a fact. Nice little tyke, though."

"Nice enough, nice enough. But the boss had class, the boss was a real player."

"Yeah. Remember when he almost hit that old lady?"

"Yeah. He was going down the road in that old V-8 of his and ran right through a red light. Those two old maids were crossing the street and Big Jim almost hit one. The other came over and tapped on the running board with her umbrella. Big Jim always said how she had a face looked like something the cat threw up. Mister! she said, you almost ran over my sister! Big Jim just smiled at her and said, hell lady, how was I supposed to know she was your sister?"

They told themselves later that they really had thought they were going to go out and mess somebody up. It's funny how you can't tell how you'll grieve.

After the hit men left, a lot of people went up to see what it looked like. There were pieces of Big Jim blown all over the bathroom, even chunks stuck to the ceiling. It was hard to clean up. They had to use a paint scraper on the walls and a rat-tail brush to ream him out of the bullet holes.

"We wanted to collect him all together for burial but an awful lot of Big Jim got rinsed down the drain."

Laughing Harold and his gang are sitting around one

of the green felt-topped tables in the back of the Rolling Ring playing blackjack. Maude is perched on a bar stool kibitzing whenever anybody's sloppy enough to give her a peek at his down card.

Harold riffles a fresh deck. "I guess it's still my deal?"

Actually Maude is only about half paying attention to the game. She's gotten herself cranked up on gin and is complaining about everybody's favorite topic the last couple of years, the breakdown that's taking place in the Inner City. This seems to be connected to the massive Urban Renewal project that's been going on. A lot of the outlying areas are completely leveled and the people have been forced to move into a housing project south of the Civic Center if they can't find a place to stay downtown.

"Dime ante."

"Raise a nickel," says Roy.

"Damn!" says Larry. "You can't raise it before he's even dealt the damn cards!"

Roy glares at him as a round of cards flicks out across the bright green surface of the table. Larry is the sharpest dresser in the gang and a very good man with a blade, although when there's any real work to be done he can be hard to find.

"For example, hooking. I told Shirley, I said, Shirley, if you're going to be a top-drawer hooker you got to get out there and really *hook*, get your teeth into it. The days when the good stuff came looking for you are gone, you know?"

"That so?"

"Used to be how we were like those what you call 'em French curtains, not curtains, courtesy-ians?"

"Courtesans?"

"Yeah, like that, you know, like dress really fine and always have regular customers that would make a big deal out of it and you'd have a nice place with a big bed and wine and spend some time at it. None of this one, two, three, see you next week crap, you know?"

"That so?" says Harold, watching Roy.

"Hit me," Roy says, and Laughing Harold flips out a king, "busted."

"Look at me. I gave as good as I got. You turn a trick you make a friend, after awhile it starts to mean something, you know? Okay, so he's out with his wife you don't know him, nothing wrong with that is there? It doesn't mean shit, he'll still come around, more if he knows you're discreet. She isn't his fault is she? No, I mean hell no, no more'n I'm his nor he mine, you know? Particularly if you're like one of these courtesy . . . , courtesy. . . ?"

"Courtesans," says Harold again. Roy is gazing up at Maude, probably dazed by all those pronouns.

"Larry?"

He thinks about it for a minute. "I'll stand."

"Moe?"

"There're too damn many whores Harold, nobody can make a good living out of it anymore. There's competition for the best corners and they get into these price wars while the johns just stand around gathering dust and pretty soon tourists start snapping photographs of them and I don't know what all!"

She stumbles back over to the bar to get another slosh. Harold flips over his down card. He's got two queens; he wins again.

"Fucking lucky bastard," says Larry. He had nineteen.

"And now how these nighthawks are, I mean what kind

of business is that? I mean if you ran a shoe store and after
you sold some guy a pair of shoes you went and beat him
up, I mean what kind of business is that? You couldn't
expect him to come back could you? You got to establish a
clientele and keep your feet on the ground and . . ."

"Keep what where?" says Larry and Roy laughs.

"You just watch! The damn place's coming apart."

Roy looks at Harold and says, "Bad cracks!" but Harold
just smiles and answers Maude. "That so?"

"You're damn right! And I'll tell you something
else . . . "

Dimes drop into the pool of light in the middle of the
table as Harold deals another round, the first card down
and the second one up. He deals himself a down card too.
Sometimes strangers complain that the dealer is supposed
to have both his cards face up, but Harold just smiles and
tells them how this is supposed to be a friendly game and
they get the point and shut up.

Maude starts in again about how the Urban Renewal
Program's going to strangle the Inner City. Larry tells her
she's got a mouth like a twenty-four-hour liquor store.

"Huh?"

"Always open!"

Roy laughs so hard he coughs beer back up out his nose
and Maude gets mad and stalks back over to the bar to
bother somebody else.

"Not exactly kind of you. She's old you know."

"Yeah, well . . . ," Larry says, and takes a hit and busts,
and Moe does too. Harold has an ace showing and Roy's
holding an eight and showing a king.

"You got the nine, don't you?"

"I mean, you know," says Larry. "All this bullshit about

Urban Renewal, I mean we've been *hearing* it, you know?"

"Sit down."

"Man, I mean, we got about zero gang left, just us and Donnard and Todd, who can't do anything but complain, and a bunch of worn-out old whores that you keep around here and . . . "

"I said sit down," Harold says, and he does.

Roy has to decide.

"I know you got it, don't you?"

"Only four nines in the deck, you remember how many've gone down?"

"I forgot."

"You got the odds."

"But he raises me every time I raise him. He doesn't even think about it; maybe he's bluffing?"

Harold smiles, taps his ace.

"Okay boss, I see your nickel and I'm upping it a nickel."

Harold just tosses in a dime.

"Damn! He's got that nine. I know he's got it."

Harold's smiling, his down card fitted under his ace. "Why nine," he asks, "and not a face card? Or an eight?"

"Eight?"

Darlene walks in. She's probably the best-looking woman on the block and considers herself a bona fide member of the gang, even though Donnard and Todd don't like the idea.

"How come he said that about the eight? He knows?"

Darlene's got on a low-cut lime green cocktail dress and black fish-net stockings, a little bit corny, but when it's a body like Darlene's that's involved, nobody laughs. She flips up her skirt and drags out a roll of greenbacks from the little silk purse she has fastened to her garterbelt strap.

She fans the wad and it's mostly twenties. Every guy at the table is watching her. She smooths them out and gets them all folded the same way so they look nice.

"You need any money, Harold? It gets to be kind of a lump and . . . "

"Jesus, Darlene, not now."

"Yeah, well okay. I was just asking."

"I don't think I need anything. I've got a good dog on tonight."

"Oh well, that's good. Yeah, that's better."

"I'll get you back that five I borrowed this morning."

"No, that's okay. And that twenty last Tuesday, and that ten that time you were drunk and . . . "

"Here, Darlene," he says, unfastening his cuff links. "Pawn these, they ought to cover most of it."

"You know I was just kidding, don't you? Didn't I just offer to loan you some more?"

"Yeah, okay, Darlene."

"You aren't mad, are you?"

"Roy, you playing?"

Roy throws in a dime so Harold does too.

"No, I'm not mad. It just hasn't been much of an afternoon, that's all."

"Okay, but you know Harold, anything you want."

Harold looks up at her and smiles thank you and she knows he means it.

"Well," she sighs, "I'm keeping somebody waiting." She strolls back down the length of the barroom, putting a touch of unnecessary hip action into her walk that even in its natural state is a show stopper.

"Roy?"

"Shit!" he says and folds, tossing his cards into the middle of the table. Laughing Harold scrapes the coins a little toward his side, leaving a dime ante.

"Still my deal then. Anybody for a beer?"

"You got to show us!"

Harold was just waiting for him to ask. He flips over his down card. It's a six.

"God *damn!*" says Roy shaking his head. "Damn . . ."

Harold asks Larry to help him bring back another round. Standing up at the bar waiting he starts talking about how there's some work that has to be done. Larry is nodding, "Yes, yes, I can do it," but he looks a little worried, like a guy getting told he's the one who has to go down and explain an abbreviated feeding schedule to a bunch of moray eels.

"You aren't scared, are you?"

"Me boss, are you kidding?" Larry grins and pats the bulge where his spring-action toad-sticker is snoozing.

"I don't think the Civic Center cops'll hassle you."

"Nothing," says Larry with a flip of his hand that's a little too quick. "A bunch of damn amateurs, man. But Beatrice hasn't been down here for a year, what if she won't come?"

Harold holds a full glass to his lips, watching his reflection in the mirror behind the bar. He still looks okay, but he has been drinking too much. It'd be nice to be down at the Fumbling Hen with nothing more to do than watch Little Eva bump through her new routine, the South Seas Boogie Woogie she's been working on. It'd be nice to be able to be there and not have to think about that dog race, and how he might have to hurt somebody, and how they might be getting ready to try to hurt him first.

"Just tell her like I said, okay Larry?"

"Sure, but what if . . . ?"

"Okay?"

Harold turns back with his beers. A tourist has crept in behind him to get a close-up, so he has to sidle around the guy while he fiddles with his flashgun, trying to figure out why it won't work.

"Still my deal, huh?"

Roy's got a silly grin on his mug, and one hand is obviously covering the jacket cuff of the other.

"Something wrong?" asks Harold and Roy snorts, "What? Wrong? Me? No, nothing," trying to conceal his excitement.

Harold picks up the deck and frowns like he was weighing it. He holds it to his ear and riffles it once, eyes half-closed, faking a mask of intense concentration.

"There's a card missing."

Roy's face drops open, then he slowly produces the ace he had tucked up his sleeve. Harold shuffles it into the deck without saying anything and deals another round.

"Dime ante. Get it up if you're in."

"Damn!" Moe laughs, tilting back in his chair, and Roy's ears turn red.

"You got something to do, don't you Larry?"

"Yeah boss, well, I was just going."

They play a few more hands but they're getting bored with the game. There's a cowboy show on TV Roy would like to watch, so they break it up and drift back to the bar, glad to see that the tour group has gone at last.

Laughing Harold has a lot of problems. The Baine Gang started falling apart on the day his father died and by the time he was old enough to inherit it, there wasn't much left. For a while he tried to rebuild it using guys from his old street gang, but it wasn't the same. The virgin urban wilderness that had lain back and spread itself open for his father was gone, with nothing much left but the grooves scored where Big Jim had thrust his fists in to tear out what he wanted. He was a man of vision who realized that poor people just needed a little pruning before they could be made to bloom into something worth having. Big Jim's power was the ability to simplify, to recognize in any situation what the raw materials were, who they owed, and how they could be induced to give up something they might not normally want to. Before he was killed he had put together a smoothly operating organization that was the envy of every political ward boss, businessman and pimp in the Inner City.

"Avoid overhead," Big Jim used to like to say. "Stay out of production. The service industry's where the cash is. It's amazing what folks will pay just to get you to let them alone."

Which is not to say that the Inner City didn't feature traditional ghetto values for Harold and his pals when they were growing up. They could still stalk through the brick and granite canyons alert to genuine danger any time they wanted to. There were always a few jerks around willing to try something a little stupid in order to pick up a rep on the streets. And there were plenty of rumbles with rival gangs, social activities that seemed to receive some sort of tacit approval from somewhere, probably because they weren't a real threat to anybody but the rumblees themselves. There were hubcaps to be stolen, and purses to be snatched, so it's not like there weren't things to do, and being involved in the possibility of getting killed at any moment helped the boy develop skills he might not normally have been exposed to. Harold and his pals kept busy, and when Donnard and Todd decided that they were old enough to start putting the Baine Gang back together again, there was no hesitation, although it must've been hard for them not to be aware of the fact that it didn't much matter what they did since the ground pattern was established and didn't encourage improvisation. They were willing to go through the motions, though. The basic directions had a kind of clarion quality that was addictive, if not actually nutritious, and like the dubious pleasures to be gotten from dominating pinball machines, you could pretend you weren't being had if you wanted to.

But it was only play, and Harold and a few of the brighter members of the gang could sense that in how easily their energies would be diffused. What should have been only distractions came to dominate their attention, and the night-town world of women and music and booze became more than just the appropriate milieu for the so-called underworld figures. It was all they had. The new Baine Gang was shaky from the beginning, and a lot of people in it were there simply because it was the best party in town.

Harold had relied upon Beatrice since they were kids, and she became one of the real powers in the gang, a fact which displeased a few of the more traditional members. Harold didn't feel that he had to explain his growing dependence on her. Everybody knew that the dog of Big Jim's death was always with him and so figured that he needed Beatrice to balance against that. She was a talker. She would always be the one who could say what something was going to mean. She would try to get the situa-ation laid out in words so they could see it, so they could understand what was going on and maybe shake themselves out of it.

The one thing the new Baine Gang had was class, they definitely looked sharp, and if all they had to dress for was the ceremony of watching their world break up and rot away, well, all the more reason to try to do so with a little style.

Harold closes the back door behind him. The wings of the alley are folded in shadows and loops of rope hang from a scaffolding lost in the gloom overhead. Down the alley two men are acting silly, passing a cigarette back and forth, while beyond them a hooker has ducked in off the street after a quick trick to adjust her make-up before getting back on stage.

"You're going to die down here," Beatrice told him just before she left. "Sooner or later you're going to be bad for business and they'll blow you away just like those wrecked buildings they're removing. And not because they're afraid of you, you'll just be in the way, just another useless piece of furniture to be gotten rid of."

"You think I like this, the way it's become?"

"Don't you?"

"What should I do?"

"Go down and look at what's happening. This place is going to come unglued. You and your gang, you're anachronisms, clowns. What happens when they take over the off-track tickets? What happens when they legalize gambling? You're running out of underground, you know?"

Harold tried to explain how he liked the Inner City world with it's old buildings and broken sidewalks, everything worn and comfortable from all the people who had been there.

"That's scenery. All you're talking about is the scenery. This is not some simple shakedown, you know. You should go down there and look at what progress will mean to the Inner City."

He went the next day. It wasn't hard to find the neighborhood that was being relocated. Everybody was running around out in the street, mothers and kids yelling for each other, their arms full of stuff they didn't know where to put down. The Urban Renewal Program had begun about a year earlier but had confined itself to old silos and warehouses so people didn't pay much attention. Then about eight months later it began hammering at the first tenements on the edge of the Inner City. By the time Harold got down there in midsummer, the project was in full operation.

Urban Renewal crews don't give much notice. The people in an area know they are going to go, but they don't know exactly when. The vans just show up one morning and the people are gone by that afternoon. The Urban Renewal crews have problems with inefficiency, but they can still manage to clear out a full city block in a single day.

Harold had settled himself in the shade of an awning to watch the action when a part-time numbers runner named Willy the Wisp asked him for help. His mother was being moved out to the new housing project that day and he was worried about it.

"Well hell," said Harold, "she's going to get a new apartment out of the deal, isn't she?"

"Yeah, but she don't want to go, nobody does."

"That so?"

"Say, Mr. Baine, she's real old, anything you could do

about getting them to leave right away after they put her in the van? Sometimes those bastard van drivers go off and drink beer for an hour or two after they get done loading. They don't care about nothing, they're on a salary and nobody's checking to see how many runs they make. It's real hot today, too."

About then, two guys came down the stairs in front of the tenement carrying his mother's bed, the sheets and blankets still rumpled from when she got up that morning. One of the blankets was dragging on the ground so Willy went over to tuck it up under the mattress, but the van driver told him to get the fuck out of the way.

Harold strolled down the row of green moving vans, trying to see if there wasn't something he could use. The whole place was in hysterics. Piles of tattered furniture were blocking the sidewalk, so he had to walk out in the street. The area contained mostly old houses that had been carved up into a lot of tiny apartments crowded with people, so the Urban Renewal crew was having a hard time keeping everything flowing out smoothly.

Harold figured the van driver was just another working stiff even though he was employed by Urban Renewal, so he stopped him as he was about to heave a cardboard box full of dishes into the back of the van. The guy was as tall as Harold, but about twice as wide, with the sleeves cut off his coveralls and big red arms hanging out. Harold explained what the problem was, laughing about how his pal Willy was worried about his dear old mom. "You know how crotchety old ladies can get, it'd be nice if you could get her out to her new home as quickly as possible, what with this miserable weather and the way the old suffer in the heat."

The guy just looked at Harold and when he finally figured out what he was talking about, told him to fuck off, he was tired of these crummy jerks with their crummy junk. He was going down to the corner tavern for a few cold ones and if Harold didn't like it he knew what he could try to do about it.

He threw the box of dishes into the back of the van carefully enough not to break more than half of them and walked away.

"Willy, do they always put the people in the back of the van? Maybe your mother could go out by bus or something? I've got a little cash and wouldn't mind springing for the price of a ticket, seeing as how it's a friend and all."

"They make you go in the van, they shut you in with your own stuff. I think they do it on purpose. Everything has a number stamped on it and they pin a plastic name badge on you that has that number on it."

"Well, I guess they want to try to be efficient."

"Yeah, but then those bastard van drivers go off and get juiced. There ought to be something we can do."

"That guy seems real mean, I don't know . . . "

Laughing Harold was waiting by the truck when they put Willy's mother in.

"Why don't you go by the tavern *after* you deliver the old lady?"

"You trying to tell me what to do?"

Harold didn't say anything, just held out a brown paper sack, smiling. The driver pulled out three cans of beer, linked together with a plastic noose.

"What kind of shit is this, only half a six pack . . . ?"

Harold held his pistol pointing right between the guy's eyes, the muzzle of the barrel about a foot from the bridge of his nose. The driver's mouth sank open. He was staring down the bore as if what was going to happen was written in there. Harold cocked the hammer with his thumb.

"Now you can get shot, or you can take the old lady straight out to the housing project. Enjoy those beers on the way, but drive carefully. I know your name and where you live, it's written on your vehicle registration. If you make a mistake, I'm going to come by some night when you're not expecting me."

"Yeah, well," said the guy but Harold just stood there looking at him with the big ugly gun in his hand and that was that. Later, after the last of the vans had lumbered away, special demolition squads moved through the buildings placing dynamite charges. The dust blown up from the explosions stained the setting sun into a huge bloody fruit and Laughing Harold waited under it, watching as it sunk vaguely from the dirty sky, trying to figure out what was going on and what it was going to mean.

Willy came back once it got a little darker.

"I didn't much like doing that. It always seems to get back to you, sooner or later."

"Hell, Mr. Baine, you scared that guy good. Big Jim himself couldn't've done it any better."

Harold looked at him then fitted a cigarette between his lips. "Who?"

"Oh, well no, I didn't say . . ."

"What's a punk like you know about Big Jim?"

"Well nothing, of course, I just thought . . ."

Harold stopped him, suddenly realizing that the odd sound he'd been hearing was the clanking treads of advancing bulldozers.

"Big Jim's dead. Don't you forget it."

"Sure, Mr. Baine, sure."

Harold never did find out if Willy's mother made it safely out to the new project or not. Walking back through the Inner City he stopped near Beatrice's apartment, but he wasn't quite ready to talk to her yet, so he continued on to the Rolling Ring. He went back out to the Urban Renewal area the next day and the place was completely deserted. The bulldozers had scraped the rubble into middens spaced about every hundred yards. There was nothing left but a dog whimpering miserably on a concrete slab that must have been a front porch.

"Here, poochy, come here boy."

Harold wandered through the leveled area until he came out at the other end, the dog trailing him from a safe distance. There were some old factories that had been abandoned a couple of years earlier. Beyond them was another open space, stretching for almost a dozen blocks, also marked by the evenly spaced mounds of rubble, some over a hundred feet high. Harold stood on the edge of that section and squinted, trying to force his eyes to focus on the black glass towers of the Civic Center. He could see the hard yellow dirt at his feet, and the nearest mounds of rubble, but the Civic Center towers were only a blur, and beyond them was nothing, a gray blankness.

The dog skulked up behind him, its tail between its legs.

"You look pretty well fed, you must be from the part that got knocked out yesterday. That was your home, huh pal?"

Harold hadn't known so many outlying districts had been demolished. The rim around the Inner City must have been completely destroyed already. There were weeds growing on the tops of these middens, which would date them from at least before the spring rainy season.

Gusts of wind moved across the deserted plain, throwing up twisters of dust clouds that would hold for a hundred yards or so and then collapse back.

"Sure is lonely out here," Harold said, and the dog caught his tone and moaned in agreement.

Harold walked out into it for a few hundred feet and stopped beside a huge midden. On the leeward side was a black circle of earth with the charred ends of burned sticks marking the circumference of a campfire. Harold kneeled down to feel if the ashes were still warm and noticed that some of the sticks were actually the burned ends of broken bones. He stood up quickly and looked around but there was no one in sight.

"Somebody out here, dog?"

There was nothing, no other indication, but Harold knew he had arrived at the beginning of something, and he was probably going to have to try to follow it out. He stood there in all that awful open space and realized Beatrice might not know the extent of whatever it was that was happening. He hurried back, pleased by the fact that he had a legitimate excuse to go see her. He let himself into her apartment, but it was empty, cleaned out, echoing hollowly as he went through it searching for some indication of what might have happened. There was nothing left in the silent rooms but a snarl of tangled wire coat hangers on the floor of the closet and a broken ball-point pen left inexplicably in the bathtub. Suddenly he realized that whoever took all of her belongings might have taken her, too. She might have been kidnapped because she was onto something the Urban Renewal people didn't want her to know. There was no sign of a struggle, but they could've surprised her. Harold slammed the door behind him and ran down the two flights of stairs to the manager's apartment.

"Miss Cotton," he said, his voice sounding like a child's, "on the third floor . . . ?"

"Yes?"

"Where is she?"

"She's not here."

"I know, I know, what happened?"

"When?"

"I don't know when! To Miss Cotton, where, did she . . . ?"

"She moved out."

"What? By herself?"

"Someone might have helped her, I don't remember . . ."

"What? What do you mean?" Harold said, again aware how unsubstantial his voice was.

"Sometimes I don't remember some things so good without a little help." The manager smiled.

"Huh? Help?" Then Harold got it and yanked his wallet out so fast he ripped his pocket.

"Well, there were two men, big ones. They could've been cops, from uptown like. They had this van and . . ."

"A bust? She got busted?"

"Well, I might not remember that exactly." He smirked, hand held out for another ten bucks, except this time Harold grabbed him and slammed him through the doorway, pushing until he was arched backwards over his television and easily scared enough to talk.

The manager told him that it had seemed pretty amicable, and although the cops had made a few snide remarks, Beatrice evidently treated them like servants and they put up with it. "So it must not have been a roust," Harold told himself, "not a roust, then, not a roust," trapped by that idea and stumbling home to its rhythm like a man on stage with his foot stuck in a bucket.

Marky's got his finger probing up his nose. He's being careful. His nostrils are raw and he doesn't want to open up any old scabs.

Maldeflour notices what he's doing and belts him in the back of the head with a bratwurst.

"Sit quiet. This here's the police office, show some respect."

Marky doesn't say anything; he just climbs back up on the chair to wait until his uncle looks the other way.

"Sometimes I'm sorry your maw died. Better it'd been her stuck with you than me."

They're sitting in the waiting room of the Police Captain's office. There's a secretary in there too, but she's staying as far away from them as possible.

They had come out to the Civic Center as soon as Laughing Harold left the dog barn. Maldeflour tried to make Marky stay home but he wouldn't do it; he kept following him. Maldeflour threw rocks at him but he was clever enough to stay just out of range. At last he had to give up and let him come.

"You ain't worth a damn, not a damn. I can't even trust you to check the coin returns on public telephones because I know you'll palm the damn dime if you find one."

Marky just kept walking behind him. He'd filled his pockets with eating sugar and so had enough to last him for several hours. On the way, Marky caught a stray cat but couldn't figure out what to do to him. "It's a cryin' shame we ain't got no gasoline," said the boy and his uncle told him he guessed he could carry it over to the river if he wasn't so damn lazy. "You might go in with it, far as I'm concerned, I never did figure to be taking care of no kid." Finally Marky took a chance and dropped it in front of an oncoming dumptruck but it landed running and made it across the street unharmed.

"Shit," said the boy, "that ain't no kind of luck."

A buzzer on the secretary's desk sounds and she tells them the Police Captain will see them now.

"I reckon he will unless he's got his eyes shut," says Maldeflour and laughs.

The secretary doesn't say anything but just smiles and presses against the wall as they go past her. Marky pulls on his uncle's sleeve. "Say, you catch a look at them big tits?"

After the door closes she gets an aerosol can of disinfectant and sprays the two chairs where they were sitting. On her way back to her desk she stops and thinks about it for a minute then takes the cap off and fogs the whole room.

"The boy can sit over there against the wall."

"Set yourself in that corner, Marky."

"I want to sit in the chair by the police desk."

"He wants to sit up here."

The Police Captain looks at the kid. He remembers the last time he was here it ruined his lunch. The boy doesn't seem to have improved any, but there's nothing much he can do about it.

"Okay, but let's make it quick."

Maldeflour places the long gray bratwurst sausage on

the Police Captain's desk. "We brung you a present. We smoked it ourselves; it tastes good."

The Police Captain looks at it. He doesn't ask what it's made of. He thanks him but doesn't move to touch it.

"What do you want, Maldeflour?"

The fat man leans back in his chair. He opens his shirt pocket and peers down into it, then pulls out a piece of cigarette and sticks it between his lips.

"Gimme one too."

"Shut your hole, Marky."

He finds a wooden kitchen match in his other pocket and scrapes it along the side of the Police Captain's desk leaving a yellow scratch mark.

"You promised. You said if I followed what the law said you'd make sure I'd be okay. I done what the law wanted me to, now you owe me one. This here dog race, it's coming out like it's supposed to, but that guy ain't going to like it."

"Who?"

"Harold Baine."

"Oh. Big Jim Baine's boy. So what do you want?"

"Him killed."

There's suddenly an overpowering smell of urine. The Police Captain leaps to his feet. "He's pissed his pants!" he yells. "He did it again!"

"More'n likely," says Maldeflour. "He ain't but barely human."

"Get out of here!"

Marky just sits there looking at them, his face serene. He's got a fistful of sugar now. The whole front of his coveralls is soaked through and drops are puddling up under the cuff of his right pant leg.

"I said get out of here!"

"Not until we get this matter agreed. I followed the law, almost six months now, you got to get me this man killed."

"We don't work that way," the Police Captain says, but Maldeflour doesn't move.

"That gang stuff is gone. He's no threat, he stays in his place."

"Killed. I want him killed dead. You remember you said I'd be okay, so you got to do it. I followed the law, now I want mine. You know he got his woman living down here in this big Civic Center Complex you got here. You can use her. She can get him to come so you can rub him out."

"It doesn't happen like that, Maldeflour. That old-style gang war stuff is bad for business. Tourists don't like real bullets."

"Her name's Beatrice. I don't know the rest but she came down here a year ago. You use her."

"No promises, Maldeflour."

"Killed dead, I want it. You owe me one."

Marky's still sitting there, dreamily sucking on sugar.

"Come on, you think you going to live here?"

Maldeflour gets the boy standing up and pointing toward the door, then busts him in the back of the head, knocking him flat in a shower of moist sugar.

"Pissin' on the police rug, I never heard of such a damn thing! Like I said, sometimes it seems like a real shame your maw up'n died on me like that."

They go out and the Police Captain buzzes his secretary to come in with the disinfectant and a pail and some rags.

"And bring a pair of big tongs too, there's something on my desk."

• • •

Beatrice is standing behind a glass door watching the rain beat into the boulevard that borders the Civic Center Complex. She's got an umbrella but doesn't feel like walking the five blocks to her apartment building yet, so she turns and rides the escalator down to the big shopping center in the basement. She strolls along the center of the corridor feeling very calm, very much at ease. She usually tries to limit herself to two joints before five o'clock, but the rain was making her feel blue so she smoked another just before leaving work and now she feels fine.

She goes into a clothing store and browses. The clothes are nice but conservative, appropriate for civil servants; they don't really move her.

"Is there something I can show you?" asks a clerk.

Beatrice just stares at him. "What?"

"Would you like to try something on?"

"Oh," she laughs, "I was daydreaming. No, nothing, thank you." She hurries out, surprised to be so stoned.

Mixed in with the shops are a few bars and restaurants and these are starting to fill up with municipal employees. Beatrice doesn't usually like to hang around after work, but she is lonely today so she glances into the dark bars, half hoping to see somebody she knows. There's a jangling in her head and everything she looks at seems somehow connected to what she's going to see in the next instant, giving her the frightening feeling that her brain is leaping forward making connections she can't quite follow.

She enters a large, noisy bar and sits down at the darkest end. She's looking at a martini in front of her, wondering why she ordered it when some guy sits down beside her.

"Say, don't I know you?"

"I don't know," says Beatrice. "Do you?"

"Didn't I see you this afternoon?"

Beatrice considers moving but there's no place left to sit and she's too stoned to feel like standing at the moment. That last joint was one too many.

"Can I buy you a drink?"

Beatrice tells him no just about the time the double martini lands in front of her.

"You're on the Press Secretary's staff, aren't you? You were sitting right behind him at the press conference. I guess you are plugged in pretty high."

"There must be some mistake."

"Sweetie, it was you!" Beatrice feels a knee moving against her leg, pushing up against her thigh.

"No, I mean I don't do anything. I'm just there."

"You were busy, I saw you. He was asking you questions. Hell, I wouldn't forget a face like yours," he says, trying to look down the front of her blouse.

"He was faking it," says Beatrice. "Complicity makes his lies seem more plausible. It's like . . . like when, you know . . . "

"Yeah?"

"Uh, what was I saying?"

"About how the Press Secretary confers with you to make his remarks seem more plausible."

"Oh, yeah. That's right."

"And . . . ?"

Beatrice tries to tell him that she has to be going. She should have known better than to pile booze on dope. She can't tell if he just wants to take her to bed or if he has something more complicated in mind.

She looks at him again and suddenly gets it. "You're a cop, aren't you?"

He shrugs. "I might be. But I'm more interested in what *you* might be."

"This a bust?"

"No sweetie, not this time." He puts his hand on her thigh and squeezes.

"You're a fine-looking big lady, but don't you be getting too wrecked tonight; I might need you."

"Who the hell *are* you?"

"You let me worry about that. I'll see you later, doll. I know where you live."

Beatrice watches him work his way out, then tries to follow him but falls. Somebody helps her up and she gets into the bathroom. She locks the door behind her and flicks on the overhead exhaust fan then sits on the toilet, trying to read the graffiti. . . .

It always comes back to the same thing: that she's lost her lover. She and Harold were together for almost their entire lives. There must've been a thousand times when if they'd have only done something a little differently, they would have been okay. Ten thousand opportunities, how did they manage to miss all of them? Where was the slight voice, revealing itself in the wind unfolding summer trees, telling them how to get clear?

It's not so much she minded being a whore, she got used to that soon enough. She was tough, born and raised in the Inner City, and it was fun being the best around.

But Harold had to keep talking about it until she would scream, "It's fine! It's fine! Just stop trying to justify me to myself!" and he'd shut up.

She takes a long hit on the joint, holding the smoke deep in her lungs. Someone knocks on the door and asks her if she's all right. She doesn't want to answer but knows if she doesn't, they'll go get a passkey.

It's not that I hated that world, she tells herself, pretending that she's also Harold. We always knew what it was like. The Floating World, we called it, and tried to pretend that nothing mattered. You understand, don't you? I just didn't want to die there. I was born there, but I didn't want to die there. You understand, don't you Harold? I'm getting older, I'm always going to be alone. You don't know what that's like for us. It's different for women. You understand, don't you?

She takes a last hit off the joint and drops the roach into the bowl. First, she isn't moving because she's listening to the hiss of the roach fallen in the water, then it's because of the action of teardrops puckering the surface of the same water. Standing before the mirror she wipes her face with Kleenex and realizes there is some connection between water and glass. She feels very strong as she walks out and finds the front door after only a single false start.

Then she's moving down the corridor and the directions are written on the walls so she doesn't have to try to understand them. She's in the central underground plaza, has been there for a few minutes without noticing. There are lovely multilevel pools splashing into each other, and brightly colored carp swim blindly in circles through the silver water. A small sign beside the main pool tells Beatrice these fish are a tough new variety that can thrive in the artificial atmosphere of the Civic Center Shopping Arcade. They're a cross between the gaudy orange and yellow Japanese carp and a variety found in subterranean pools in Venezuela whose eyes have atrophied from centuries of living underground in total darkness.

"Venezuela," she pronounces the beautiful word, "Venezuela, Venezuela . . ."

She sits by the edge of one of the pools, trying to get things sorted into some kind of structure. Nearby are machines that sell packages of scented food and some kids are feeding the fish, floating the white spheres lightly on the surface. The carp detect them by smell, nosing up and swallowing them whole without nibbling and hardly ruffling the water. The kids sit quietly and watch the fish feed. Beatrice realizes she's only pretending to look at the fish and is actually just staring at the smooth surface of the water.

"Venezuela . . ."

You understand, don't you? It's not so much that I was afraid of dying, but I didn't know what to do about being alone. I didn't seem to have myself. I'd be sitting in an empty room and get the crazy feeling that there was *nobody* there, *nobody at all!* You understand, don't you darling?

Beatrice touches her hand into the water and the surface shatters into broken mirrors of white light. She jerks back as if she'd been burned.

"You'll scare the fish."

There's a kid staring at her with glasses so thick his eyes seem like enormous jellies. She looks down at her wet sleeve and starts laughing. She's discovered another conjunction. "Venezuela . . ."

Then she's on the escalator, surrounded by kids with cameras. They're riding up and down and up and down, taking pictures of each other as they slide past and handing the developed photograph across on the next trip. Beatrice stands at the top of the moving stairs and watches, sensing that there are patterns before she can actually distinguish them. The kid on the way up always poses, standing stiffly, occasionally with one hand raised as if waving, while the kid on the down escalator does the photographing.

In an alcove under the escalator is a knot of kids squatting in a ring, going through handfuls of photographs. They pluck out particularly interesting ones and show them to each other, the colored rectangles stuck up from their pudgy fists like the barbed plastic tags that indicate price per pound in butcher shops.

Between her and them are the advancing stairs, and it's here that Beatrice begins to sense she's touching into ritual. Because those kids are showing the same picture again and again, and each time the other kid duly nods approval, agrees it's interesting, even though he must've seen it a dozen times already.

This happens occasionally in the Civic Center Complex. The moment is often couched in the form of play, and is always illusive, as if it wanted you to think that all you would have to do is just allow yourself to be sucked in a little closer. From up here Beatrice can't tell if the kids really look at the picture or just fake it, and for some reason that distinction seems like it might be important.

"Venezuela."

She sees the steel teeth of stairs rising toward her like frozen water, frightening in its orderliness. She doesn't seem to be able to move; she doesn't seem to be able to go back down there. It's as if she's afraid she might hear them chanting, might hear their childish sing-song voices reciting the mindless words of some grotesque cabal, the poems of a dying empire preserved in the petrified language of its nursery rhymes.

Then Beatrice is in the rain, walking fast so she doesn't
have to deal with the tears on her cheeks. The rain falls
steadily down between the tall silver buildings, filling the
city with a false twilight. If it wasn't for the irregular red
and green eyes of the traffic signals counting themselves the
length of the boulevard, if it wasn't for those reds and
greens, it'd be like living in the milky canyons of the moon.

By the time she reaches her apartment, she's running.

Harold realized he had underestimated Urban Renewal.
Walking back into the Inner City that day a year ago he
could feel that there had been some sort of subtle shift and
he wanted time to work out the implications. Block after
block of wasteland was bad enough, but beyond that was
the idea that Beatrice's disappearance was somehow connected to the Civic Center's program.

He got back to the Rolling Ring hoping for some kind of
message but all they told him was that Maude's cat had
thrown up in his shirt drawer. He sat up at the bar with
a water glass full of straight rye whiskey. Donnard and
Todd were the only people who could get near him.

"She told me she was going to do it, but I always figured
I'd be able to stop her when the time came."

"That so?"

"I thought it might take care of itself."

"Your father was always very direct. He always went
straight for the throat."

"That's a fact, Harold. It's a shame he died before you
were old enough to know him."

"He was crazy about you. He said you were going to
become something legit, probably a lawyer."

"I guess you don't remember him?"

"Not well, like in a dream, him standing in a doorway telling me good night, a couple of whores trying to hurry him but him just standing there looking at me. Except I can't see his face because the light is behind him, just the huge dark shape of his silhouette, with the glowing coal of his cigar burning like a single eye."

"He was shot down in cold blood, Harold."

"I know that."

"Something's got to be done about it."

"I know. I'm working on it."

"We're getting old. We want to be in on it but we're getting too old. We owe it to the boss."

"Big Jim's been dead for . . . "

"For his memory then, Harold, in honor of his memory."

"But he still *is* dead. It doesn't matter."

Donnard and Todd looked at each other, their faces cool and as patient as snakes.

"But Harold, the guy that ordered the contract on him isn't dead yet."

"You think I don't realize that? You think I have any chance at all of not thinking about that?"

Donnard and Todd didn't say anything, just sat there waiting and watching him drink.

"I'm working on it, all right?"

"We know you're not afraid, but we worry about the delay."

"I said I'm working on it."

"We know, Harold, we know."

Harold spent days trying to discover what had happened to Beatrice. He felt stupid wandering around asking people if they knew anything, but he didn't seem to have much choice. Roy suggested that he might try Tony Pizzicato. Harold didn't care for the idea since turning to an outsider like Pizzicato was the same as publicly admitting he was losing control, and there was already a lot of grumbling about the breakdown of the Inner City.

"He's a real nice guy though."

"You know him?"

"He just asks me questions."

"What kind of questions?"

"Just questions: what I like to eat, what are my favorite TV programs, like that."

"Why?"

"He said he's just interested."

"And he writes all this down?"

"Naw, he says he just remembers. He's real good at remembering things. It's what he does."

Harold figured if he could run into Pizzicato by accident it wouldn't look too bad, so he got back out on the streets again. Tony Pizzicato was one of the few people to move into the Inner City at a time when most people were talking about leaving. He set up a private detective service that was rumored to specialize in all kinds of unconventional work. Harold didn't know if he was an actual private gumshoe or just some fancy new breed of con man. One thing that everybody could agree about was that Pizzicato always knew what was going on. Harold wandered around for a couple of hours but couldn't seem to make the connection. He did find out that most of the locals were dealing with Pizzicato.

"You get the weather?"

"So I know how the track will go, make odds for the mudders."

"Why don't you just watch the TV weather report?"

"No man, Pizzicato *knows*, in fine detail."

"And you pay for it?"

"That's what's nice. He just says he's doing me a favor. Some day I can help him back."

"That so?"

"It's like this service. He's real friendly."

Pizzicato's apartment was on the roof of the Bijou Theater. There was a long steel staircase fastened to the back wall of the building with a sign that said: TONY PIZZICATO, EXPLANATIONS & GLOSSES. The alley behind the theater abutted an empty section of the river bank, and since nobody was around, Harold took a chance and went up.

"Come in! Come in! I know who you are, glad to meet you at last! Company here, Arabella," Pizzicato shouted over his shoulder. "Make yourself presentable."

Harold was surprised by how short Pizzicato was. He looked at lot bigger when he was dealing on the streets.

"I know what you want. Don't hang back. Come in and shut the door. It's always drafty up here, wind blows off the river, you know."

"Yes, I suppose so."

The inside of the place looked like a TV repairman's idea of a seraglio. The walls were lined with all kinds of electronic gear, oscilloscopes and banks of vacuum tubes piled on each other, many of the units linked together with insulated cable. There was about an equal amount of ostrich plume fans and pornographic bric-a-brac, some of it evidently instructional, and parts of the room were obscured by diaphanous veils hanging from the ceiling. Harold noticed a strange smell in the apartment, like a mixture of incense and marijuana and burned insulation material.

Seated in the corner on a pile of silk cushions was the largest woman Harold had ever seen. She was draped in layers of veils and long silk vests. When she reached over to stub out her joint, an immense left breast swung into view with all the weight and authority of the history of Islam.

Harold slowly removed his fedora.

"Mr. Baine, allow me to introduce Arabella Barella."

Harold nodded. He didn't trust his voice yet. She was wearing a lot of costume jewelry, some pieces of which were actually small electronic devices. There was one little machine she wore around her neck like a choker and whenever she spoke, the looped filaments in a row of vacuum tubes behind her glowed like fiery worms.

"Arabella used to be with the circus."

"That so?"

"There's one of her old posters pinned to the back of that door."

Harold looked at a picture of Arabella lying naked on a beach. She was somewhat younger then and couldn't have weighed much more than three hundred pounds.

"That's fine," said Harold politely, "a good likeness."

Tony indicated a cushion and Harold sat down cross-legged, his hat in his lap.

"Joint," offered Arabella. "Pill?"

Harold declined. A bundle of insulated cables was protruding from the mountain of pillows she was reclining on. They disappeared under a bank of veils so he couldn't tell what kind of devices she was plugged into, but from the thickness of the bundle there must have been a lot of them.

"You can always tell a saucehead," Arabella said. "They get nervous easily."

"Arabella!" said Tony shaking his head. "When she's high she gets the giggles. It's something to see, the whole room trembles."

"That so?"

Pizzicato seemed genuinely glad to meet him and so Harold gradually lost his distrustfulness. The man's enthusiasm was infectious and Harold found himself explaining his situation with a lot less hesitancy than he would have thought possible.

"You want to find your woman, I can understand that. I'd be lost without sweet Arabella," he said, fumbling around in a pile of veils until he found her foot and gave it an affectionate squeeze. "But I don't do much missing persons work anymore. Not that there's no business, mind you, sometimes I think half the population's missing."

He disappeared behind a heavy silk drape to get a couple of bottles of beer.

"I'm running a detailing service now," he continued, "providing glosses. There's a staggering amount of sludge out there that people have to deal with and a hell of a lot of them are foundering. It's largely a case of too much information, so I try to help my clients develop methodologies for sorting through the bulk of it in order to try to figure out what they might have to be able to know."

"I don't exactly understand."

"Tony can explain it to you," said Arabella.

"I used to do it mostly with computers, but now I'm depending more and more on stacking it up here," Tony said tapping his head, "because detailing has become largely a matter of explication and sorting."

"The Philistines got Tony booted out," said Arabella, sucking on another joint.

Tony looked a little troubled.

"They didn't understand the leap that had to be made," he said. "They were trapped in the concepts of the past. I was working with the new super-omnicomputers. They're incredibly delicate, high-strung, sometimes they have to be wheedled before they'll even open up enough to start the information retrieval process."

"The others were all hard-hearted men. Tony was the only one willing to pamper them. The newest machine in particular needed a great deal of attention."

"Uh," said Harold, "what I had in mind was finding where this woman went and maybe getting a message to her."

"There are those who doubt that our computers can love us," Tony said. "I am not among them, I assure you. The problem is in the rigidity of the scientific mind, always insisting on verifiability as the only measure of value. Proof! Proof! What dog shit! They think that what is real is what can be proven. Stupid! Hopeless! I have spent rainy autumn evenings alone with the newest super-omnicomputer, leaning with my cheek pressed tenderly against its console, and actually *felt it yearning for me!*"

"Because it knew you were simpatico," said Arabella.

"Or," said Harold, "maybe just her address . . . "

"It's their neurotic craving to deal only with the 'real' that is the culprit. They're constipated! They simply want something they can hold in their hand and point at and say, 'That, god damn it, at least is *real!*'"

Arabella laughed. "Tony, you're a card!"

"Picky, picky, picky!" Tony said, ignoring her, starting

to get himself worked up. "As if something that 'appeared' to be *out there* could be the only arbiter. I tell you, Harold, it's a habit formed from childhood, taking physical properties too seriously."

"Tony's beyond the hardware side of it."

"Not true! Not exactly true, there's a pleasure to the gadget I don't deny, but the so-called smart boys place too much emphasis on the merchandise. They ignore the implications of nonactual entities."

"Nonactual entities?" said Harold.

"Those aspects of information that haven't stumbled into the stupefying rigidities found in your average 'X is—and only is—Y' type of proposition."

"Tony thinks logic sucks," said Arabella.

Harold didn't look any less puzzled.

"He was forced out of the Academy."

"By idiots!" Tony said getting more excited. "By the same clowns that walk around denying that electrical devices can have a sense of humor when the fact of the matter is we simply haven't been able to discover what they think is funny!"

Tony was on his feet, rubbing his hands together and stalking back and forth between two pink veils. Little white patches of spittle were forming at the corners of his mouth and Harold was afraid he might be going to have some sort of fit.

"That's right!" Arabella started clapping her hands, huge slabs of flesh hanging swaying from her arms. "Yes, that's right!"

"I ask you, Harold," Tony said more calmly, "what love is if not the process of distinction followed by selection, plus," and here he paused dramatically, "the ineffable that makes it glow!"

Harold nodded.

"And *that* is the very crux and central jelly of computer science! Just because the machines don't choose to secrete . . ."

He stood looking out the window and shaking his head slowly. Beyond him Harold could see the eastern mountains glowing in the afternoon sun.

He turned and looked at Harold beseechingly. "Could it be that I've misunderstood the true nature of love? We distinguish shapes, colors, and attach labels: these are arms, legs, this is a head, and then arbitrarily select one head and decide to call it beautiful, desirable. Why?"

"I don't know," Harold said somberly. "That's just the way it is."

"And then to deny that elemental process to anything that is not living, it doesn't seem fair."

Harold looked at Arabella and she smiled reassuringly. "He'll be okay, he's a very emotional man. So few people truly love them, he feels they're just being *used*. He'll be better after awhile."

"But why does he take it so personally?"

"He's been denied access to systems he helped to design. There was a prolonged court battle but in the end the judge found against him. He was declared unfit. It was a question of reciprocity. Court was convened in the computer center but he couldn't get the newest super-omni-computer to respond. When he asked it if it loved him, the print-out was evasive. His lawyer tried to argue that it was just being coy and that *that* was prima facie evidence of emotional involvement but the judge didn't agree. After the trial he was a broken man. He still had rights to use the standard models, but the one that was the heart of his heart was forever denied him.

"But come back tomorrow, he'll have your information for you. He's just a little overwrought now."

Harold stopped on the way out and patted Tony sympathetically on the arm, saying he was sorry. Tony just nodded and continued staring out the window.

Harold went back the next afternoon and everything was fine. Pizzicato opened a fifth of bourbon and they drank the whole thing. Somewhere near the end of the bottle Tony took Harold into his bedroom. There was a hole bored through the floor that came out right above the theater's movie screen. He'd devised an upside-down periscope and told Harold how he and Arabella used it when they were balling.

"Hell," said Harold, "the location's all wrong. The way you've got it you can see everything in the theater *but* the damn screen."

"Yeah," Tony said, "that's the way we like it. That's what turns us on, the mystery of the thing. All those suckers lined in rows, the silvery light flickering against their faces, lost in illusion under that empty space while I'm here high above them, whooping it up on sweet Arabella!"

"You're bitter!" Harold said. He tried to imagine what they must look like but he couldn't do it, he was too drunk.

Later on that night they ended up down at the Rolling Ring drinking beer. Harold doesn't remember how they got there, although there was some sort of scuffle on the way. Tony had started yelling at a sidewalk peddler who was hawking automatic onion slicers, shouting that utilitarianism was a betrayal of the promise of the imagination. The guy didn't know what he was talking about, but he didn't like Tony's tone and was about to bust him one when Harold intervened and said that Tony was under his protection.

The rest of the night is vague. At one time Tony tried to explain to Darlene about some ex-colleague of his who wanted to teach computers to literally copulate, using tubes and valves and motor-drive units, and how *that* was a complete misunderstanding of everything he had been trying to do. Darlene didn't seem to know what was going on, but she was attracted by Tony's energy.

"Everything is a metaphor for something else," he told her drunkenly, "and literal-mindedness is the only heresy. A computer doesn't *really* have a memory, it *metaphorically* has a memory. The same is true of love. Trying to teach computers to *fuck!* Intake ports and rubber nozzles, that's dis*gust*ing!" Darlene agreed it was unusual.

"Damn right," said Harold, not following the conversation but totally convinced of the correctness of his new friend's explanation.

Much later they were stumbling arm in arm through dark alleys, trying to find Roy. The plan was that they'd get some muscle then go find the heretic who had misinterpreted Tony's theory of computer love and beat him up. Nothing came of the idea since by the time they actually got under way they'd been drinking long enough to guarantee that they were only marginally mobile.

Harold woke up the next morning with the worst hangover he'd had in months. Crumpled in his jacket pocket was a piece of paper with Beatrice's new address written on it. She'd moved to the new developments, practically in the center of the Civic Center Complex itself. It was one of the few places in the entire city that he really couldn't go without risking a bust.

He sat staring at that paper with his head pounding, trying to remember if he had realized the night before that the whole point of her new address might well be to let him know that she was finally out of reach.

Harold's getting bored sitting in the Rolling Ring. He's got a couple of hours before the dog races start so he figures he might as well take a walk, get a little exercise.

"Roy?"

"Yeah boss?"

"You busy?"

"Well, I'm watching this cowboy show and it's real good. See, this clodbuster's wife and kids get all killed by these guys so he gets all crazy and . . ."

"Okay, Roy. Forget I asked."

Outside it's still misty. The twilight sky seems a lighter gray now and wisps of clouds veil up the slopes of the hills east of the city, fit themselves into dark pine-filled canyons and dissolve between the fingers of dripping trees. . . . Not that Harold can see that far, for him it's just a smooth crepuscular wash of distant blues.

He strolls down the bank watching the thumping brown waves on the swollen river. Caught in the support pillars of the Fifth Street Bridge is the corpse of a red cow. Harold spends a moment with the idlers who are speculating on what ought to be done about it, then crosses the bridge and comes back up the alley that runs behind the Third Street Station. Lots of business down here too. There's something about this weather that gets the citizens on the bottle.

He stops in front of the Fumbling Hen. The photographs of the girls are beaded with rain but he can pick Little Eva out easily. A group of tourists slip in behind him, snickering at the pictures. He turns to leave, but there are three nighthawks coming right at him.

"Hey slick!" yells the one with the sore on her mouth. "Don't waste your money just eyeballing it!"

"Ten bucks! Ten bucks, cheap!"

Harold gets through the door. He can still hear them laughing at him. They know better than to try to hustle inside bars, but it's bad luck running into them twice on the same day. The stage is empty except for Little Eva's cardboard palm tree in the corner, so he sits at the bar to wait for her next number. He could go back to the dressing rooms and look for her, but there are always a couple of chorines hanging around half-naked and he doesn't feel like getting involved with them.

He shakes a pair of tabs out of his aspirin bottle and notices that it's almost empty. He'll have to remember to get some more. An unfamiliar girl steps on stage with a boa constrictor and a clear plastic tub full of whipped cream. Harold motions the bartender over.

"Nope. Haven't seen her."

"She hasn't been here at all? No phone call or anything?"

"Nothing. The manager's not real crazy about her missing work like this. Stick around and wait if you want, that snake's fun."

"No thanks, I never did care much for animal acts."

Harold checks a couple of places on the street, but nobody has seen her. Little Eva has come in late before, but never more than a few minutes, and tonight she's already missed her first three sets. He feels a little strange going through the process of searching for her since it was almost exactly a year ago that he did the same thing for Beatrice.

The trouble with looking for Little Eva is that there isn't any place she wouldn't be. Harold has always been a little puzzled by the ease with which she seems to get along. He was the one who found her a room in the Rolling Ring, telling himself he'd be like a big brother to her. He tried to explain to Beatrice how there were so many runaways flocking to the Inner City that the least he could do was help with lodging. Then one morning he woke up and Little Eva was sitting on the edge of his bed without any clothes on.

"You must've enjoyed that."

"No, well Bea, you know . . ."

"You don't have to say anything. She's a lovely young woman."

"Well sure, she's young, sure."

"And her figure is marvelous, those thin hips and tiny waist, her behind is no bigger than a boy's, and yet her bust is certainly very fully developed, isn't it?"

"Yeah, well, I didn't really notice. You see she was just . . ."

"Didn't notice?"

"Well, noticed a little maybe, was noticing some and then maybe wasn't so much noticing as, as . . ."

"As what?"

"You know, Bea. I mean . . ."

"But I don't mind, Harold, really I don't. I might even try sleeping with her myself."

"Oh, now Bea. I was just sort of sleepy and she was just sort of naked and . . ."

"How interesting! And how are you just *sort of* naked?"

"You know, Bea."

"Then you wouldn't care if I just *sort* of slept with her too?"

"Oh, now Bea, she's just a kid."

"Oh really?"

Harold spent the rest of that day wandering around the Rolling Ring getting absolutely nothing accomplished. Beatrice was clever enough to continue to point out to him that she understood perfectly, which of course was a lot worse than if she'd have gotten mad and made a scene. Little Eva didn't seem to be aware of any complications, and if Beatrice ever did try to make love to her, Harold never found out about it. Harold wasn't worried about Beatrice forgiving him since she always did sooner or later, but there were a couple of awkward days when her usually comfortable cynicism was a little brittle and her smile a little too pointedly ironic. Harold knew enough to stay away from Eva for awhile.

He tries a place down by the river where a lot of runaways hang out, but he can't find anybody who knows where Little Eva is. He figures they might not tell him even if they did know since a few of them still have problems with parents who want them back for some reason.

The search is probably hopeless, so Harold lets it slide into being nothing more than another stroll through the Inner City. This is how he has been spending a lot of his time recently. It's a kind of incantation for him, this aimless wandering through the downtown alleys, as if it were some sort of ritualistic reconstruction of the lady he's been searching for since she left a year ago, and maybe from even before then. He remembers Beatrice in terms of these weathered old buildings. It's not so much a direct connection as a shared element, as if both reflected whatever it was he had hoped was going to nourish him. But it's hard now not to realize that they are empty shells, and that the quality of the old way of getting along he finds in them might be nothing more than a reverberation from his own yearnings.

Her voice is still with him, although the timbre is vague. It's liquid, lilting, shifting mixtures of blues and greens, telling him about drifting, saying, "Harold, you're nothing but a water plant floating through the world, a broken bit of duckweed on the current, don't you even care?"

There was nothing he could say to her. He wanted everything to stay the same. He pretended to think that she was still mad about Little Eva, but they both knew that wasn't the case. If Beatrice had any deep misgivings about the girl's addition to the Rolling Ring, they didn't last long. Little Eva's energy and youthful enthusiasm drove everything before it, and having fun became infectious. She would wake up early in the morning, leap out of bed and slide down the banister in her baby-doll pajamas. Pretty soon the whores were doing it with her, everybody ending up in a pile at the foot of the stairs, giggling like schoolgirls. They wanted to put in a jukebox. They wanted to hold sock hops on Friday afternoons, but Maude put her foot down on that. She would be the last one to have anything against nostalgia, she said, that's obvious. But the Rolling Ring had a reputation to uphold, and decorum was important.

"A honky-tonk needs decorum?" asked Darlene, and since Laughing Harold wasn't around, somebody else muttered that a bunch of tinhorn gamblers weren't exactly high society. Maude was adamant. "There may be a place in the trade for children," she said. "But not here."

A group of the younger hookers appealed to Beatrice to help them but there was nothing she could do.

"Maude's all business," she told Harold in bed later. "I wonder if that's because she's so old. She doesn't seem to take much pleasure in anything else."

Harold looked up from her ample breast to explain again that he really had been surprised by Little Eva's precocity. Beatrice laughed and shoved him away, telling him to get out if he was going to fantasize about somebody else on her time. Harold was sincerely trying to make it up to her, so she sighed and settled back, giving him her nipple again.

"For somebody raised in a bordello," she said, "there sure are a lot of things you don't know about women."

Harold turns into the twilight gloom of the alley behind the Roxie Theater and stops in front of the body of a dead dog lying on its back against the wall, all four legs pointing stiffly at the sky. Harold hunkers down and watches it. It looks real dead, no question about that. Its eyes are crusted over with dry papery scales.

Up there in dog heaven, I guess.

He feels the weight of his revolver pulling him down, the clear smell of its oil coming up complicated with that of the decaying corpse. There's something alive in the dog's mouth, something white and shiny that's crawling out of the throat. Harold stands up abruptly and turns away from the dog.

Being dead. That is not the way to get along.

He moves down the alley heading for a main street. He wants to be out walking with people.

"Evening, Harold," says Todd, and Donnard nods, takes

off his fedora and wipes his bald head with a handkerchief. "Muggy enough for you?"

Harold doesn't say anything. He's been trying to avoid them lately.

"We're going over to the Buckingham Palace Hotel. We got some business there. For you, Harold, we're helping you."

"That so?"

They both smile up at him, just like two old grandfathers except for the gaudy suits, and their cool eyes inexpressive as clams.

"Mr. Donnard has not been well. He's having trouble keeping food down and his stools are bloody. It's time, Harold, it's time. It should've happened years ago. What if your father's enemy should die of a heart attack? How would you feel then?"

Harold doesn't say anything. He just stands there watching the people walk by.

Donnard starts coughing, deep broken gasps racking his whole body.

"It's time," says Todd, "time to get that son of a bitch now."

"I'm working on it."

"Tonight or tomorrow. We're helping you. We think we have a guy for you."

"A guy?"

"A torpedo, an out-of-towner, somebody nobody up in the Civic Center knows."

"I don't work like that."

"We figure he could be used to make a direct frontal assault and while they're trying to stop him you could get in the back way."

"I don't like to work with people I don't know."

"We'll call you about it later. You'll be at the Rolling Ring?"

Harold nods.

"Sure you will. It's time."

"Aren't you going to invite me in? I told you I knew your address."

Beatrice unhooks the safety chain, steps back out of the doorway. She isn't really surprised to see him.

"This is a nice apartment you have here. Lovely view of the city. The Press Secretary must pay you an excellent salary."

"I work hard."

"I thought you said you didn't do anything?"

"I don't know if I do anything or not."

"Ah," he laughs, "the strain of that? Still, I've been on the Force for fourteen years and my apartment stares into a blank brick wall."

He eases himself down into a chair and tells her his legs ache. He's on a semiofficial visit. There've been complications that she might be able to help them resolve. A complaint has been made against Harold Baine. There's been a long-standing unwritten agreement between the Force and the Inner City of mutual tolerance that for their part they would like to see continued. When he saw her this afternoon, he recalled that she had had strong connections with the Inner City. Perhaps she could arrange a meeting?

Beatrice stands with her back to him, looking out over the rainy city. He comes up behind her and she feels his breath on her neck.

"We want to help you," he says, one hand resting lightly on her shoulder. "We know you haven't been as happy as you might have expected. But before we begin, perhaps you would like a drink?"

He shuffles over to the bar. "I like this kind of gin, too. Did you know that the secret of the great gin and tonic is to pour the gin through the slice of lime?" He smiles at her, then turns back to the bar. "Unhappiness," he says, "is a psychological problem. More than fifty percent of most psychological problems are caused by causes in the sufferer's own head. Documented fact. More than fifty percent. Other causes are accidents, diseases, birth defects at being born, and unusually severe external conditions such as torture or prolonged imprisonment.

"Lifers," he continues, "are inevitably nuts. When we were students at the Police Academy we were required to do field work in the prisons. It was an experience I'll never forget. At that time they could be viewed from two o'clock in the afternoon until four. It was a sobering spectacle."

He hands her a drink. "Here's mud in your eye."

Beatrice takes a small sip. She's afraid she might throw up.

"I always thought you ex-hookers drank a lot. There's still things about being an inspector that I haven't learned. It's a challenging life."

He limps back to his chair.

"You're probably wondering about my injuries. See that knee? The patella is one hundred percent stainless steel. You know what a patella is?"

She shakes her head. Her hands are trembling.

"It's the kneecap."

He sticks both legs straight out in front of him. "Each tibia has an axial pin reinforcing it. The right fibula here is attached with gold wire at the top and at the bottom. The femur's sixty-six percent stainless, too."

He looks at her, waiting for her to say something.

"That's awful," she manages. "What happened?"

"Two motorcycle accidents, hit by a bus once, fell down a flight of stairs. Got beat up by a couple of junkies one time; got shot with a hand gun in this leg on two separate occasions. Approximately two years ago, I sustained severe wounds in both legs from a twelve-gauge shotgun, pellets in the groin too, superficially wounding the penis and the scrotum." He stops, smiles at her. "The penis was pierced," he says carefully, "but thanks to alert action by the emergency ambulance crew, it was saved intact. Almost exactly one year ago, I got thrown down an elevator shaft by a suspected felon who was resisting arrest. I had to spend three months in traction.

"As you can see," he says clinking the ice cubes in the bottom of his glass, "the life of a police officer is filled with peril."

"You should be more careful."

"Oh, don't worry about me. I'll die in bed. Ninety-two percent of all police officers die in bed once they pass the rank of sergeant. Cigarettes, booze, a high-calorie diet, those are the real hazards."

He gazes reflectively into his empty glass so Beatrice asks him if he'd like another. He laughs and says, "Sure, what the hell, you have one too."

He sits watching her make the drinks. His heavy thighs are spread apart loosely, his slacks stretched tautly over the soft clot of his genitals. He fishes a small metal tool out of his pocket and is tapping it against his leg when she comes back. It looks like a thick gold fountain pen except there are a couple of levers on it and some sort of calibration around the barrel. At one end is a steel loop and Beatrice realizes that it's actually a hook with the barbed point tucked safely behind a little metal flange.

"A present," he says holding it up, "from the Captain." He presses a lever on the side of the barrel and the hook springs out on the end of a four-inch shaft. "It's very sharp. It's supposed to be some sort of fisherman's tool but I have other uses for it."

He tastes his drink. "Did you remember to pour the gin through the lime? You forgot, didn't you? Weren't you listening to me?"

Beatrice says she's sorry.

"How can I help you if you don't pay attention? This is a very complicated business and if we don't help each other there could be unfortunate consequences. This Mr. Baine is an acquaintance of yours, isn't he?"

"I haven't seen him for a year."

"Do you have any reason to believe he's involved in any illegal activities?"

"No, I don't."

The Inspector laughs. Beatrice stands in front of the window again, leaning until her face is pressed against the glass. She can see the rain beating against the outside but it's perfectly silent; she doesn't even get a sense of moisture. The window is sealed and for some reason she realizes that it's probably unbreakable.

"I'm sorry," he says. "I shouldn't have laughed. But I get the feeling that you don't trust me. There's so much of that now, it adds to the breakdown in the dialog between the community and its police force."

Beatrice doesn't look back at him.

"This Mr. Baine, it's possible that in the past he may have been involved in prostitution or gambling but that now he's pursuing some other line of work, don't you think?"

"I have no idea."

"You have no idea." He opens a small case containing a portable polygraph tape recorder.

"This is just a formality, this machine. We like to use it whenever we interview someone. It helps the interviewee avoid errors in recalling information and frees the police officer from the need to try to remember where the inconsistencies occurred. It's one of our most valuable tools."

He tells Beatrice to lie down on the couch. He attaches a small wire to the inside of her elbow, brushing the back of his hand slowly against her breast and then looking her in the eye and saying, "Excuse me."

He gets the machine running and tells her to answer two questions in the negative.

"Is prostitution legal?"

"No."

"Did you ever work as a prostitute? Did you?"

"No," she says at last.

He turns off the machine and asks her if she'd like another drink before they begin. He tells her she should relax, she has nothing to be afraid of.

"What do you want?"

"It's not what I want that's at issue. It's what you want. People evidently have a very high opinion of you. I have been asking questions and your conduct is irreproachable. There is the consideration of your personal happiness and in this we have been willing to be patient and allow you to work through your anxiety. Sometimes we wonder if part of your problem might be the fact that you possibly have not broken from your emotional past as cleanly as you would have liked. This is understandable.

"Things are complicated by this charge against Mr. Baine. We had hoped that he too might be persuaded to join us, but he has evidenced no interest in civic affairs. It troubles us when official police matters become contaminated with emotional entanglements, so first we must help you understand what you are doing and why.

"Try to relax and not worry too much about this. These things happen in human lives but it's best to begin working on them as quickly as possible.

"We understand you, we want to help you, all you have to do is trust us."

A kid comes into the Rolling Ring and says he wants to talk to Mr. Baine. The bartender asks him his name and he says Tom Buck.

"So, Tom Buck," says Laughing Harold, "two guys? But you don't know who they are?"

"Just two old guys. They said they seen you around. They said you'd know who they are. They gimme two bits and said you'd gimme two bits too."

He has his hand out. The palm's clean but from the wrist up it hasn't been washed much recently.

"It must be Donnard and Todd. I thought they were going to phone." He gives the kid a quarter. "Behind the old Vogue Theater?"

"Yeah. They said as soon as possible. They're waiting."

Harold tells Roy to stick around for about twenty minutes in case Larry gets back and then to come over looking for him. They're going to synchronize watches except Roy's has stopped. They try to borrow Darlene's but she doesn't want to do it, so finally they decide Roy will just have to keep an eye on the grandfather clock behind the bar.

Harold starts working his way down the alley behind the old Vogue, not exactly sure this is what he had in mind for the evening. It's dark back there, and lonely. He'd much rather be back at the Rolling Ring watching the dog races. There's a bare light bulb burning down at the other end of the alley, but beyond that he can't see a damn thing. Those shadows back there are just garbage cans, right? Funny how from this angle it looks like they're moving.

"Mr. Donnard? Mr. Todd? You in here?"

Harold never has cared much for this kind of clandestine stuff. It always seemed to be mostly play acting to him. He moves around a couple of crates.

Wham! It feels like the whole building fell on him, smashing him flat. There's a lot of weight back there, but it's grunting a little bit too much to be bricks, and those things grinding into the middle of his back feel an awful lot like knees. He's pinned down, one arm crushed under his chest and the other jammed against his side. His coat gets ripped up over his head and something, a foot or an elbow, slams into his back and then his gun is gone. He even hears the *whang* it makes as it lands among the garbage cans on the other side of the alley. He moves slightly, trying to feel how much room he's got, rocking both ways to find out which direction is softest, but he's not real cocky, these guys are all over him. It'd be nice if Roy showed up right about now.

A guy on TV used to carry a little derringer tucked

behind his belt buckle and when he got caught in a jam he'd wait until the right moment, then flick it out and get the drop on the heavies. Harold wanted to do that too but he had trouble keeping the thing stuck behind his belt. He'd get a little juiced and forget it was there and go into the bathroom to take a leak and shake it out, *plunk,* right into the urinal. Guys pretended not to notice of course, but he'd still have to reach in, fish the damn thing out and wash it. When he'd go back into the barroom, everybody'd have a real straight face but they all knew. He'd have to say something like, "stupid little *pea*-shooter," so they could let it off laughing.

Harold hears a piece of piano wire being uncoiled. If he doesn't make his move pretty soon, it's curtains. One guy is kneeling on his back but now the other is squatting in front of him, getting ready to loop the wire around his neck. He knows this is a real poor way to do it, you ought to always use a garrote from the back. Harold twists up to the side and shoots a knuckle chop into where he figures the guy in front of him's eggs are. He has the geography right except the dude has on some kind of hard plastic jockstrap and Harold just about breaks his hand. He realizes that these guys must be cops, nobody else would go in for a dumb piece of gear like that. Now he's twice as mad at himself because this kind of dark alley rub-out is typical of the off-duty cop style and he was stupid enough to fall for it.

The guy he cracked does go over though, and Harold manages to get his thumb deep enough into the other one's eye to loosen him up. He jumps up and is hot-footing it out of there while they're still rolling around with their pain waiting for it to settle so they can figure out how badly they've been injured.

He's running with a nice even stride, heading deeper into the alley, when he hears the first slug sing past him. Silencers, he thinks. These guys are careful, choke wire and noiseless gats three blocks from where anybody might be listening. They must've come out of some kind of P.R. school. He half expects to run into Roy along here but it's real empty so he figures it's just going to have to be a foot race.

He cuts down another alley, hoping to shake them with a sudden change in direction even though it means he's got that much farther to go before he hits civilization. This is all old Ruby Red Viper turf so he knows the landscape pretty well. A couple of blocks over is Roy's old place and just beyond that is the corner grocery store where Beatrice used to live with her mom. When Harold was a kid, he stole fruit there. He was small and used to wear a pair of baggy trousers that were just right for shoplifting. He was so young nobody ever suspected him and he could carry off stuff that bigger kids wouldn't even dare to try for. The first time he met Beatrice she stopped him waddling out of the store. She was three years older and a lot bigger, with a reputation for being a fast runner and a fierce fighter. She was tall and bony and always had skinned knees. She kept her hair braided so she wouldn't have to comb it. If you thought you'd look better with a black eye or a bloody nose, a good way to get there was to yank one of Beatrice's braids.

She dragged Harold around into the alley behind the store. He was scared; he knew he was going to get hit. She reached down into the front of his pants and pulled out a couple of fresh peaches. He tried to act surprised, he didn't know how the hell they got in there, but he also started crying, he was real guilty. She told him to stop being such a baby, she wouldn't hit him. He stood there snuffling with two pearls of snot drooling down his lip. She used the hem of her skirt to wipe his nose and he caught a glimpse of white panties. He was only seven but he'd had a lot of education and he knew there were certain things you were on the lookout for just like there were certain words you could get a lot of mileage from, even though you only had a vague idea of what they referred to. You took seriously what the bigger kids were interested in, it was as simple as that, although growing up in a whorehouse made it hard to catch on to the throat-choking mysteriousness of the whole business.

This time, though, all Beatrice wanted to do was play house. She'd make him a peach pie, he could be the daddy. She arranged some orange crates into a table and chairs and made him sit down. He was a funny-looking little kid with big ears and a dirty face but he was better than nothing. She said wait a minute, she'd get a knife and a pie plate. She hummed a song as she skipped back into the store. As soon as she was around the corner, he grabbed his peaches and scrammed. He didn't stop running until he got to the hole in the fence behind the Rolling Ring, a hide-out he used when the whores got too sloppily sentimental over him.

Two blocks later he takes a peek over his shoulder and they're still back there, still right behind him, and he's got a good four blocks to go before he hits a place where any people are. He ducks down into a narrow alley that leads through a bunch of abandoned warehouses out toward the edge of the Inner City and for a minute thinks he might've ditched them. He slides along, staying in the darkest shadows, trying to catch his breath and realizing he never would've made another block running full speed. He doesn't have the wheels anymore—too many cigarettes. Just when he's starting to feel good about it he sees them, two dark shapes trotting steadily up each side of the alley, checking doors to make sure he's not hiding in one of the buildings. Christ, those guys are *careful*. He's too tired to do much more running, why the hell are they trying so hard? He's got about one more good idea left, so he figures he might as well get to it. He turns left at the next corner, kicking an empty garbage can as he goes by to make sure they know where he is.

Clogging this alley is a lot of old junk that he has to climb over and that's a good sign because it means people don't come down here. He finds the place he's looking for and tugs out a loose brick. The trip wire is still coiled behind it, rusty and covered with dust but in one piece. He pulls it out and attaches it to the cleat one foot above the ground, then stretches it across the alley and carefully hooks it to the ring of the spring trigger on the other side. He looks up at the big bin hanging over the alley, but there's no way to tell if it's still full of the junk they'd prepared for a rival gang one afternoon years ago. He runs another thirty yards down the alley, then hides in a doorway until he sees them again, trotting along, sniffing at the shadows.

"Yeah, flatfoots, your mothers suck dogs!"

They stop, and then start running again. The first one stumbles over the trip wire.

Harold had just assumed that if they ever used it, it would be during the daytime and they'd be able to see how well it worked, but it's so dark here that all he gets is the sound. It's possible that they might've been able to jump out of the way, but somehow he doesn't think so. The roar was a little bit too short and too loud, the shudder that ran down the asphalt a little too high on the Richter scale.

He edges back over to see what it looks like. There's no sign of anybody, just a heap of rubble. Right on top of the pile is the engine block of an old Ford flat-head six and he thinks how he hasn't seen one of those in years. He seems to remember that they'd put a transmission in too, but he can't see it anywhere and he knows he couldn't move any of those big slabs of concrete to look for it.

There's a foot sticking out of the pile. The shoe is gone, popped off with the force of the impact, and there's a little runnel of blood dripping out of the pant leg.

He looks at the engine block again. It's funny how you can get attached to old things, even old parts of cars, how things that were made years ago seem to have more character than the things that are being built today.

Beatrice believed that antiques had value because they'd survived so many possible accidents. She said museums were a mistake since all they did was attempt to stop an object's normal trajectory, to muscle in on its fate. As soon as you take something out of circulation to protect it, it becomes like a seashell, beautiful enough, but lifeless, and actually a lot more fragile because it has lost its soul.

Harold tugs on the foot but it won't move, not that he wanted it. He was just curious. A gust of wind moves the bin door and it squeaks, the hinges are rusty, it has been years. He can see the evening sky behind the empty bin. He had meant to ask Beatrice if she thought that objects had real souls, like people, but she'd removed her blouse to wash and the heavy curve of her breasts had distracted him.

He pulls some concrete blocks down over the foot, then starts back up the alley to look for his pistol. Son of a bitch, he thinks, glancing up at the night sky again, this just isn't any way to get along, not at all.

"The drink first, Maude."

"It gets infected, then where'll you be, huh?"

"Maude."

She goes over to the bar and grabs of fifth of bourbon and a glass.

"Roy?"

He doesn't say anything. His face is screwed up feeling bad.

"Did you forget the time?"

"I couldn't find you, boss. I got lost, it was real dark in there."

"Okay, Roy. That kid Tom Buck, somebody find out who he is and who bought him. Be polite but firm. It probably wasn't his fault, but he ought to get a little bad luck for not being smarter."

"You want me to go do that boss?"

"No, stick around, Roy, I'm going to need you later. Where's Larry?"

Nobody's seen him.

Maude starts working on his face with a wad of cotton and Mercurochrome. He's clenching his teeth, trying to pretend it doesn't hurt.

"That's enough." He pours himself another drink. "How about the race, you guys see it on TV?"

They all look at each other guiltily. They were watching a cowboy movie and completely forgot about the dog race.

"God damn it!"

"I'll call the track," says Darlene quickly. "I know somebody there."

She listens for a minute then hangs up, her face blanched white with shock. "Awful!"

"Well, what happened?"

She shakes her head and sits down. "They were preparing the track," she says, "getting it ready for the last race. They run over it with rakes to get out the dog turds and also the bottle caps and junk people throw from the stands. That tears up the surface so they have to harden it down again with a steamroller, one of those heavy ones."

Somebody pours her a drink.

"So what happened?"

"The Silver Wringer was in his cage waiting right over the section they were rolling. Somebody left the cage door unfastened." *Sniff!* A tear's forming in the corner of her eye. "Just as the steamroller was passing under the rail . . ." The tear spills down her cheek and she wipes it away with a hankie. *Snuffle!* "He fell!"

"My god!" says Maude. "That's awful!"

"Fell?" says Laughing Harold grimly. "Or was pushed?"

Beatrice slides into the warm water of her bath. She wants to forget the interrogation, forget everything, just empty herself into the hot water. She wonders if they are going to try to kill Harold, and if they expect her to try to warn him.

She moves her legs apart, the bath water is cooling. The dark patch of her pubic hair is fluffed like seaweed beneath the surface. She used to love the way Harold would kiss her down there, massaging her clitoris until it felt so good she almost had to make him stop. He said he could smell her on his mustache for hours afterward.

The bathroom door swings open and the Police Inspector

comes in. Beatrice sits up with a start, splashing water over the edge of the tub. She folds her arms over her breasts, trying not to show how scared she is.

"I realize this is rude of me, but you didn't answer when I knocked, so I let myself in with a passkey. There are a couple of problems I can't seem to get squared away and I'm sure you would want to do everything in your power to help clear this matter up."

He lowers himself on the closed toilet and lights a cigarette, smiling at the way she is covering herself.

"Don't you have an ashtray?"

There is one on the window sill behind her. She hands it to him but he takes her arm instead, his eyes squinting and his face flushed and moist.

"This wouldn't be the first time that a man has seen you without your clothes on. But I suppose you think you've left that life behind you, don't you?"

He takes the ashtray without releasing her arm. She tries to wrench herself away from him but his grip is too strong. She drops her other arm so he can see her breasts, and that surprises him enough to let her go.

"Free from the past," he says slowly, his face slightly puzzled. "Doesn't that have a fine ring to it. Free from the past. I wonder if it could be true?"

Beatrice sits up straighter and hugs her knees to her chest. She asks him if his superior would approve of this type of questioning, but he ignores her. He still seems a little off balance.

"But at least you are no longer involved in that unlawful behavior. Or rather you're not a victim of that corrupt social subculture where the men prey on the bodies of the women."

"Does that bother you?"

He holds his cigarette in his mouth and begins to remove his coat, grunting with the effort. Tucked under his armpit is a tiny automatic pistol.

"Your friend Mr. Baine takes money from prostitutes, I believe."

"That's not true."

"He forces them to pay protection."

"No. And he never has. He's a gambler, and the games are usually small-time."

"White slavery is an abomination."

"So what do you care? You're not in vice. In fact, I don't think there even is much of a vice squad, is there?"

"Then you admit that he was involved with prostitutes?"

"Sure. Half the hookers in the Inner City had a crush on him at one time or another. Whenever I'd turn my back there would always be somebody ready to rub up on him."

The Police Inspector smiles, his eyes drifting down her body. "You see," he says triumphantly. "You protect him like a mother, or I should say a past lover that is not quite past enough. Of course it's not unusual for there to be some residue of a past affection, but in this case it seems to be a particularly thick crust."

The long ash from his cigarette curls and then drops onto the bath mat. He slides awkwardly down to his knees and tries to flick the bits of ash into the ashtray but only manages to rub it deeper into the pile of the mat.

"I'll be quite frank with you. There are people, very unsavory people, who want to harm Mr. Baine for selfish reasons of their own. We wish to protect him, but cannot do so directly. We had hoped that he might accept a position here in the Civic Center, something with managerial responsibilities."

He places both thick hands on the edge of the bathtub and leans in toward her, his face closing on hers until she can see the little plugs of congealed oil oozing from the pores of his nose.

"He doesn't trust us. It hurts me deeply when we do everything in our power and yet people don't open their hearts to us."

"This water is getting cold. I want to get out."

He forces himself heavily to his feet, his old injuries obviously bothering him. On the rack by the door is a big fluffy bath towel and he holds it open waiting for her.

"You look lovely," he says. "I'll dry you."

Beatrice abruptly stands up, her arms at her sides, facing him boldly. The Police Inspector is again caught off guard. He falters momentarily, his face betraying the fact that he hadn't expected her to accept his offer. Beatrice steps out of the bathtub in front of him, her feet apart and her hands on her hips, waiting for him to make up his mind. Finally he hangs the towel over her shoulders, draping it down over the front of her body like a man covering a mirror.

"I might have to ask you to take a ride," he says in a weak voice. "To answer further questions."

"Why don't you leave me alone?"

"Beatrice?"

"What do you want?" She begins drying herself, watching his reaction as she rubs the towel under the weight of her breasts.

"I can't always do what I want."

"Neither can I."

"Perhaps we could help each other?"

"Perhaps we could."

"This Mr. Baine . . ."

"Why don't you forget about him?"

"You want to help us, don't you?"

Beatrice drops the towel down and runs it between her legs. He turns away, picks up his coat and opens the door. "There may be some problems later. We may have to take you downtown. The D.A. might be preparing charges."

"Charges?"

He still has his back to her. "No matter what happens," he says at last, glancing back at her quickly, "I want you to know how fond of you I'm becoming."

A formal party is under way at the Poole mansion. Everyone's dressed in tuxedos or ball gowns, everyone except Maldeflour, that is. He's wearing an old brown suit highlighted with the scattered white lace of acid burns down the front.

"What the hell's *he* doing here?" says the host.

"Shhh!" Quellabia says. "He'll hear you."

"I don't care if he does hear me! I want him to hear me! He doesn't have any right to be here. He'll ruin the victory party. I'm going to ask Jameson to show him out."

"No, daddy, don't do that, please? For me? Please?"

"What about the sterling? And my Persian miniatures?"

"You can get more. I'll tell Jameson to have one of the waiters keep an eye on him."

Her father doesn't like it but in the end she gets her way as usual. She calms him down and walks him over to where a bunch of bankers are talking about money. She holds his arm and makes sure he can feel her breast pressing against his elbow, a simple enough gesture but one that rarely fails to get her what she wants. She points out that at least the nephew isn't around and that makes him feel a little better. Quellabia doesn't mention that Marky is in the kitchen gorging on clots of confectioner's sugar she cleverly left in a big mixing bowl on the floor for him, hoping he'd make himself sick enough to pass out.

Quellabia Poole is the richest broad in the Inner City. Like most society dames, she has a taste for the low life, although this doesn't mean that she'd be interested in Maldeflour for himself, not for a minute. A lot of the Poole family money originally flowed out of somewhat unsavory sources but Quellabia doesn't know anything about that, she's strictly on the spending end. She likes slumming because she's titillated by colorful down-and-outers, thinks degenerates are stylish. She gets cautious among the lower levels, though, and not even Quellabia's kinky enough to handle a hard-core subspecies like Maldeflour. She wants him to stay because she thinks he's pals with Laughing Harold, and he's the one she's really after.

Everybody's on their feet making toasts as Pigeye is led whimpering into the ballroom, his tail tucked up between his legs.

"Sweetie!" coos Quellabia and runs over to grab the bony dog.

Pigeye looks up and recognizes her and that makes him feel a little bit better. He slings out his long tongue and licks her elegant fingers, his eyes saying something like, I'm sorry, I'm sorry.

"Precious lover!" She bends over to hug him, making sure the men in front of her get a nice long look down the front of her low-cut gown. Quellabia's always been a crowd pleaser, what with her prevalent décolletage, her aversion to underwear, her tendency to produce herself as an ongoing montage designed for public consumption.

A group gathers around her, holding up champagne glasses, toasting Pigeye.

"Fine-looking dog, that Pigeye."

"A great sprinter."

"Good wind, a very deep, deep chest."

"Yes, deep."

"Long legs, lovely thigh muscles."

"Very impressive."

"Deep . . . "

Quellabia is down on one knee, trying to hug the squirming dog. He's wiggling and shivering at the same time, trying to lick her face and in general going about three different directions.

"That there dog's a crackerjack," says Maldeflour.

"I beg your pardon?" says a dignified old gentleman, the president of a large investment brokerage house.

"Yessir, an A-number-one speedball, moves quicker'n piss pops on a hot griddle."

"Are you addressing me, sir?"

"Yep. You get you a dog like that you can run you up some money."

"Are you referring to capital gains?"

"Nope. I'm referring to dogs. You get you a speedball like that that has a long pecker on him and stud him out and always demand you first pup. You going to win you some races, run you up some money. Particularly if you get some help from a friend."

He reaches into a pocket and hands the president a filthy business card that says: *A.A. Maldeflour, Dog Work.*

"You can't keep it. I only got but the one left."

Just about then Pigeye glances over Quellabia's shoulder and notices that his trainer has moved into the circle of people around him. Maldeflour spread some kind of pungent salve on an infection he's got on the left side of his head and maybe that's why the dog didn't recognize him sooner. Pigeye cringes and tries to hide behind Quellabia.

"I don't reckon the Silver Wringer could've took him anyway," says Maldeflour. "Old Pigeye's a damn fine dog. You look and you see a dog's asshole," he says to the president. "You measure the amount of scar tissue. A layer equals a year of help."

Pigeye can't take much more; there's no place to hide. He starts whimpering and tangling his leash around his mistress.

"Pluck up that dog's butt, missy. I'll show you a ring of callous so hard you could shine it up with a rag and see your face in it. Mark of a champion."

Pigeye collapses. A combination of post-race jitters caused by guilt at having once again failed to catch the little mechanical bunny and raw fear at the memory of Maldeflour unglues him at last. He pisses all over Quellabia's fancy ball gown.

"Damn!" She jumps back too late. Her dress is soaked, the silky fabric sticking to her skin. She doesn't really get mad. It's nothing more than a good excuse to go upstairs and change clothes again, just about Quellabia's favorite pastime. She's already gotten about as much attention in this slinky ball gown as she could hope for anyway, particularly since the crowd is mostly businessmen and bankers. She knows their sense of lust has a severely limited shelf life, no doubt partially due to their unnatural grubbing for paper profits. Quellabia's got a little-girly organdy pinafore she wears over a transparent blouse that ought to get some of the financial wizards drooling again.

"Take him into the billiard room, Jameson, and have one of the waiters give him some water."

Upstairs, Quellabia steps out of her dress and is ready for a quick shower. She wraps her hair up in a bath towel and turns on the hot water, leaving her dress wadded up in a corner. Somebody will pick it up for her later.

After she dries herself off, she walks back into the bedroom. Laughing Harold is lying on her bed, hat pulled down low over his eyes, a cigarette dangling from his lower lip.

"Hiya baby, long time no see."

Quellabia is so surprised she forgets to act jaded.

"H-how'd you get in here?"

She wraps a big white bath towel around herself, still slightly uncertain. She would've liked to have lured him a little, used her clothes on him, getting him hoping for it so she could refuse it a few times. It isn't fun when it's not all snarled up with rules.

"What do you want?" she asks, but Laughing Harold just smiles suggestively.

Quellabia's met him a couple of times before and has noticed him noticing her although she's been careful to pretend not to. There was always something about him that made her feel vulnerable, as if he knew she was noticing his noticing.

She strolls over to her dressing table and starts brushing her hair, stalling for time. She wants to give him what she thinks he wants, but doesn't want him to know she wants to do it. She doesn't want him to think she doesn't want to since she wants to, but she thinks that if he thinks she wants to, he might use her wanting to to make her do something she doesn't want to.

Laughing Harold pats the bed beside him. "Come over here, baby. Let's have a little chat."

She sits down obediently on the edge of the bed, about as cagey as a rabbit getting sold a used car by a snake.

"Cigarette, sugar?"

She nods, so he lights another one and reaches up to place it between her lips. She looks at him with big moony eyes then exhales heavy blue smoke out over the bed. She figures she's been playing hard to get long enough so stubs out the half-smoked cigarette, leaning forward over him to let her hair hang down in front of her face.

Laughing Harold smiles, then casually reaches up and opens the front of her towel, smoothly pulling the whole thing off with a twist of his wrist.

Harold is lying under the silk coverlet, resting. He still has his fedora on but his clothes are piled on the chair beside the bed. His shoulder holster is hooked over one elbow, the pearl-handled butt of his Colt sticking out where he can grab it. Quellabia is sitting naked at her dressing table, busily writing in her diary.

"There's something I got to ask you, Quellabia."

"Just a minute. How do you spell 'cunnilingus'?"

"Damned if I know, sugar. But listen, a guy is here, a kind of ex-friend of mine. I want to talk to him, but I don't think he's going to like it so I need a quiet place, see?"

"I guess I could just put 'eat out.' But that sounds too crude, don't you think?"

"Sounds okay to me. But like I was saying, a place where nobody could hear us, even if we get a little noisy."

" 'Eat out' does have a nice punch to it, though."

"Quellabia!"

"Darling," she coos, turning to him with an expression of sincere admiration on her face, "I've never had it so good before. It was meaningful, profound."

"That so?"

"A sheltered life is such hell," she sighs. "You're lucky to have been born in a slum and raised in a bordello. I've been trapped like a bird in a gilded cage."

"Well, a ghetto isn't just good times, you know."

"If it hadn't been for my chauffeurs and my butlers and gardeners and houseboys, for the mailmen, the grocery boys and service station attendants, and teachers and psychiatrists and gynecologists, I'd have pined away a virgin, shriveled up like a raisin."

"About this guy I was telling you about . . . "

"There was never a chance to do anything. If it hadn't been for accidental encounters on trips, in airplanes, on trains, cruise ships, in the back of tour buses, under the grandstands at football games, tennis tournaments, soccer matches; if it hadn't been for occasional meetings in the darkened booths of fashionable restaurants and bars, or hidden corners in permissive boutiques, hair salons, jewelry stores, to mention only a few and to ignore the various chance conjunctions on street corners, at rock concerts, in vacant lots, in elevators and on stairs and once even briefly on an escalator, I never would have had an opportunity to learn about sex."

Laughing Harold excuses himself and goes into the bathroom to get a drink of cold water. When he comes back she is lying on the bed again, the silk sheets kicked onto the floor. It's not hard to figure out what she has in mind. "You aren't paying attention," he says sitting beside her. "I got to fix this mug, see? And it's got to be a surprise to him."

"There's a game room in the basement, all kinds of games. Daddy has funny tastes when it comes to love," she whispers, her tongue licking up the inside of his thigh.

"Maybe I could take care of this guy and then get back to you. You say this room is quiet?"

"It's soundproof. Daddy's friends get sort of silly sometimes. There's even some antique French dungeon furniture that he thinks is *nouvelle vague*."

"What's that mean?" Harold says, trying to ignore the fact that his penis is stiffening again.

"I like complications, too," Quellabia laughs. "But I don't go in for the pain part of it all that much. There's a closet full of women's clothing in large sizes, Nazi uniforms, even a six-foot papier-mâché phallus costume, except it isn't very erotic. It looks more like a blighted turnip."

"Well," Harold says trying to pull himself away from her. "It's hard to work with papier-mâche. . . ."

She climbs on top of him, licks her lips into a big wet O then blows him a kiss. "How about you honey, you like S-M? A little bondage and humiliation maybe?"

"Nobody ties me up," says Laughing Harold thoughtfully. "Particularly none of you moneybags whackos."

She's holding herself over him with one hand, using the other to realign the angle of his erection. It slides up into the warm moisture of her pussy and she smiles, closes her eyes and relaxes her weight on his chest, riding with the rhythm.

Harold doesn't know if she has an orgasm or not. His is not much more than a sputter compared to the one earlier. His face in the mirror over the bathroom sink has heavy bags under the eyes. He lays his penis in the warm water but he's too tired to wash it. The medicine chest is full of pills. He looks a little wistfully at the high-priced downs, but tranquility is the last thing he needs right now, so he settles for a couple of aspirin.

He can hear Quellabia at her dressing table, scribbling furiously, filling pages trying to describe something that's basic, but illusive.

"You guys down in the ghetto ever do anything out of the *Kama Sutra?* I've got a copy of the secret illustrated Prajna-prong text that Daddy found after the war. Some people who used to work for a man named Goebbels gave it to him. It was banned everywhere."

Harold is back on the bed with his face buried in his hands. His voice is muffled but she can catch enough of his reply to understand that he has simple tastes.

"Fine," she says. "What could be simpler than the *Kama Sutra?*"

Harold looks up at her. "I always thought the *Kama Sutra* was some kind of curry restaurant."

Quellabia giggles, agreeing that food and balling make a nice complement. "We could lick chocolate mousse off each other's genitals, but I guess you'd prefer something a little plainer, like tapioca pudding."

"That's disgusting."

"Not your style, huh? How about the Sleeve, then. Ever try that position? Or the Arabian Birthday Cake? Peeling Donald's Duck?" She's reading from some sort of calendar in the front part of her diary.

He shakes his head.

"The Airplane? The Five of Clubs? The Shiva Twist? Around the World in Eighty Licks? Absalom and Achitophel? Three on a Match?"

"Never needed them," he shrugs, sitting up.

"Wow! You must really know something." Quellabia straightens herself, limbering up her shoulders and shaking her arms to get the muscles loose. Harold explains to her his basic feelings concerning copulation. In order to insure access to the game room downstairs, he is willing to plow through the act once again, although his heart isn't in it. Fortunately the pulmonary organ is not the one in question. He begins to outline what he has in mind and when the girl realizes that he is talking about the missionary position, she blushes. She says she feels like a new bride. She says nobody has tried to do that to her since she was a kid. Harold wonders why she gave it up in the first place and she says, "Well, I guess just curiosity, to try other things, because they were there."

Harold nods sympathetically. He suggests that in her oversophistication she may have mistaken intricacy for worth. He could refer her to a friend of his named Pizzicato who could explain the wider implications. It is perhaps the simplicity of the act itself that admits tenderness. He states quite bluntly that he is talking about affection between two human beings, and the girl blushes again, points out that the very idea is making her nipples stiffen.

He lays her back gently and stands over her with his hands on his hips and his hat on his head and his penis sticking out true before him, as stiff and unbending as the Protestant sect's insistence on justification by faith alone.

"Magnificent!" sighs Quellabia, and Laughing Harold smiles as ironically as possible.

The night rain is beating in the empty black streets, none of the drunks will sleep outside tonight. The bridges are awash with rain and Duck River's rising, only the hind legs of the dead red cow under the Fifth Street Bridge are still above the surface.

People are tired now, the evening's over. Conversations in the Rolling Ring have settled into a heavy repetitiousness, and most of the drinking has become mechanical. Anybody who had any other plans has long since left the bar.

The sun will come up behind rain clouds in three or four hours but everybody will have given up by then and gone home to try to sleep.

The bartender is restocking for tomorrow's business and a few waitresses are sitting down at the end of the bar smoking cigarettes and going through their receipts. Some sections of the barroom have been closed, the chairs placed upside down on the tables, clearing the floor for the janitor.

Laughing Harold is sitting exhausted at a corner table, dealing out hands, playing five-card stud against himself.

Maude is a couple of tables over. She's getting ready to work on the bar ledgers. Roy and Moe are out on the streets, trying to see if there're going to be any serious repercussions.

Harold did a job on Maldeflour, but he didn't kill him. At the beginning it could have gone either way, but Maldeflour was clumsy and Harold realized how scared he was and felt sorry for him. Harold knows that the last thing you want to do is sympathize with your victim, but he couldn't help it. He cornered Maldeflour in the basement and found him hiding behind a pink pillar. Harold realized that this must be the papier-mâché costume and the absurd incongruity of the situation was too much for him. In the end, he just warned him to get out of town.

A couple of guys come up and ask Harold if he wants a game. He's played with them before; they operate sausage-stuffing machines in a meat packing company on the other side of town. They come around once a month or so to lose their pay. He doesn't feel much like playing with them, but he needs the money. Usually he makes secret rules for himself so he won't clean them out right away, such as throwing out any spade no matter how well it would've fit in.

"Pull up a chair, gents," he says and starts shuffling the cards.

Maude's totaling up the accounts receivable column and grumbling about how much credit some of the more persistent customers have managed to float. She doesn't usually work on the books until late at night. It's not exactly a secret that she's the owner of the Rolling Ring, but she tries to keep it as quiet as possible. She likes to complain about what a tough life she's had and probably figures that being the owner of one of the most successful joints in the Inner City might make it hard for people to sympathize with her, particularly when the drinks get a little watery.

Harold's having a difficult time staying interested in the game. The two sausage-stuffer operators are bluffing each other, bumping a nickel each time, probably two pair against three of a kind. Harold folds, "too tough for me," and the stuffers both grin.

Darlene comes in and shakes her head at Harold. "I tried a lot of places, nobody's seen her."

"I guess she didn't come."

"Larry might've screwed it up. He's gone."

"Yeah, I know. Look, Darlene, why don't you stick around here tonight, okay?"

"Sure."

Harold sits back into the game. "What happened?"

"He had three treys," says the loser.

"My deal," Harold says, and neither of them objects.

They play a couple of hands and Harold is solidly ahead when the front door slams open and Floyd Cloudfinger's standing there dripping wet. He points a long finger down the length of the barroom.

"You Harold Baine?"

Laughing Harold doesn't look up. He just riffles the cards a couple of times, then passes them left for the cut. Seeing that big Indian has the sausage stuffer a little nervous, which he shows by getting tangled up in some kind of complicated cut that involves dividing the deck into about eight stacks. Harold casually slips his .44 out and lays it in his lap. The stuffer finally gives up trying to get the deck shoved back together and pushes it in a loose pile toward Harold.

"I said, you Harold Baine?"

"Who wants to know?"

The sausage stuffers slowly push away from the table, not trying to get out of their chairs yet, but just sliding them backwards until they're about fifteen feet away from the table. Harold deals out a hand anyway.

Floyd starts coming down the middle of the room, staring at Harold all the way. Nobody says anything.

"I want my sister."

Harold looks up at him but doesn't answer. He can't

quite make out his face, but he knows he's never seen him before. He glances back down at his hand. A straight flush in spades, impossible odds to deal something like that. He throws the cards face down in the middle of the table.

"I don't know what you're talking about."

Floyd's standing on the other side of the table, his head and shoulders lost in the darkness beyond the hanging lamp.

"Gloria Cloudfinger. You g-got her somewhere in this city. I want her b-b-back."

"Like I said, I don't know what you're talking about."

Wham! The Indian slams his fist right through the top of the table, smashing it in half and blowing cards and coins all over the room. One of the stuffers is so surprised he tries to jump around behind his chair but gets his ankle caught in the rungs and falls over on his ass. Nobody pays any attention to him.

Harold is still sitting behind the broken table, but his .44 is up now, not exactly pointing at the Indian yet, but just out where he can see it.

"Who the hell are you?"

"Name's Cloudfinger."

"I don't know your sister."

"You b-better find her."

"If I don't?"

The Indian draws a thick forefinger across his throat in a slow slicing motion, a steady grin on his face.

"That so?" says Harold, and cocks back the hammer on his Colt.

"Not you."

"Not me? Who, then?"

Floyd just smiles. Harold watches him, then yells at the

bartender to call the Fumbling Hen and see if Little Eva made it in to work.

"Don't b-b-b-bother," says the Indian.

Harold's got his pistol pointing at the Indian's heart. "You better not have hurt her, you son of a bitch!"

"All I want is my sister back. She's family. I don't want her b-b-being a whore."

Harold lowers his pistol. "I don't know her."

"You b-better find her. You got a week."

"Listen, it isn't Little Eva's fault, she's only a kid."

"It isn't nobody's fault. That don't mean shit. You still got a week."

Harold looks at him for a minute then sticks his pistol back under his arm. "Maybe we ought to talk about this, you want a drink?"

He gets up and strolls over to the bar, keeping an eye on the Indian's reflection in the mirror.

"I don't drink with strangers."

"That so?" Harold brings back a fifth of rotgut and a couple of tumblers.

"I don't even know what your sister looks like."

"She looks like me."

"That right? And she got a job as a hooker?"

Nobody in the room laughs. There's something about the Indian that keeps things from being funny. He stands in the middle of the room, water dripping off him and dropping into little puddles forming on the floor. He doesn't try to dry himself off; it's like he didn't notice he was wet, or that being wet is anything to remark on.

"Sit down," says Harold "take a load off." He puts the glasses on a table and pours out two stiff drinks, but the Indian doesn't move.

"A little late to be starting on this stuff, but what the hell." Harold takes a sip, whistles, "*Whew!* Bad shit this whiskey." Floyd doesn't even look at his glass.

"When do you think your sister might've come into the city?"

"Twelve, maybe thirteen years ago."

"Oh man," says Harold shaking his head, "you have any idea what the turnover is in a place like this?"

"You g-get me my sister and I won't hurt your girl."

Harold sloshes the half inch of whiskey left in the bottom of his glass, watching the ripples.

"How do you know your sister even wants to be with you? You haven't seen her for a long time, maybe she likes what she's doing? Suppose I do find her, what if she doesn't want to be with you?"

"You g-g-get her if you want your girl."

"She's been gone for so many years, how come you're just starting to look for her now?"

The Indian smiles for the first time, a slow grin notching up the corners of his face.

"I been in the slammer," he says, "doing time."

"What for?"

The Indian's still holding that smile. Nobody in the barroom's breathing.

"Murder one," he says slowly, "murder one."

There's nobody left but Harold. The rain has stopped again and the sky has broken into black hollow spaces laced by blowing clouds. The street is completely quiet, all the bars and bordellos are closed, the neon lights extinguished.

Harold has dragged a chair out onto the sidewalk in front of the Rolling Ring. He likes the city when it's empty like this because it's the only time he can completely relax and let everything slide. Darlene made it plain she wouldn't mind sharing her bed with him tonight and he almost accepted, but he knew he was too tired to sleep. Now, watching the pale clouds sail silently down the night sky, he feels like a witness, like a man on the edge of the world. . . .

Then gradually the sky is less black and the eastern edges of the clouds are lit by morning. In twenty minutes he'll be able to distinguish the silhouette of the hills east of the city, and that's usually a signal that it's time to go in and try to sleep. There's something in the ambiguity of very early morning that's soothing to him. He senses a kind of safety in the blues and purples of twilight, as if the uncertainty of the world itself was at last rendered viable in the shadowy period that is neither night nor day, but only changing.

A man moving ponderously crosses the street. Harold watches him draw nearer, feeling strangely calm, an inevitable product of his total exhaustion.

The figure shuffles tiredly as he walks and Harold senses that it's Roy before he can actually see his face. He realizes then that he's been waiting for Roy, that subconsciously he's been anticipating his return.

The big man stops in front of him. He holds his hands out from his sides in a despairing shrug, his face still showing traces of surprise. Laughing Harold offers him a cigarette but he brushes it away with an awkward gesture.

"It's Beatrice, boss. They busted her. They said she snuffed a couple of weasels. They said it's first degree, open and shut. They told me to tell you to think about it."

Harold doesn't answer. The top layer of clouds is lightening, gliding above the length of the sleeping city like the exploded blossoms of huge translucent flowers.

"I guess it's not just Maldeflour, is it, boss?"

"Who were the guys that got hit?"

"They took me down to the morgue to see the bodies, but the heads were in paper sacks. They just showed me quick and then took me away. It was just two guys. They looked like they'd been machine-gunned. Maybe they were cops, I don't know."

"Did the cops who showed them to you seem upset?"

"No, they seemed okay about it. But you know how they are."

"You sure they were shot and not crushed?"

"They looked like bullet holes. I couldn't see so good, though."

"Well, Roy, maybe we better try to get some sleep."

Harold stands up to go in but Roy doesn't move. "What's it mean, boss?" he says, his voice cracking. "What are they going to do?"

Harold looks back up above the buildings. The sky is a soft gray now and the sailing clouds are edged with gold.

"I don't know, Roy. I really don't know."

Part Three

• • • • • • • • • • •

Sons
of the
Pioneers

A dog is feeding on carrion in the clear predawn quiet. It is alert at first, but gradually becomes so intent upon gorging itself that it can be approached from downwind.

A man with a homemade spear hides behind the charred skeleton of a minibus, waiting.

The dog stops eating, cocks its head up as if it has heard something, nose trying to pick up the scent. Three hundred feet away is a mound of rubble and above that the morning star hangs in the cold sky. The dog turns back and continues bolting chunks of rotted flesh.

Far down the barren stretch of Urban Renewal desert the eastern hills suddenly blacken as the edge of the sun emerges from beyond them, expanding like a burning eye from the dark earth crust.

The dog looks up again and is momentarily blinded.

The man runs right out of the rising sun, silently sprinting the last fifty feet until he's within range, then hurling his spear like a javelin, catching the dog in the side just behind the ribcage. It spins with a yell and shakes the spear loose from its body, runs a few steps, and stumbles, slamming its bloody jaws into the glittering sand. It struggles to its feet again but this time throws itself sideways and turns in circles, snapping at its own entrails that ooze out blue and squirming from the wound in its side.

The man circles the thrashing animal until he can get in from behind. He pounces, pounding its head with a piece of iron pipe until it stops twitching.

He squats back on his heels, the sunlight glowing on his face, and deftly rolls a cigarette. He pulls out a tiny magnifying glass in a copper case and focuses it until the end of his cigarette smolders. He tilts his derby hat farther back on his head to watch the sunlight spread across the flat expanse of sand and asphalt and rounded piles of rubble.

"Sure is pretty," he says to himself, then binds the dog's legs together with a piece of cotton rope and slings it over his shoulder. He picks up his spear and starts back the way he came, being careful not to get too close to any of the middens.

A group of children appears. They stand in his path but he ignores the confrontation and keeps moving, his spear grasped firmly in one hand and his iron pipe in the other.

They follow him, walking silently in ragged single file. He expects to feel a knife blade slash into his kidneys at any moment but pretends to be unconcerned, knowing that they'll jump him if they sense his fear.

Ten minutes later he sees a thin wisp of smoke curling up into the pale blue sky and knows his pal Henry has got the morning fire going. He's within a quarter mile of his camp so takes a chance and glances behind him. The children are gone, they must have disappeared under one of the middens.

Beyond the smoke he sees the black glass towers of the

Civic Center gleaming coldly in the morning sunlight like huge malignant quartz crystals.

"Hey Henry!" he shouts. "Breakfast comin'!"

Little Eva shakes Floyd awake.

"Stop that!"

"I want to go home."

"Go b-b-back to sleep."

"I'm not sleepy. I'm hungry. They don't have anything to eat here except bowls of warm water with barley."

"You stay here."

She gets up and starts wandering around the room. On three sides are bins full of old Christian paraphernalia, sorted according to subject.

"That old man's crazy, you know? Did you see this stuff? They keep it because they think tourists are going to want to come and look at it. This box here is full of nothing but broken Jesuses, some of them when he was a baby and some when he was pinned to the cross and some where you can see his heart out on his chest, all bloody and on fire with a crown on top, weird, huh?"

Floyd rolls over and tells her he wants to get some more sleep.

"That old man tried to make me do something really dirty last night, Floyd, don't you care?"

Floyd just grunts.

"How come you're keeping me if you're not going to stick up for me and get me something to eat?"

Floyd doesn't answer so she gets up and starts going through his trenchcoat looking for cigarettes.

"You don't smoke, do you?" she asks, but he's snoring again.

The door is open so she strolls out into the corridor. The stairs down at the other end lead up to the main floor of the warehouse. The door at the top is usually bolted but this time it's open too. She moves carefully across the cold stone floor. Blades of sunlight stream in from barred windows just under the eaves, occasionally illuminating a gigantic scowl or the bunched muscles of a dusty wooden shoulder. Little Eva didn't really have time to look at the gods last night, she was too busy running, but she moves through them now and her face is solemn.

A bright rectangle at the other end of the hall is the front door standing open and she hurries toward it, glad to be getting past all these creepy statues. Little Eva hasn't had much in the way of religious training and it's hard for her to distinguish between metaphorical incarnations of the divine and the monsters from Mars that regularly traumatize cities on television.

Outside, under the morning sun, Mrs. Poppy is having a bath. She's sitting in a low wooden tub while her guardian pours a pail of water over her head. She seems to like it, her hands are waving in front of her face and her croaking sounds a lot like laughter. There's a cauldron over a low fire and her guardian mixes this carefully with cold water from a mossy spigot. He tests the temperature by splashing a little on the inside of his elbow before dumping it on her.

"Mrs. Poppy is particular about her bath water. She doesn't like it when it's too hot," he says.

"Do you always give her her baths?"

"No one else will, poor dear. Whenever the weather's nice and warm I like to bring her out and wash her."

"Oh. Listen, Floyd asked me to go get some cigarettes for him so I'll just kind of go out there and get some . . ."

"Fine, but don't get too near Pinky, he bites."

Eva looks at the gate. There's a big German shepherd sitting in front of it with his tongue hanging out. He's not exactly looking at her, but she gets the point.

"I'm hungry," she says.

"Do you like pie?"

"What kind of pie?"

"Fruit pie?"

"*Proak?*"

"No, Mrs. Poppy, I said pie. There's a pie," he says to Eva, "on the counter of Mrs. Poppy's kiosk. Please help yourself, although it would be nice to save some for Mr. Cloudfinger."

"A real pie?"

Mrs. Poppy's guardian smiles at her, puts the bucket down, and starts toward her. Eva backs up until her heels touch against the porch. He stops in front of her.

"*Cro-groak!*" says Mrs. Poppy and her guardian laughs and tells Little Eva that she must be jealous.

"She was sexually active as recently as forty years ago, parts of her still must remember, although she's totally incapable of any sort of meaningful congress."

"How old is she?"

"She'll be a hundred and twelve in November."

Little Eva nods. "That's kind of old to be fucking, all right."

"She's forgotten what goes where, but she still feels yearnings. I suspect it's the spring weather."

Eva can see her hanging on the edge of her tub, one hand

held out toward them, her blind face pressing toward the sound of their voices.

"I should get her dried off, we don't want her to catch a chill."

Eva checks the wall. It's a good ten feet high, with a row of spikes on the top.

The old man pulls a plug and the bath water starts draining out onto the sand of the courtyard. He asks Eva to help him dry Mrs. Poppy and hands her a rough white cloth. Eva touches her arm and it's like a bird's leg, nothing but bone and yellow skin that flakes off in opaque scales if she rubs it the wrong way.

"With the grain," the old man tells her, "stroke her with the grain so she won't lose so much skin."

Eva stares at him with her mouth open.

"It's psoriasis," he says, "an interesting variant. Her epidermal cells are something like those of an iguana. She can go for days without water, but she can't stand the direct rays of the sun for more than an hour or so."

He has Eva hold her up while he fastens the clothes back on her, then winds her with layers of black shawls.

"And don't think about that wall. Pinky has been trained to guard the entire perimeter."

Eva looks at the dog again and he whines and wags his tail this time.

"Does he like to chase tennis balls?" she asks.

"I don't know, I've never tried him. But let's go enjoy some of that pie, shall we?"

"Hey, Harold, come on down!"

Maude's standing in the alley behind the Rolling Ring looking up at the roof. "Hey, come on, okay? Come on down."

Darlene comes out yawning. She's wearing a black silk kimono with golden dragons embroidered on the back.

"Harold!"

"What's he doing up there?" says Darlene.

"He climbed up there as soon as he woke up. He didn't want any coffee or anything."

"Hey, something the matter?" yells Darlene, and they both listen. No answer.

"Hey, what do you want?"

An empty beer can rattles off the tile roof and lands in the road.

"He took a six pack up with him."

"Watch that stuff!" says Darlene. "You could hurt somebody!"

"Let's go back inside. He'll get hungry pretty soon."

"What's he mad about?"

Maude just shakes her head. "Damned if I know. . . ."

If Harold's eyes were stronger, he'd be able to see the forests on the eastern hills from up here. As it is, they're nothing but a soft green smear. Beatrice loved the forest, particularly on a day like this after a lot of rain. She said the way the rain swelled the duff underfoot made you feel the heaviness of death, the layers of dead leaves pressing down into the earth as mulch for the living weeds. When you're dead, you should be buried in the mountains, she told him. Your grave should be covered with moss and decaying plants. Those shallow rows of bins lined up under suburban lawns are silly. No wonder people are afraid to die. There's not much dignity to an eternity of lawn sprinklers and power mowers. Who'd want to lie under all those neurotic metal blades?

"I'll drink to that," says Harold to himself, and tilts up his can. He's sitting on the peak of the roof, wearing only his underpants and an old wide-brimmed fedora. He climbed up with his Colt hooked over his shoulder, but it became a nuisance so he left it hanging from a flue.

The skyline of the eastern hills is supposed to resemble the contour of a reclining woman, her body stretched the length of the Inner City. Harold wants to be buried on the slope that would correspond to her womb, with his head pointed toward heaven and his feet toward the streets and bars.

He should've gotten glasses, ones shaped like pilots wear, with tinted lenses. That would've been sharp.

Buried up there on those mountains, he'll have wild azaleas growing over him, their roots touching down into his bones. When they blossom, it'll be him again, his life in those gaudy flowers.

"It's stupid."

Beatrice said they should just go away, head so far back into the mountains nobody could find them. There's no reason to do anything he doesn't want to do. There's no reason to put himself in the position where he could get killed.

Beatrice is in the slammer.

Stand up and throw the empty can all the way to the river? And probably fall off the roof.

"Hell, I should've killed Maldeflour . . .

"I should've gotten glasses . . .

"It's stupid."

By early afternoon Harold is in motion. He's got on a good-looking gabardine suit and has traded his white fedora for a genuine panama hat.

"It's summer, girls," he says with a swagger, "the silly season."

"You look fine," says Darlene. "But we heard about Beatrice getting busted. We think you ought to do something about it."

Harold smiles. "I'm on my way."

He figures Tony Pizzicato is the logical place to start and tries his apartment first but he's not there. He works through a couple of likely alleys until he finds him dealing near a bank of phone booths down in front of the Third Street Station.

"What're you doing, selling guided tours to tourists?"

"Naw, some guy wants to know about the bureaucratic structure of the Civic Center so I agreed to meet him. He said he'd be wearing a blue and red Hawaiian shirt and leading a tame baboon."

"He could be anywhere," says Harold, peering into the motley crowd. "Is that all you've got to identify him?"

"Yeah, but he's still got ten minutes."

Harold tells him what he needs but Tony says, "You know, Harold, I'm really out of the missing persons business. Lately, I've been working strictly in distinctions."

"Distinctions?" says Harold. "Isn't that what you were doing before? That stuff about love? How first you realized that the smear you were looking at was a head and then you decided it was beautiful and then you decided that you loved it?"

"I'm beyond that."

"That so? I thought that was pretty good stuff."

"The point of the distinction making process is in the breaking down of the ramifications of interpretations implicit in the given unit of information itself."

"Oh yeah? Well . . . so I guess that guy who was trying

to get those machines to fuck each other isn't so much a problem anymore, huh?"

Tony looks at him like he doesn't know what he's talking about, then tries again.

"You keep slicing the sludge into smaller and smaller globs until you're touching into the basic crystalline structure of the syntax itself."

"That so? And people buy that?"

"People don't know what they're doing. They're scared. They're involved in processes that they can't see either end of. It makes them feel insecure. They believe that if it can just be made simple enough, they might be able to understand it. It makes them feel good, Harold, like they mattered."

Harold flips out a pack of cigarettes, offers one to Tony, and takes one himself. "What a racket. And you can do this? Day after day?"

"Sometimes they *don't* matter. Then it's a lot like faking an orgasm, but you learn to do that too. It gets to be more like the shell game than Occam's razor, but as long as the john doesn't know it's not real, who's hurt? I can turn a dozen tricks on a good day. A lot of the rubes are *bound* to be superfluous, but there's no reason that they have to know it."

Tony sees his customer and tells Harold he has to go.

"But what about my Indian? And the other stuff?"

"Meet me in an hour at the Rolling Ring. Christ, look at the rainbow ass on that baboon, who'd want to walk around with a thing like that? You suppose it bites? Some guys don't have any sense of proportion."

Harold leans against the phone booth until Tony makes the connection, then moves back over to the other side of the river. He stops in a couple of places and asks if any-body's seen little Eva but nobody has, that Indian must really have her. He doesn't feel like heading over to the Rolling Ring yet so he just strolls around looking at the people.

He wanders into the Fumbling Hen even though he knows there's not going to have been any contact. A new girl is on stage dancing so he stands in the back and watches her. She's not as pretty as Little Eva, but she's got a lot more meat on her. Harold always thought Eva was a little on the skinny side to be a real hootchy-kootchy dancer.

"We're going to have to replace her," says the manager. "Our basic clientele is mostly eyeballers. We can't wait much longer."

"That's okay."

"Me personally, I'd have been willing to give her a couple of days, but there was a lot of complaining last night."

"I understand."

"That's Prudence Penderecki up there now, we're lucky to get her on such notice. She's not much of an artiste, but the customers are going to be interested in her big tits. You understand, don't you? We don't want any trouble."

Harold smiles at him. "No trouble," he says, "not your fault." He watches the stage for a minute. Prudence is somewhat amateurish, but her sincerity is obvious.

"She does have a kind of charm, I'm sure she'll be popu-lar."

"Well," says the manager quickly, "she isn't Little Eva, nobody could ever replace her. That act with the flaming batons was a real crowd pleaser. Something about bare breasts bouncing to John Philip Sousa that gets folks up. Likely there's an appeal for the war vets who'd always felt vaguely that *that* was what they were fighting for in the first place but then when they came back home, all they got was married."

"People are patriotic," Harold says. "They like a little scrap of flag in everything they do. Eva used to say that she thought it was the Shirley Temple imitation that they liked, the curly fright wig and the dimples and the baby talk and the lollipop on the G string."

"The people are fond of children, no question about that. You can see them on the park benches in the afternoon waiting for school to let out."

Harold laughs. "So that's where you get your customers?"

"Down-range from the swing sets, bored and lonely."

Harold strolls back out on the river bank again. The river looks green under the clear sky, the water still seems clean. It'd be nice to go swimming in it, or just wade in the shallow parts and feel the little silver minnows nibble at your ankles. It'd be nice not to have to do anything, to just lie back and watch the seasons change, farm a little maybe, or at least put in a garden. Keep a couple of chickens, nothing complicated, a small place far back up in the mountains, overlooking a stream, with fruit trees, he could learn to be quiet, to look at the world carefully, learn about plants and insects, learn the names of wild flowers, learn how to recognize trees in the winter without their leaves by looking at their shape and bark . . .

Nuts, Harold thinks and flicks his cigarette butt into the river. I'd last a couple of months and then get bored, come back down into the city, come back down to see the ladies, play cards, drink whiskey, move around down in here with the people.

He gets up and starts walking toward the Rolling Ring.

Just because you know what's good for you doesn't mean you'll bother to try to do it. It may not be the way it ought to be, but it sure as hell is the way it is.

"How was the dude with the monkey?"

"Not a monkey, Harold, a baboon, a mandrill from western Africa. And the guy had a lot of problems. He didn't seem to be plugged into the information glosses he needed, so he couldn't do his job. He didn't even know what his job *was*, for christsakes, and he couldn't tell anybody because he hadn't known for a long time and hadn't been doing anything. He said he was afraid they'd notice they didn't need him so he just kept going through the motions. His desk's in the middle of a big room with dozens just like it all around him. For awhile he got by because he did what everybody around him did. He figured that by doing that, he must be touching down into essential procedures."

"That sounds like a pretty good system."

"He had to give it up. It started to dominate him. He got to the point where he'd go through the motions of lighting up a cigarette every time the guy he was watching did."

"Smoking's very suggestive," says Harold.

"Yeah, but he didn't smoke, he didn't even have a cigarette or a lighter. There was a woman right in front of him he used to copy until he realized he was miming putting on lipstick."

"That's no good."

"Yeah, he also realized that he was beginning to try to copy two or three people simultaneously. It was only a matter of time until he suffered some kind of breakdown."

Harold shakes his head. "You putting me on, Tony? I don't need it today, I really don't."

He calls the bartender over and orders another drink.

"You have carrot juice?" says Tony, and the bartender laughs.

"Just orange juice then."

"I feel like a sucker, but I'm going to guess that when the guy realized he was in trouble, he tried calling you, right?"

"No, this happened years ago. He went into a kind of collapse, spent a lot of time in bars when he should have been at work. But that's what rescued him."

"Nothing wrong with spending time in bars."

"In his case, it was the mirror behind the bar that saved him. He was watching his reflection in the glass when he realized he could solve his problem by imitating himself. Actually, he was doing it already. He said the way he was sitting there with his head down and his glass in his hand looked a hell of a lot like the way somebody in his fix ought to look. All he had to do was practice with a mirror at home. He managed to isolate little nervous mannerisms he assumed might belong to somebody like him and pushed them and pushed them until they began to form up into a kind of counterfeit personality. . . ."

"Wait a minute! Imitate himself?"

"Yeah, it worked perfectly. Transferring the system to his office was simple once he'd discovered its principles."

"But he still wasn't doing anything?"

"No, but he was busier than hell. He'd get to work and sit down at his desk and then immediately try to imitate the sitting down in terms of what might logically come after, the settling in, say, and then the settling in could be followed by a mock preparation as someone like him might fake it. He said it was the busiest he'd ever been in his life. He'd get home exhausted, knock back his half-dozen martinis and collapse into bed. He said he slept like a baby; he had a kind of strange peace, certain that nobody would cut through the layers of imitations of imitations to the very core."

"So he was getting along, wasn't he? Why's he want to change now?"

"He'd refined it too narrowly. Some jerk took home movies of their section of the office and showed them at a party. My guy was standing in the bathroom at the time, talking to the reflection of what he considered to be a brilliant imitation of a man carrying on a conversation with himself in the mirror when he heard people laughing. He came out and saw himself on the screen. He was in constant motion, jiggling and babbling as he very, very, very carefully adjusted the sensitivity of the ERASE button on his pocket calculator, honing it to the point where the slightest shadow of the little electric numerals lingered, only gradually fading away."

"Yeah, well, that sounds bad."

"He left the party blinded by tears, doesn't remember the rest of that night, but suspects he did nothing but stalk through the city. The next day he called me."

"So what did you tell him?"

"Nothing, just to sit tight. Somebody in his section owes me a favor. I'll use him to set an input that'll alter the flow of the information glosses in such a way that some'll start dropping by my customer's desk. He doesn't need to know everything, just enough to measure where he is so when he decides to try to fake a suicide attempt he'll have a pretty good idea which way he'll be shifted."

Harold orders another drink and tries to buy one for

Tony, who refuses, mentioning something about optimum intake and the degeneration of gratification.

"How much is all this going to cost the guy?"

"Nothing, but now he owes *me* a favor."

"Does it ever end up in money?"

"No, that'd break the relationship. Now I've got two links in that section, one owes me and one doesn't, but both are part of a chain. The pleasure's in having the chains extend until two that have been growing independently for years finally cross and both neutralize and encyst themselves in a splendid explosion of emotional sparks. Their instant of juncture is called a 'hatch,' and there's enough power in the gloss of a single hatch to direct the secret psychic life of the city for years."

Harold's holding up his glass for the bartender. He finally gets impatient, "I'm waiting here, god damn it!" he yells. "And make it a double this time, for christsakes.

"Well Tony," says Harold trying to get a grip on himself, "that's very interesting, but what do you do for money? For food and stuff like that?"

"Arabella deals dope."

"Oh."

"What do you need on this Indian woman, just raw information on location? That's pretty dull, you know. How about the relationship between wherever she is at X instant to wherever she is at X plus Y, Y being a unit of time, if you like, or a unit measuring her degree of involvement in reality at time X plus one, or some sort of combination package?"

"I don't exactly understand what you're talking about. You see, this big Indian's got Little Eva some place and if I don't find his sister for him he's going to . . . ."

"You told me. Try not to say the same thing twice, it isn't economical."

Harold apologizes.

Tony stands up. "I'll get you the location, with a complete probability breakdown on the likelihood of her being there on any given second of any given day, including Sundays and holidays."

"Maybe you could just find out her address? Or where she works? Something simple? I need it pretty quick."

"Nothing's simple, Harold, it never was." He puts on his hat and starts to leave.

"Aren't you forgetting something, Tony? Don't you want me to tell you the woman's name?"

"Not necessary, there are other ways in. I told you location is basic. I've got a lot of nets out, even if you don't tell me her name, I'll arrive there anyway."

He struts down the length of the barroom with a jaunty air, his hat tilted on the back of his head. He stops in front of the door and looks back at Harold.

"You realize," he says, "that in a sense I've already got her. That in a sense I always knew what you were going to need and knew that I was going to have it, have had it, always will have it. I was *born* knowing that name, just like you were. The difference is that you sit around and wait for it to hit you in the face, like a custard pie thrown by a clown."

A good-looking hooker walks up behind him, cocks out a hip and lays a long tit against his shoulder. "Hey, short stuff, how about you and me taking a little stroll between the sheets?"

Tony doesn't even hear her.

"Everything that's going to happen already has. That's

the first law of omniology. And the second law is, even though everything is caused by everything else, that in itself doesn't matter. Even accidents have antecedents, it's a question of distinction. Power is in knowing. The simplest event, a plane crash in Peru, when properly understood becomes a metaphor for the history of the universe. It's all in the arrangement and, of course, the accessibility to information glosses."

He goes out, the whore looking after him like he was crazy.

Harold jumps up and runs out into the street, pushing through the crowd until he catches up with Tony. He grabs him by the shoulder and spins him around, his fist clenched.

"Even the *date* of the plane crash," says Tony quickly, "the time of day, becomes freighted with meaning if you're just plugged high enough up in the teachings of omniology."

"What the hell's that?" says Harold threateningly.

"This system. It's like an ongoing astrology crossed into a mathematical progression. There are places up there where any single event is fondled in its most basic unit, the most delicate boundaries exist, and the whole thing teeters on the brink of perfection!"

"Then," says Harold, "how do you *know* I'm not going to bust you in the mouth right now?"

"I just do," he smiles. "And I always will."

"I don't like this," says Harold, shaking his fist in front of Tony's face. "I really don't."

"I know you don't."

"Will you *stop* that, god damn it!"

Tony just smiles.

Harold's fist falls to his side. He looks at him for a minute, then lets him go. Tony walks away through the crowd, bouncing up on the balls of his feet, six inches shorter than everybody else but unwaveringly commanding the middle of the sidewalk.

"You want to talk about it?"

Beatrice doesn't say anything.

"You have the right to remain silent, but it won't do you much good. You have the right to counsel. If you wish, the court will supply you with a lawyer, an expert in criminal jurisprudence."

Beatrice lies on her stomach in the dark tank, her face buried in her arms. Two bulls picked her up a couple of hours earlier and told her she'd be charged with homicide.

"Perhaps there's something I can get you?" The Police Inspector smiles, but she still doesn't move.

"This, for example?"

He's holding her silver dope case pinched between his thumb and forefinger like it was something he didn't much want to touch.

"There must be a dozen joints left. How long do you think they would last you?"

Beatrice looks up at him. "What do you want?" Her voice cracks.

"Why did you kill those guys?"

"What guys? I didn't kill anybody."

"Perhaps not. But you will seem guilty."

He stands up and taps the edge of the silver case against the bars until a matron comes to let him out.

"How long am I going to be in here?"

"This is just a holding cell. You'll be moved to the Women's Correctional Facility in a day or two."

"Where's that?"

"I have no idea."

"Listen," says Beatrice, coming over to stand behind the bars. "What's going to happen to me?"

He looks at her for a moment, then shrugs and walks away.

Beatrice is dreaming that she's swimming in the river. A man is standing on the bank holding her clothes in one hand and a huge black umbrella in the other. There seems to be some connection between the wetness of the river and the need for the umbrella. She feels she could figure it out if she had to, but she doesn't bother. Then she realizes that the man is Harold. He's watching her but he's not going to say anything. There's a huge house and she's inside and people are being asked a question, one by one. If the question is why a certain door either has or has not been left open, she won't know the answer and this makes her feel anxious. . . .

A man is shaking her shoulder roughly and she jerks awake. She can smell whiskey on his breath. He leans down close to her and hisses something she can't understand, his hands fumbling for her breasts. The tank is pitch black and completely deserted. She slashes out with her fingernails and rakes him across the face. He finds her head then knots his fist in her hair to hold it steady. He hits her a short sharp chop to the forehead with the base of his hand and she's suddenly dizzy. A tiny diamond of light in her brain shines briefly like a beacon miles away in the darkness. . . .

Then she's awake and her knees are on the cold cement floor but her chest's pressed flat on the bed and he's fucking her from behind, dog style. He grunts as he bumps against her and she'd like to hurt him but her body's drained, almost paralyzed. He starts jerking faster and just before he comes, he makes a sound in his throat like an old man hawking up snot. He pushes himself off her and stands beating against the bars with a piece of metal. Somebody lets him out. She feels his semen oozing back out of her and crawls across to the corner where there's a roll of paper on the floor by the toilet bowl. She pulls herself back up on her bed and tries to go to sleep but her head is pounding from where he hit her and she can feel another line of his slime draining down her thigh.

"Disrobe please," says a matron with a stiff face about as friendly as shoe leather. Beatrice takes off her skirt and blouse.

"Your brassiere, also."

"Why?"

"To prevent you from using it to hang yourself."

"Why would I want to kill myself?"

"Your brassiere."

Beatrice unhooks it and hands it to her and the woman puts all her clothes in a plastic sack with a tag on it. It's cold in the room. The walls and ceiling are shiny white tile and the whole place looks like an abattoir. The floor slopes toward one corner where there's a drain so it can be washed out with a hose.

"Sign this receipt."

"Can't I have anything to wear?"

"Sign this."

She signs it. She was going to complain about being assaulted in the tank last night but she realizes that this woman is obviously not the place to start.

"Will I be allowed to phone someone? Or at least get a lawyer?"

"Go through that door."

"Isn't there some sort of preliminary process? I haven't had a hearing or anything."

The woman points at the door behind her.

"Without any clothes on?"

"You'll be issued the appropriate institutional garment."

"Appropriate to what?"

The woman just points.

Beatrice goes through the door and there's an identical room with another tough-looking matron in it. At the far end of this room are racks of faded denim dresses.

"Name?"

"Beatrice Cotton."

"Number?"

"I don't know. No one told me."

"Stupid!" says the matron, and hurries out of the room.

Beatrice stands in the middle of the room until the woman comes back in.

"You're 207-7493."

"Oh."

"Size?"

"Nine."

"Sign this receipt."

The woman hands her one of the denim dresses. Beatrice puts it on but a couple of the buttons are missing in front and it won't close properly over her chest. She asks for another one but the woman tells her this is the one she has been issued and she has to wear it for three days at which time she will be issued another.

"But look, you can see, it's open in the front. I can't go around like this."

"Your name is Beatrice Cotton number 207-7493?"

"Yes."

"That's Civic Center Temporary Detention Unit dress number 9-39, is it not?"

"Yes."

"Then that is the correct dress."

"Could I have a safety pin or something?"

"It's against all Unit regulations to allow detainees any sharp or pointed object which could prove potentially dangerous to themselves, or to any members of the staff."

Beatrice is waiting in a lovely, sunny room. There's a white cloth on the table and a low blue glass bowl of pansies.

"Those flowers are pretty, aren't they?" says Beatrice, and the matron behind her grunts in assent.

"There's an ashtray here, does that mean I can smoke?"

"Unh."

"But I don't have any cigarettes. They took them away from me when I was brought here."

"You buy them."

"Where?"

"From other detainees."

The matron bites off the ends of her words as if she didn't like the idea of her voice being in contact with Beatrice.

"But where do they get them?"

"From the staff. As rewards."

"For what?"

"Helping."

Beatrice tries to ask her more questions but the matron tells her to be quiet. She sits at the table and fingers the edge of the cloth. She counts the flowers in the bowl but can't figure the number exactly because she might have missed a couple on the back side. All she can see out the window is blue sky. There are no cracks on the wall to make maps out of, nothing to do.

"Do you like your job?"

The woman doesn't answer and Beatrice wonders if it's permissible to turn around and look at her. Probably not, since the chair she's sitting in is bolted to the floor. Beatrice pushes slightly against the table and realizes that it's bolted down too.

"How can I get a cigarette?"

"Be helpful."

"To who?"

The matron refuses to answer again. Beatrice tugs gently on the white cloth and it moves slightly. She pulls again and the bowl of flowers moves. That means it isn't fastened to the table.

"What are you doing?"

"Nothing."

"Well, stop it."

Beatrice folds her hands in her lap. She needs something to settle her down. She laces her fingers together then unlaces them.

"Isn't there any other way to get a cigarette?"

The matron doesn't answer. Beatrice tries to imagine her sitting there with her mouth squeezed tightly shut, a pink pucker like a dog's asshole. She giggles nervously.

"Quiet. You think it's funny?"

"No."

Beatrice asks her what's going to happen but the matron still won't answer her. She'd thought it might be a good idea to try to make friends with somebody who could help her and then tell about the rape. But that might be a mistake, and anyway she doesn't want any more trouble. All she wants is to get out of here. This matron, obviously, is not going to help her.

Beatrice sits with her legs crossed, tapping her toe against the table leg.

"Stop making that noise."

"Why am I here?"

"You're waiting."

"Why? What for?"

There's the sound of the door behind her opening and closing.

"Are you still here?"

There's no answer. She takes a quick glance over her shoulder. The room's empty. She jumps up stumbling against her chair and runs to the door. She listens, then eases it open half an inch but there's nothing to see, just a vacant hall lined with other doors like hers.

She crosses the room and tries to open the window but it's stuck. She's pushing against it when the door opens again and the Police Inspector comes in.

"Would you sit down in your place again?"

She's staring at his face but it doesn't seem to be marked. He waits for her to return to her chair, then sits across the table from her. He has a large folder that he places in front of him.

"It's stuffy in here," she says, gesturing toward the window. "But it seems to be jammed."

"I should hope so. Would you like a cigarette?" He places a fresh pack beside the ashtray. Beatrice's hands are trembling as she tears off the cellophane wrapper.

"Do you have a light?"

"What?"

"A light, a match." She holds up her cigarette.

"Oh, no, I'm afraid that I don't."

"But you smoke, I know you do."

"Never in the morning." He smiles at her and she thinks she can see streaks running across his cheek, like bands of face make-up.

"I need a light," she says, realizing how weak her voice sounds. She doesn't want to plead.

"Smoking's bad for your health."

She doesn't say anything but just waits with the cigarette between her fingers and finally he laughs and pulls a pack of matches out of his coat and hands it to her.

"Why did you kill those guys?"

"I didn't kill anybody."

"You'll fall. Murder one, with malice.

"The jury won't want you on the streets, shady past, underworld connections, you'll get life, no chance for parole in twenty years. You have any idea what the slammer will be like for a good-looking lady like you?"

He plucks a flower out of the vase and crushes it between his thumb and forefinger, rolling it until there's nothing left but a moist smear. He drops the dead wad in the ashtray.

"You haven't exactly told us the truth about your feelings for Harold Baine. There's nothing wrong, but it's becoming more and more evident that it's to everyone's best interest if he rethinks some of his present ideas."

"What do you want? You want me to set him up? Is that it?"

He shakes his head. There's a line on his cheek from his mouth to his ear that's slowly darkening into a grayish purple.

"We don't seem to be able to communicate with each other. We could have been close friends, but you don't trust me, I can tell. That's a shame."

"What do you *want?*"

"You insist on trying to oversimplify everything. We did not make this world, we inherited it. Things aren't nearly as neatly arranged as we might like. Progress is being made, social structures are being redesigned. But nothing is as simple as we might like it to be."

He takes a cigarette out of the pack and lights it. Beatrice is staring at his cheek. Another purple line is beginning to emerge, parallel to the first one.

"We do our duty, no man can do more. The best that we can hope for is to get everything out in the open where we can examine it, decide what should be allowed to remain and what should be allowed to conclude. Identification, examination, evaluation, and controlled extension," he says, counting them on his fingers. "It seems to me there was a fifth point to the Police Captain's program. Euthanasia? No, he wouldn't have used the word, a high degree of negative associations are attached to it."

"But what do you *want?* What do you want from *me?*"

A thin line of blood has seeped out of the bottom of the deepest groove on his face. He doesn't seem to notice it, his cheeks may have been deadened with a local anesthetic. In the bright sunlit room, the viscous blood has a greenish tinge, like cheap motor oil.

"I suppose evaluation is the key," he continues more slowly, watching Beatrice's expression. "The relationship between the Police Force and the Academy is essential for promoting harmony. Some day, the inspector and the professor will be no more than two aspects of the same man. Evaluation. We will be able to evaluate everything. And then, when two things are in conflict, it will be possible to decide which one would be better off in a state of permanent nonexistence."

"I don't understand what you want," Beatrice says flatly, no longer trusting herself to stare at his bleeding face.

"Peace. Total, constant, continuing peace. An end to crime, an end to war, an end to unhappiness and disharmony. We will make you happy at last, all of you."

Beatrice snatches up the glass flower bowl and hurls it at him, but he ducks just in time and it smashes against the far wall. The door slams open and two matrons jump on her and wrestle her back into her chair.

"There's a chance you'll be released," he says, his voice a little hurried, the left side of his face a thin sheet of dark blood. "Perhaps new evidence has been uncovered, or perhaps in the course of another investigation a voluntary confession was obtained. The details don't matter."

"They do to me!"

"When will you finally understand that we're trying to help you?"

"Gloria must be hungry, Henry. I believe it's your turn."

"I fed her yesterday. It's Tom's turn."

"Tom?"

"Hell," says Tom, "I don't see how come she can't come and get it like everybody else. There's some that are cracked worse than her."

"Gloria needs understanding."

"How come it's just Henry and me has to do this understanding?"

The man wearing the derby hat looks at him for a moment, then tells him there are rules.

"Goddamn rules aren't fair!"

The man with the derby hat ignores him. He unfolds his pocketknife and cuts a sliver of meat from the dog haunch they're barbecuing over a low fire.

"Turn the spit once, Henry. I believe this is just about fit to eat," he says, still ignoring Tom.

The three of them sitting around the fire look like hoboes dressed in ragged coats and broken shoes. The one named Tom has a wide-brimmed hat he's proud of. The crown's stove in but he's got a good-looking hatband made out of a chain of beer-can pop-tops. Henry is not quite as distinctive, except for his baggy pants, which are a dozen sizes too big. There are about fifteen other people arranged around the edge of the midden, but they won't approach the fire until they're told to. The group is nomadic, they'll stay at one midden for a couple of days and then move on, but even so some of the more overtly insecure members inevitably claim territorial prerogatives, and for this reason the fire area is declared out of bounds.

"You're a camp warden, aren't you?" says the man in the derby hat. "Camp wardens look after the loonies. It's been decided."

"How come I can't be a hunter, too?" Tom says.

" 'Cause you don't know how to hunt!" says Henry, then

laughs at his own joke and slaps his thigh. "You don't know shit about hunting!"

"It isn't fair," says Tom, and Derby Hat says, "maybe not, but it's the way it is. And besides, I always work best alone."

They have a pot of dog stew cooking over another section of the fire and Henry slops a load of this into one of the old hubcaps they use for plates and hands it to Tom. He gets up reluctantly and shoves his hat down tighter on his head.

"The goddamn stupid rules!"

"Maybe you'd rather live by yourself?" says Derby Hat quietly and Tom shuts up.

He goes around to the other side of the midden and stops in front of a kind of cave Gloria has made for herself out of the piled-up rubble.

He tilts his hat back and kneels down at the opening, trying to see her.

"You okay in there?"

She doesn't answer so he places the food in front of the opening.

"You want to come out and talk a little today?"

He squats back on his heels and smells something familiar. There's a pool of fresh shit right behind him.

"God damn! You aren't supposed to go to the bathroom here, you're supposed to go out there in the desert, gentlemen on the sunrise side of the midden and ladies on the sunset side. That's the rules."

"Dogs," she says, her voice like a low moan coming out of the darkness.

"You afraid of the dogs?"

"Dogs . . ."

"You go in pairs, buddy system. The dogs'll stay away. Hell, better the dogs than the men coming for you. You want the men?"

"No!" she says, her voice raw and dry. "No men."

"You don't want to come out and talk? It's okay with me if you don't want to, but I'm supposed to give you a chance. But I guess you don't want to so I'm going to go back and get myself something to eat."

She doesn't say anything.

"That okay with you, Gloria? Okay if I go back and get me something to eat?"

He waits for a minute, but it's still silent so he leaves.

"She didn't want to talk, huh?" says Derby Hat.

"No, nothing but dogs, dogs, she's still scared of the dogs."

"I guess she just had a bad experience," says Henry.

"Indians are nuts," says Tom. "I don't know why we have to drag all the goddamn loonies around with us."

"Maybe you want to leave them out here alone?" says Derby Hat.

"Well, no, hell, I don't know. But we don't seem to do anything but just keep moving around."

"You got something else you'd like to do?"

"Yeah," says Henry, "you think maybe you got something else you can do?"

"Hell," Tom says, "gimme some of that stew. I had the roast yesterday. Seems like we could at least get some variation in the menu."

Derby Hat leans back against the burnt shell of a television, picking at his teeth with a little piece of copper wire.

"Tom has himself a hard time getting satisfaction,

doesn't he, Henry? You suppose maybe he'd be happy if he had more responsibility?"

Henry laughs and Tom says, "Oh no, you're not sticking me with anything else."

"He doesn't even know," says Henry. "He hollers before he's bit."

"You're trying to stick me with the loonies!"

"Wasn't thinking of the loonies, Tom. You know that campfire we saw the other day?"

"You said it was children."

"That's the one. Well, I don't think it was. A pack of them met me today, and they looked pretty hungry. They hadn't been eating meat, or anything else, for that matter."

"So who's the fire?"

"That's what I thought you might like to find out."

Derby Hat slouches farther down and closes his eyes, getting ready to take a nap.

"You mean, go look?"

"You like to try something like that?"

"Hell, yes!"

"Get back before dark."

Tom jumps up and runs over where he keeps his gear. He's got a short-handled spear with a long steel blade.

"How come you sending him?" says Henry.

"He might learn something seeing what it's like out there."

Floyd's gone for food so Eva is under the floor, tunneling. She found a big silver crucifix with a stout wooden handle that makes a pretty good pick, particularly after she got the Jesus pried off. She's going to dig out, just like they do in the prison movies on TV. She's got floor boards wedged open with a couple of plaster Virgin Marys.

She's shifting dirt when she hears a horrible yell. She climbs up out of her hole and pushes out the two supporting Virgins and fits the boards together neatly.

The upstairs door has been left unlocked again. They're doing a real poor job of keeping her kidnapped. She wonders why she should even bother with the tunnel if they aren't going to try harder.

Down at the other end of the warehouse floor is Mrs. Poppy's guardian on his knees, his body bent and racked with violent sobs. Before him lies a crumpled bundle rolled in a tangle of black rags.

He looks up at Little Eva, his anguished face dark with pain.

"She's gone!"

"Who? Mrs. Poppy?"

He nods his head, then covers his face with his hands and bursts into loud whooping sobs.

"Ah, gee. That's too bad."

"She's in a better world," he says, his eyes spurting tears.

"What'd she die of, old age?"

"I didn't think she'd ever die!"

"Well," says Eva patting him solicitously on the shoulder, "well, well . . ."

He raises his face to the heavens and shakes his fists. "Why her?" he demands, his voice hollow with agony. Suddenly he runs over to the emergency fire-fighting gear and snatches up a red ax.

"Oh, hey," says Eva, "let's be a little careful."

He ignores her and dashes behind Mrs. Poppy's kiosk, then with a single blow severs the rope holding the hanged angel from the rafters. The angel lands with a crash and Mrs. Poppy's guardian begins furiously hacking at it, screaming that it shortened her life span.

Eva kneels beside Mrs. Poppy and stares into her face. She may very well be dead, but she certainly doesn't look particularly different to Eva. She waves her hand in front of her eyes, then remembers she was blind anyway. She touches her skin and it's cool and lizardy, just like before.

"Maybe she's only sleeping?" Eva says, but the guardian doesn't hear her.

There's not much left of Mrs. Poppy. She must have been shrinking steadily for the last few years so that now that she's actually dead, she looks like a mummy that's been baking in the sand.

Her guardian has begun chopping at the row of angels on the benches beside the kiosk, bellowing in rage and remorse. Eva starts walking slowly backwards, hoping he won't notice that she's trying for the door. She doesn't want him coming after her with that ax.

It's a long way to back up but she finally makes it after bumping into statues a couple of times. The last thing she sees before slipping through the door is the exhausted guardian sinking gradually into what looks like a cord of firewood, except here and there is a wooden head or arm sticking out of it, melancholy reminders of the inevitable collapse of sanctity.

Little Eva gets into the courtyard and is heading for the main gate. Pinky's there waiting for her but she's ready for him. She's wadded a couple of white veronica veils into the size and shape of a tennis ball and when the big dog growls, she holds it out and shows it to him.

"Here boy, come here boy."

Pinky looks at her, puzzled. No one's ever challenged him before and he's actually more of a pet than a watchdog. Besides, he's always had a secret soft spot in his heart for chasing balls.

"You want to fetch, boy?"

He does, darn it. He knows he shouldn't, but he can't help himself. His tail starts wagging.

Eva throws the wadded-up cloth ball into the middle of the courtyard and he dashes after it, yelping happily. She starts fumbling at the gate trying to get it open, but he's back with the ball immediately and drops it at her feet.

She ignores him and he starts barking.

"Shhh!" she says. "Quiet! Here." She picks it up and throws it again and off he goes. She gets the gate open this time and is in the alley moving fast when she hears him coming, the wadded cloth unwinding in his mouth. He cuts in front of her and drops it so she stops and tries to fix it into a ball again, but he's bitten through the strings she used to form it.

"I can't fix it," she says, and starts to walk past him but he growls threateningly so she stops.

"You have to have it, huh?"

He wags his tail.

She pulls up her blouse and tears a narrow strip off the bottom then uses that to reform the veronica ball. She throws it back toward the warehouse and as he charges after it, she runs the other way.

She makes half a block before he catches her and drops the wad of veils at her feet again, his tongue hanging out and his ears perked up, just a hundred and fifty pounds of police dog having fun.

"Why don't we just walk along together?"

She tries to move past him but he growls meaningfully again. He must figure since he's abandoned his post, he might as well get his pleasure while he can. She tears another strip from the bottom of her blouse and he waggles around, getting excited.

Seven blocks later her blouse just barely covers the bottoms of her breasts, but she's standing in front of a sporting goods store with a tantalizing display of tennis equipment in the window. She doesn't have any money so she's going to have to figure out some way to steal a can of balls. By now it's not so much that she can't get rid of the dog, she's grown really fond of him, and his affection for her is obvious.

When she gets back to the Rolling Ring, she's going to ask Harold if she can keep him. She can predict the usual objections, but she'll promise to take care of him herself, and Harold will give in. She likes him so much she's already renamed him.

"Wait here, Duane," she says, and saunters into the sporting goods store.

Roy's sitting at the bar with a can of beer watching a movie on TV. The guy on the screen is blazing away with a pistol, although he never seems to hit anything.

Darlene and a couple of her pals are lounging around in their kimonos, waiting for the evening. The joint's empty except for a gang of leather-jacket ramblers down at the far end of the bar, washing the dust out of their throats and telling each other lies. The conversation's garbled, but occasionally shouted phrases float out, appraising the merits of various motorcycles or women.

Darlene gets up and strolls over to the bar. She's not wearing a bra and the motorcycle jockeys stop talking to watch the heavy roll of her breasts under the thin silk kimono.

"Where's Harold?"

"I don't know," says the bartender. "He said he'd be right back."

She sits down at the bar and he pours her a cup of coffee. "What do you think about that Beatrice deal?" she says. "You think she could've done it?"

"Sure she could have."

"I couldn't do it."

"No," says the bartender, "I couldn't either. But we aren't Beatrice. She's a very tough lady."

Harold walks in. "No sign of Tony yet, huh?"

"Hey, what're you going to do?" says Darlene.

"About what?"

"About Beatrice getting busted."

"I'm working on it. Give me a beer," he says, and sits down to watch TV with Roy. The same show is still on and the guy's still shooting his pistol. He runs and dodges and hides behind old barrels and crates, shooting over the top. One time he even hides behind a horse, firing out from under its belly and making it nervous.

"Jesus," says Harold with disgust, "you ever try to shoot from behind a horse?"

"Well, it's a trained horse and so it knows if it wants to eat, it'd better not kick him or anything."

Harold looks at Roy and shakes his head. The camera still hasn't shown what the guy's shooting at, nothing but his pistol going off again and again.

"That's no way to do it," Harold says.

"No, you're right there, you got to reload."

"I mean the style of the thing. He hasn't got any class; he's just slinging lead. Why do it at all if you aren't going to do it right? There's enough noise as it is."

"Her face'd make you go blind," says one of the ramblers, "but her pussy's practically prehensile and she can clean and reassemble a carburetor in about ten minutes flat. I don't know what more you could ask of a woman."

The door slams open and guys dressed like cops charge into the room, each one carrying an automatic rifle and wearing a flak jacket.

"This a roust?"

"Shut up!"

A couple of them run upstairs and pretty soon people start stumbling down to the barroom, mostly half-naked whores, some with a boyfriend or an early customer trying to hop back into his pants.

"Everybody up against the wall."

They start the frisk but nobody's got any iron except Harold and Roy, so all they do is drain the bullets out. When they work their way down to the ladies, the frisk is a lot more like a feel-up, particularly since most of the girls from upstairs aren't wearing enough to cover themselves, much less a weapon.

"All right, get them in the back, everybody but Harold," says the Police Captain, standing just inside the door, posing as if he was waiting for someone to take his photograph.

"So," he says coming forward, his eyes hidden behind mirror lenses, "so you think you want to be a cop, Mr. Baine, you think it's easy to be a cop."

"I didn't say that," says Harold.

"How come you want to be a cop then?"

"I don't. But I don't have any choice. The cops are going to win."

"Of course we are, of course we are, so what?"

Harold doesn't answer. The Police Captain laughs, the overhead light glinting off the steel frames of his sunglasses. He looks down the room to make sure everybody's watching him.

"I want them face down," he says and straightens his long leather coat.

"You don't think we're cops, Harold? Is that the problem?"

Harold shrugs. "You're probably cops."

"Of course we are, of course we are, we always are."

Harold doesn't say anything.

"You know what we heard, Harold? We heard that you wanted to bump off the guy that ordered the contract on Big Jim. We all know who ordered that contract, don't we?"

"I might not."

The Police Captain laughs. "Is that why they call you Laughing Harold? Because you make jokes? Did you ever stop and think that we're caught in an untenable situation just like you are? Look at those guys," he says indicating a couple of the men he brought who are standing stupidly in the corner. "You think I like associating with those assholes?"

Harold just shrugs.

"Who's going to keep the damn peace, if not us? All guys like you think about is not getting killed, isn't it? Isn't it?"

Harold doesn't argue.

"If we wanted to kill you, we'd blow you away right now, pull the plug, nothing could be simpler."

He slides out his pistol, a big .457 magnum.

"A drop-gun, Harold, stolen from the Force and so unregistered. It'd blow a hole in you you'd notice. Any one of those jerk-offs back there'd do it for a dollar. Hell, they'd probably pay me for the pleasure."

He leans over, his elbow braced against the green felt of the card table, the pistol pointing right at Harold's heart. He's waiting for him to say something.

"So, you don't want to kill me?"

"Did I say that? Did I say I didn't want to kill you? All I was saying was how easy it is to do, nothing about if or when it's happening, or where, or how, or whether I want to do it or not. Don't be naïve, Harold. We don't deal in personalities."

He slips his gun back inside his coat and sits down.

"You called me, right, Harold? You said you wanted to talk, about yourself and a woman we allegedly have in detention, Beatrice Cotton, right?"

Harold nods.

"I was going to save this, but maybe you need it now. Hey," he yells, "get me those photographs."

He shuffles through a few big glossy eight-by-ten enlargements and finally tosses one on the table in front of Harold.

"The end of an era," he says. "I assume you'll be able to recognize those two turkeys."

It's a morgue photograph of a pair of dead bodies lying piled next to each other on a single narrow dissection table. Their eyes and mouths are cracked open and they've been tied together by a piece of wire twisted around their necks. The bodies are naked and there are nasty little red puckers all over them where they were hit by bullets. A guy dressed like a cop stands behind them posing with an automatic rifle braced against his hip like a big game hunter. The bodies are Mr. Donnard and Mr. Todd. They look like little old men now that they're dead, they look completely harmless. It's ugly how skinny they are, all ribs and knees and elbows, their dead cocks hanging down.

"Evidence," says the Police Captain. "And we can produce a witness if we need to."

Harold looks at the photograph carefully. Their necks are bloody and torn from the wire. They must've been fastened together before they were shot.

He places the photograph carefully on the card table and with one finger slides it across the green felt to the Police Captain.

"I've never seen these men before."

"Ha ha," the Captain laughs, shaking his head in mock amazement.

He gets up and, still shaking his head, walks to the back of the barroom. Everybody is lying face down spread-eagled on the floor and the Police Captain walks in among them.

"You're free," he says, turning back toward Harold. "You don't have to do anything now. She's saved you."

He stops, looks down for a minute, then touches the shiny black tip of his boot against a hooker's bare thigh. "Roll over," he commands. She doesn't move so he pushes at her again harder and says, "Roll over." Now she's lying on her back staring up at him but he's pretending not to be interested in her anymore. He stands straddling her, his leather coat hanging down over her like stiff black wings.

"It doesn't happen like it used to in the old days," he shouts. "Those two old weasels were just out of sync, that's all. There's going to be peace and prosperity. Nobody who's in touch with the program will be in any pain. Everything is under control.

"You hear me?" he yells back to Harold, not really expecting him to answer. He looks back down at the woman lying between his boots and tells her to get up. He doesn't move and she has to pull herself awkwardly out from under him.

Then he's back at the table, friendly again. "Look at this," he says, and unrolls a large map of the city. He has the hooker stand on a chair and hold the top of the map so Harold can see the whole thing. He's colored the sections of the metropolis that border the Inner City area with different shades of blue and green.

"This illustrates the progress of the Urban Renewal Program over a one-year period. The green areas are mostly last spring and summer. This long dark forest-green band is last autumn. Winter, as you may have guessed, is reserved for the consolidation of effects. Blue is this year. These spots of turquoise here and here are April and May. June as you can see is royal blue and I'm going to do the rest of the summer in indigo, reserving purple for fall."

The colored sections form an irregular band completely encircling the Inner City like a saw-toothed zero. He shows Harold different places on the map he might remember, most of which no longer exist.

"It began here, and here, and here," he says nostalgically, "and spread in every direction. One of the techniques we learned as we went along was to remove all names of locations, particularly the names of streets. This helps to unify the renewed area. It's helpful to remove the streets entirely when feasible, or at least to disguise them in order to aid in the escape from what we like to refer to as the tyranny of landmarks, the corpses of the past unburied.

"It's absurdly easy." He smiles and leans back in his

chair, his heavy leather coat creaking with the motion. The hooker says her arms are getting tired from holding the map but he ignores her.

"Some places are five or six miles wide, particularly down here near the Civic Center, and we aren't finished yet."

He sits musing for a moment but then from the back there's a bark of harsh laughter. A clot of his men are kneeling in a circle around one of the hookers, doing something.

"Stop it!

"Assholes," he mutters to Harold. "Even with training these hirelings seldom rise above themselves."

He leans over the table. "They stink of garlic sausage, too!" he whispers, then his face opens into a crazy grin. He stands up and takes the map from the hooker and starts rolling it up. "Why don't you join us, dear," he tells her. "Wouldn't you like something to drink?"

She sits down next to Harold, looking scared. She's wearing a filmy peignoir with a short nightgown underneath it and her hair isn't combed. She shakes her head.

"You're being shy, aren't you? What do you usually like to drink? Wine?"

He purses his lips, trying to seem pleasant. She glances at Harold, but he can't help her.

"A nice glass of white wine? Harold, another bottle of beer?"

He comes back from the bar and places a glass of wine in front of the woman and hands Harold a beer.

"They aren't real cops?" says Harold.

"Real? What's that? Legal distinctions, terminology, bullshit. Real is who's got the drop on you. We need wider conceptual laws and less specificity. Ambiguity happens, that's why we want you."

"Why?"

"You're mostly there."

Harold doesn't understand. The Police Captain squats down between him and the woman and puts an arm around each of them, squeezing them to him, then nuzzles the hooker on the cheek, rubbing his dry lips on her in what for him must pass as a kiss.

"It's so easy to win, Harold, that even with the likes of those dumb mercenaries, we'll be able to do it. Empty buildings and old silos, that was the way in, those first bombings were just popping the cherry."

He jams the point of his tongue into the little hooker's ear, then leans back and laughs as she jerks away.

He moves back around to the other side of the table, tapping the rolled-up map against his palm like a billy club, little bits of steel trim on his leather coat jingling against each other. He stalks the length of the barroom and moves a few of his men to guard the front door. He polishes his silver sunglasses with a white cloth, hooks them back on, and pulls a pair of black leather gloves out of his coat pocket.

"It wouldn't be a bad life if they'd let you do what you want!" he says, his voice oddly shrill. "Just let you alone to do whatever you want. Efficiency! That's the word, efficiency, that's the name of my muse. She's sometimes a cruel muse, but she's mine."

He squats behind the hooker again and puts both gloved hands on her shoulders. "Efficiency." He buries his face in her hair at the base of her neck, sending a shudder down her body as she arches her back involuntarily trying to escape him.

"She's a tall white woman, Harold, a nursing baby at one nipple and the other oozing blood, yeah!"

He stands slowly, pulling the little hooker up by her shoulders, and moves around to the other side of the table, holding her in front of him. He sits back down in his chair, forcing her to kneel between his knees, pushing her down until her head disappears beneath the table top. He removes his sunglasses again.

"I won't tell you what it looks like between my muse's legs; you aren't ready yet."

He's staring directly at Harold, his pale blue eyes like two icy stones.

"But make no mistake about it, she's going to be the muse of anybody who wants to survive. There're too many people, there's not going to be enough food, not enough fuel, ten years from now, thirty, it's going to be a lot different. And you're going to have to decide, you're going to have to do it."

Harold feels cold. "Do what?" he finally asks. "Decide what?"

"Just who it is you're going to love, what hole you're going to kiss."

"Oh man," says Harold, and looks at the table. The Captain's hand is resting on the green felt. Harold would have thought that it'd be calm, but it's trembling so hard even the black leather glove can't disguise it.

"You don't know what it means," he says, hooking his sunglasses on, his voice urgent now, a little shaky. "You don't understand. And it's so simple!"

He hunches forward leaning in and shoves the woman abruptly down away from him. He brings both hands back slowly up above the bright green surface, appearing on each side of the table like two black suns rising out of a flat dead sea, the gesture of a priest celebrating the mystery of a mass Harold suspects he couldn't even begin to imagine. The palms slowly open toward the ceiling and the fingers flutter like burning birds as the Captain reaches across the table and takes Harold's face in his hands. He holds him intently, forcing Harold to see himself reflected in the distorting silver mirrors over his eyes.

"You don't know," the Police Captain croons, "you don't."

Then he pulls Harold steadily across the table, dragging him out of his seat, pulling him over the smooth green sea of the table into a kind of embrace until their noses are almost touching and Harold thinks for a moment that the Captain is going to kiss him, his mouth moving, still forming the sentences he wants to say but also quivering with a nervous tic twitching up his left cheek, gradually taking over his mouth.

Harold is suddenly aware of a complicated system of odors emanating from him, the heavy obvious leather and greased steel he would have expected, mixed with a cheap cologne and the subtle, clearer machinist oil he uses to lubricate his pistols, but beyond these there's a solid base that Harold can't quite identify, something he's smelled before. . . .

And then he remembers that it was the time when, as a child, he wandered away from the guided tour of the telephone company. He got lost and ended up back deep where all the circuits were, finally trapped in a section that had been abandoned years earlier. He was in a huge room filled with bank after bank of severed wires, each little blue copper tip like an accusation of broken connections, the wisps of past conversations whose producers had long since died, the words sloughed off into the electricity that bore them.

The boy pushed back through the broken twigs of torn wires until he found the chamber of the dead telephones themselves, the graveyard where they crawled off to die, their black-and-white skulls grinning baldly in the gloom. It was the smell of that funeral mound that scared the hell out of Harold, the smell of inorganic decay, of the deaths of machines, the decomposition of instruments he'd always thought just went on and on.

And Harold had started bawling, really howling. He was just a kid and that was the first time he realized he was going to have to share the world with the possibilities of a lot more events than he'd imagined.

"Harold," the Police Captain is saying. "Can't you understand?" His voice is a metallic rasp, the silver knot of a vein thuds, beating time beneath the translucent skin of his forehead. "Harold, Harold, Harold, I don't ever want to die! Not ever! I'll do anything, absolutely anything to keep on living!"

Then he lets him go, opens his hands and lets him slide back into his seat, sits back himself with his hands firmly on the table and carefully calms his breathing.

Harold knows for the first time why they really are going to win. He's never wanted anything that bad in his whole life.

"You see now why I say you're easy to kill?"

Harold nods.

The Captain pulls the hooker out from under the table and tells her to get Harold a whiskey. He doesn't even look at her this time, and Harold wonders if the whole thing was just an act.

"You think we were serious about those two jerk-offs in the alley? We never doubted you. We figured we'd use you as a kind of natural-selection agent. We hope you don't mind."

Harold takes a stiff drink of whiskey. The Police Captain smiles, drums his fingers on the table.

"How many of those traps did you have set up?"

Harold thinks for a minute. "Three? Or four? I don't remember."

"We found three. The one you used was the best, the other two needed minor repairs. On one the trigger bar was rusted too badly and on the other the trip wire was missing, probably some kids swiped it, there's lots of petty crime down here. We had a hell of a time finding an old piece of wire to replace it with. We thought if we put in a new piece it might spook you. I wonder, would it? Would you have still used it if you knew it'd been tampered with?"

Harold stares at the green felt table top. He says he feels like a guy that found out he has to spend the rest of his life living in a public toilet, and the Captain laughs, gets up and stalks around the table, laughing and rubbing his hands together.

"I sure hope you join us, I sure do. We need somebody with a sense of humor down there. Funny things happen Harold, but nobody laughs."

Wham! The front door slams open and Cloudfinger springs into the room. A cop lands on his back and Floyd turns and throws him off into the bar. Two others try to jump him but he catches the first by the neck and beats him against the second and they both go rolling across the floor, smashing over tables.

"Harold!" Floyd yells, but the last two guys at the door

finally realize what's going on and grab their rifles. Floyd cracks one across the eyes with his tomahawk, but the other gets his rifle flicked on to automatic and climbs a burst right up the wall, missing the Indian by six inches. He stands there frozen, jerking as his rifle empties itself into the ceiling. The Indian crouches, measuring him, then buries the blade of his tomahawk in his throat, an inch above the rim of his flak vest. The guy totters backward like a broken toy, his eyes wide with surprise.

"Harold!" Floyd yells again, then sees that the cops in the back are starting to pick up their rifles so he jumps back out the door and disappears down the alley.

Nobody tries to follow him.

"Well, god damn," says the Police Captain with a look of candid curiosity on his face for the first time. "Who was that guy?"

He walks to the door, his fists jammed into his leather pockets. Two of the cops are still alive, although one seems to have a broken back. He moves around them being careful not to get any blood on his boots, then stops and yells back at the cops in the rear of the room, telling them to get out to the truck. They drag the dead bodies out by the heels, leaving dirty swaths of blood on the floor, and pile everything into a big gray paddy wagon parked in front of the bar.

The Police Captain stands in the doorway after the others have gone. He still looks a little puzzled.

"Who was that guy, Harold? What's going on? Why are you changing it?"

Harold shakes his head. "I've never seen him."

"He called your name?"

Harold shrugs. "So I'm famous."

"You're making a mistake. I don't know if this is your idea of a joke, I don't know what you're up to, but if you know what's good for you, you'll get off this kind of anti-social behavior. All that old cops-and-robbers stuff is over. Get smart, Harold, you don't owe anybody anything. Live for yourself."

He turns and goes out and the people in the back start getting up, moving around the room quietly, ashamed of what happened to them. Roy comes up and sits silently beside Harold.

"Shit," says Darlene, "this is awful! They can do whatever they want. I feel dirty all over."

Harold drains his glass and stares into the ice cubes.

"What's that crazy Indian got to do with it?"

"I don't know."

"There's nothing you can do, is there? We just have to take it?"

"I don't know, Darlene. Donnard and Todd are dead, so the Baine Gang is as good as finished."

"Donnard and Todd?"

"That's who they say Bea killed."

"That can't be right. Beatrice wouldn't do that, would she?"

"I don't know, Darlene."

"So that's why they said you don't owe anything? And you believe that? After the way they do, coming down here putting their hands all over us!"

"What if they aren't cops?"

"So what? You want everything neat," says Darlene, "but it's a messy world. You worry too much about making a mistake, but even a mistake is better than nothing. I'm going to take a bath," she says angrily.

Roy watches her walk away. "What do you want me to do, boss?"

"I don't know. I guess you better stick around. We're going to be busy tonight."

"This is Duane."

"Hello, Duane."

"Can I keep him? Huh, Harold?"

"What happened to your clothes? Did that Indian do that to you?"

"Aw, this happened rescuing Duane."

"Rescuing? I thought you said you found him?"

"Well, I did, sort of, you see there was this mean old man and he was really cruel to Duane, made him stand in front of this gate night and day at this crazy warehouse and . . ."

"Okay, but the Indian didn't do anything to you?"

"No, he couldn't. He had psychological hang-ups."

"I should say so."

"You met him?"

"He was in this afternoon."

"Unh, he didn't get mad, or anything, did he?"

"We didn't discuss it."

"I sort of left without saying good-bye."

"So I gathered."

"Aw, come on Harold, can't I keep Duane?"

"He doesn't really belong to you. What are all those tennis balls for?"

"Duane kind of likes them."

"You didn't get mixed up with those photographers again, did you?"

Little Eva giggles, then lays her arm up over her head

seductively so that her blouse pulls up exposing her left breast.

"Can I keep him? Please? Pretty please?"

"Eva!"

"Puh-*lease* . . ."

"Well . . ."

"Yippee! Come on, Duane. Let's go down to the kitchen and get you something to eat!"

"Put some clothes on!" Harold says and Little Eva glances back over her shoulder coyly, then struts off swinging her hips in an exaggerated motion that's as much a parody of being slinky as anything else.

"Jesus," says Harold, shaking his head. "I wonder if I've done the right thing with her."

Harold is strolling through the sunset streets, his hands in his pockets. Occasionally, he gets bumped by a group of tourists, but he hardly even notices. The place has been crowded for the last couple of hours; it looks like it's going to be a big night.

People are hustling by, heading for bars or restaurants; the show's about to start, the curtain's about to go up. The sun is stuck stupidly like a flat orange disc above the dark buildings at the far end of Fourth Street. So go down, Harold thinks, get it over with, and has to laugh at his own bitterness. It's still hot and the sky is hazy. It's still the first real day of summer.

What a dumb idea calling those cops. All that did was make it messier.

Harold figures that the collapse must have been implicit in the optimism of the founders. The naïve city fathers

laid it out straightforwardly so that they might live in the
safety of concrete without the chance of anything crawling
out to bite them, so that they might sit in rows with their
sisters without the need to make anything, without the
need to do anything, to add anything, but just to wait lined
up like bullets patient in an automatic's magazine, talking
to their sisters, saying yes, yes, yes, yes. . . .

But Harold knows he's lying to himself again. To get
killed or not is what matters. Everything else is the polite
decoration that comes with domesticity, and won't be his
affair much longer.

The sun is gone. Bats used to feed from the shadows, but
they're gone too, probably because there aren't any insects
around here anymore. The darkness and decay of old alleys,
the smells inside moldy buildings like insidious tongues
saying feel sorry, feel sorry for yourself, feel sorry. . . .

And he knows he's still lying. Perhaps it's because Little
Eva is so obviously able to survive that he's oddly happy
and his self-pity seems largely theatrical. She wasn't even
scared, he thinks. How does she keep her head so clear?
She dances through the rubble of this place like a butterfly
and never seems to get dirty. She's probably going to get
along, no matter what happens.

Prudence Penderecki on stage at the Fumbling Hen has
brought the audience to their feet, whistling and clapping
and hollering for more. Harold's in the back of the bar
with Pizzicato. Tony's telling him how much trouble he
had trying to pin down Gloria Cloudfinger. She stops somewhere between the Inner City and the Civic Center. He's
come in at it from a dozen directions, even tried a Ouija
board, but it always works out the same.

"She's off the grid," he says puzzled, "and that doesn't happen. Evidently there are people out there without any place in society. She might be with them, but it's amorphous. I've never known information sources to be so vague."

"That so? Maybe she's dead?"

"No, I think I'd know that, being dead is simple."

"But maybe murdered? A victim of a nut in a dark alley?"

"Well, there's always something left, bits of the corpse, a wad of clothing, dental work found in the furnace, a vengeful mother badgering the investigators, a loyal dog whining beside the suspicious steamer trunk trying to make himself understood."

Tony wonders if Harold wouldn't be willing to take a little field trip into the Urban Renewal area. He doesn't like this sort of collapse to occur in his system. Harold agrees, he was going that direction anyway this evening.

"That's fine. Then I'll owe you a favor for helping me. See how things can interlock?"

"Nothing to it," says Harold. "My pleasure. But did you ever think that your way of doing business was nothing but a lot of talk?"

"I'm glad you asked me that," says Tony and is gone, starting with the basic relationship between philosophical thinking and language, and driving forward through Greeks, Christians, Rationalists, spinning loops of explanations around Harold like a spider winding a fly up in silk, saving him to be eaten later.

Harold stops him. "Man," he says, "that is the kind of stuff that's keeping me whole."

"Because you believe?"

"No. Because you do."

"How come they tear up the roads?" asks Roy.

The three of them are standing on the rim of the Urban Renewal desert, gazing out over the silvery lunar surface. The whole expanse is shivering and glistening in the starlight like the slick phosphorescent skin of a gigantic dead body.

"Homogenization," Harold says and Tony asks him why.

"They said they want to get rid of the old landmarks. They said it's easier to get along if you can forget the past."

Tony kicks at the skeleton of a dead radio half buried in the sand, the top of it bleached white by the desert sun. "They want to sentimentalize history," Tony says.

"How come?"

"Get rid of guilt. Help the citizens forget about some of the mean tricks they've pulled."

"That's not so good, huh?" says Roy.

"Come on," Harold says. "Let's get going."

"You know about evolution, Roy?"

"A little," Roy says doubtfully, "not too well."

"The whole point is in the situation of diversification . . ."

"Come on!" says Harold, and they start walking.

"Look at it this way, if everything was exactly the same, the world would freeze over and die. Why do you think there are two sexes, Roy?"

"Gee, I dunno. For fucking?" Roy says, and laughs.

"For christsakes!" Harold starts walking out in front of them. "Let's go!"

They walk silently in single file for about fifteen minutes, then stop in front of the first big midden of rubble. It's mostly broken bricks and bits of plaster with smashed beams and lead pipes sticking out at crazy angles. The whole thing is about fifty yards in diameter and as high as a three-story building.

"First time you've been out here?"

"Yeah," says Tony, staring up solemnly at the huge midden.

"Me too," says Roy. "It's sort of messy, isn't it?"

They walk past it slowly, watching the shifting nets of shadows unfold in the pale gray light. At the far side of the midden is an unbroken bathtub thrust twenty yards above the rounded crown of rubble, swaying in the gusty wind on the end of its white lead stalk like the deformed skull of a flower.

"I don't guess there's any reason to keep going in a row," Harold says. "We couldn't be much better targets if we had on neon signs."

"You think somebody's waiting for us?"

"What do you think?"

They stand in the shadows of the midden. Nobody much seems to want to be first to step out onto the starlit desert again.

"Hell," says Harold, "I guess it's up to me." He pulls down the brim of his panama hat, sticks his hands in his pockets, and strolls out onto where the road used to be, aiming at the black glass towers of the Civic Center. It's going to be about a five-mile walk. Harold's got a flask of whiskey that'll help, but he's at the end of his energy and knows he's going to start feeling the last twenty-four hours pretty soon.

Tony and Roy are right behind him, a little nervous about being out in the open.

"How about this, if every organism is exactly the same, then what'll we eat?"

"Huh? When?" says Roy, and Harold tells Tony to quit explaining everything.

The earth around them is dried into a flat gray clay, hard and hopeless with scattered blooms of bottle caps and tufts of insulated wire cracking through the surface.

"Where exactly are we going, boss?"

"I don't know."

"What'll we do when we get there?"

"I don't know that either."

It seems windier out in the open, and somehow brighter. They draw closer together until they're almost arm in arm.

"I don't like this much. I don't like not knowing."

"I don't either, Roy. How about you, Tony, you still okay?"

Tony nods. He looks a little scared though.

"You can go back," says Harold. "You can too, Roy. This whole trip is actually just more or less my business, and I don't mind working alone. I'd like to find that Indian's sister because I said I would, but my main action is going to have to be down there in the Civic Center."

"Well, maybe if we didn't have to walk?" says Roy.

"The roads are watched. It might be okay to go in directly, or it might not. I'm just being careful."

"Can't Tony tell you what's going on down there?"

"What do you think, Pizzicato, I'm getting set up, right? They're trying to get me down there so they can bump me off."

"It may not be that simple. I'd have to do a little work

on it, but my general feeling is that they don't ever really have much of a plan. There are troubled people in high places. Whims get fanned into programs by overeager subordinates. A major effort is made to appear to be in control, but they have problems too.

"You know, Harold, we've always known the answers; it's the proper questions that elude us. Or rather how to frame the questions. We can know anything we can conceive of if we can just figure out how to formulate the request. Our computers want to help us. If we can get them to teach us how to ask the right questions, we'll have it made."

"Tony?"

"Now, the trick of course is figuring out how to ask them how to ask them. It loops back onto itself so the cut-in will have to be arbitrary. Perhaps by discovering what would be the metaphorical electronic equivalent to poetry, and thus woo them with binomial blandishments . . ."

"We have things to do," Harold says, reaching for his flask. "Do you suppose you could get to the point?"

Pizzicato observes him for a moment with a slightly bewildered expression on his face, then draws a deep breath and starts again.

"You see, it's hard because it gets into such odd corners up there. People have power, but there doesn't seem to be any top end, ultimately nobody's in charge, it just blurs out, the higher you go. There are levels of bureaucrats in leadership positions said to be insane, although this might be an error in interpretation. I, for one, hope so. Insanity's such a precarious attitude, it's a shame we have to rely on it as often as we do."

"Shall I hit him, boss?"

"Let's just walk away. He can't help himself."

"It's a tool!" Tony says, a little quicker now. "Hot little brains, fizzing and popping, turn out blocks of information that are often useful. They're just like us except more so. Wait!"

Harold and Roy break into a slow trot. Pizzicato starts after them.

"Wait!"

"You going to answer my question?" Harold shouts and tells Roy to keep running.

"I was coming to it, wait!"

"Or at least shut up?"

"No, listen," Tony says, and they stop. "Like I told you before, everything's a product of everything else, so everything's a product of essentially a single source, since there's unity in a perfect multiplicity."

"Oh yeah? Says who?"

"They think that way too, except they take it literally. They'd probably like to roll up all the tag ends of misfits and oddballs and squeeze them into a kind of metaphoric suppository gel that could be shoved back up the anus of that source."

"What the . . . ?"

"They're more thorough than thoughtful, but when they finally understand something, they can be tenacious."

"What're you *talking* about?"

"Death's tidy. They might be tempted."

"Meaning me?"

"They can't see much beyond on and off, one and zero. Things get simple when everybody agrees, they've been spoiled. . . ."

Harold stands there looking at him with his arms hanging down. Tony's managing to mill around all by himself, obviously hoping that Harold understands, although he's not looking real cocky about it.

"I guess it doesn't matter," Harold says at last, shaking his head. "It must just not be my style. Even if I knew what you meant, I'd still probably do the same thing."

"Sure," says Tony, off the hook.

"Hey! What do you mean, sure?" Harold says and then stops him. "No, no more, don't tell me, don't explain anything. Simple hand signals, calm conversations, and whenever at all possible, nonverbal communication, you understand?"

Tony just nods.

"Good," says Harold, pleased. "Good. It's nice to know there's still a place in this world for intimidation."

They hear the rock before it hits, hear its lyric of smashed brains as it whirs past Roy's head, missing him by six inches. It slams against the ground fifty feet behind them and skitters off into the blank silver sands, nobody really noticing where it goes, too busy with the hard flatness of the trajectory it had coming in.

"You see anything, Roy?"

"No, boss, it came out of the side of that big mound, but I don't see anybody."

"Damn! but I wish I'd have bought glasses."

They see the second rock just in time to hit the dirt and come up running, heading for the other side of the midden. They make it into the shadows, then drop down behind a big slab of concrete, pistols pointing back out over the top, ready to shoot it out with whatever it is that's out there.

"Man," says Roy panting, "that motherfucker throws *hard!* You see the size of that second rock? That was a chunk of brick was what that was!"

Harold tells him to cover his side, the guy could come
around either way. They wait, but there's nothing to see.
It's flat and empty, an abandoned stage with nothing but
the glittering black night sky of stars above the wasteland.

"What're we going to do, boss?"

"I don't know. He must've thrown that first rock two
hundred and fifty feet."

Roy looks at him and Harold holds up his Colt.

"This old smokeless .44's only accurate for about a hundred feet or so, then the bullet starts wandering. How can
that guy do that?"

"Don't ask Tony," says Roy.

They decide they'll have to try and take the guy. They'll
circle around both sides and trap him. "The trick is not to
shoot each other," Harold says, "in case the guy's gone."
Tony decides to stay behind and guard that slab of concrete.

Harold keeps against the shadows as much as possible,
trying not to make any noise. He's not too happy with the
situation, but they don't have much choice. If they tried
to make a run for it, the guy could just bust them from
behind. Harold's moving pretty slowly, and if anything
jumps out, or leaps up, or makes any kind of sudden motion, he's going to drill it. He hopes Roy is thinking the
same way.

"Unh, say . . . ?"

Harold spins around, his pistol way out in front of him
gripped in both hands, but it's only Tony.

"What the hell are you doing?"

"I thought maybe I'd be more useful if I was with you
after all."

"Okay, but be quiet, for god's sake."

Harold figures they must've come almost halfway, although it's hard to tell. The edge of the mound forms an

irregular wall and trying to search it is like continuously peeking around corners, waiting for the blow. Every black pocket that their quarry isn't in makes it that much more likely he'll be in the next one.

"This is knocking the shit out of my nerves," says Harold. He squats down behind an upended bathtub and cracks open his flask. Pizzicato presses up right behind him.

"You want some?"

A gigantic shadow rears out of the sand on the other side of the bathtub and Harold knows it must be Cloudfinger, he can see starlight glinting off the upraised tomahawk.

Wham! Harold's pistol goes off more or less involuntarily and the Indian yells, turns, and is running across the open desert in an awkward lope, his left arm hanging down like it's broken.

Harold jumps out into the open and sits down with his elbows clamped between his knees for support.

Wham! He squeezes the trigger and kicks up a puff of dust right in front of the Indian. *Wham!* He shoots again and this time the bullet hits on the other side and about ten feet behind him.

"Damn good shooting!" shouts Tony. "That must've scared him!"

"Scared him, hell. I was trying to hit that son of a bitch."

The Indian disappears behind a distant midden. They continue on around another fifteen feet and find Roy lying on his back with his eyes open staring at the stars. The side of his forehead is crushed. Harold crouches down beside him, looking into his lightless eyes.

"Gee," says Tony, "he's dead."

"Get out of here. Go on back to the Inner City."

"But, I don't . . ."

"Get out of here!" Harold shouts and Tony backs up, then turns, and starts away.

"Wait. Here," Harold says, holding out Roy's pistol. "Take this, you might need it. Shoot anything that gets in your way."

"I don't know how to . . ."

"Figure it out," says Harold, and turns his back on him. He drags Roy over to where he was before and tries to fit the bathtub over him but he's too long and his feet stick out. There are a lot of broken bricks, so he covers everything with them until he's made a small mound next to the big one.

He brushes the dust off his hands and knees.

"If I come back, I'll take care of you. I can't do any better than this right now. I'll get that Indian for you. I'm sorry this happened. I don't know what else to say. You were a real pro."

Beatrice is released shortly after her last interview. The process is the reverse of the one the day before, although much quicker. She watches herself go through the hurried formalities, mildly noticing the fact that she has evidently lost the ability to register surprise. The two matrons are as irritable as they were yesterday, but clumsier now, and easily flustered. It is obvious that they want to get rid of her as quickly as possible. She signs what they put in front of her. The documents are probably fakes, but she doesn't bother to worry about that. Her power to distinguish among the various implications inherent in her situation has atrophied, leaving her with a numb acceptance that things might as well be working out as they are.

She wanders through a series of corridors connecting empty offices, suspecting that she wasn't really being held in the Civic Center Detention Facility. This building is too blatantly deserted. She sees the Police Inspector waiting for her in an empty foyer and realizes she had been expecting to meet him again. He asks her if she's lost and, since she doesn't know whether she is or not, she just smiles and shrugs, and continues past him, willing to let him follow if he wants to.

"I'm sorry you threw that at me, those flowers."

"That's okay. Forget it."

"I really feel badly about it."

Beatrice stops against a pillar of crated typewriters that have been stacked precariously to the ceiling. She doesn't face him directly.

"Of course we don't know as much about anger as we'd like to. Or about a lot of other human emotions, for that matter."

"Who doesn't?" Beatrice asks in a careful voice. "Who are you?"

"But we keep trying. Crimes of passion are of course often highly emotional and thus a particular problem for us in terms of prevention, or rather preventive detection."

"You know I didn't kill anybody."

"Well, as I was saying, we are optimistic concerning the future that lies before us in this field."

"The police are, you mean?"

"Why, yes, of course."

"Why do you keep after me?"

"I told you I was very fond of you."

Beatrice leans tentatively against the stacked typewriters. They shift slightly, although they aren't as unstable as they look. She could try to brace her hip against the wall for leverage, but she would feel silly if she missed him.

"You have to try to understand that in today's complex modern society we can't always do what we want."

"You mean the police can't?"

"Well, of course, and the nonpolice can't also."

She looks at him carefully for the first time. The wounds on his cheeks have become infected and even though he has covered them again with make-up, the festering is obvious. His swollen face is disfigured with an expression of grotesque candor that she realizes is very probably sincere. She watches him methodically unfold a damp handkerchief, pausing to study each configuration of the cloth like a man reading entrails.

"I know how horrible it must have been for you when they put their filthy hands on you and made you do things."

"Who?"

"The perverts who paid you to let them do disgusting things to your body."

Beatrice turns away from him abruptly and crosses into an empty office, hoping that her haste doesn't betray the twist of fear that has found her again. The inside of the office hasn't been painted yet, although the sheets of plasterboard are sealed together with careless strokes of white primer. She holds on to herself, wraps her arms under her breasts and forces herself to breathe regularly. Gallon cans of wall paint are lined along the back of the room and she counts them, then counts them again, starting at the other end.

"If you can make yourself understand that there isn't any practical value in your continuing this irrational fear of the police, then perhaps . . ."

"What do you want?" She says sharply.

"It's not what I want. It's what you want."

She writes her name on the dusty lid of the nearest paint can, then rubs it out and wipes her fingers on her skirt. She can hear his breath rasping behind her.

"What I want?"

She follows him obediently through a warren of public housing projects. Many of the buildings have already been condemned and abandoned, while others haven't been occupied yet. Sometimes it's hard to tell which is which. They walk past row after row of identical apartment houses lined up like men waiting to be shot. The Police Inspector tells her about his childhood. He never had any friends. Once his father pushed him down a flight of stairs and later cried in remorse while his mother tore a bed sheet into long feathery strips as if she was going to fashion it into some kind of rope ladder. He tells her how as a kid he used to play in the new buildings and how sometimes you could find little piles of burned underwear in dark corners and how that made you aware of the presence of other people.

"I always wanted a dog. I had an old piece of rug I used to drag around, pretending it was a dog. We went everywhere together. I named the rug Buster.

"You'll like my apartment," he says, steering her into one of the buildings. "You'll see all my things."

"Is that where we're going?"

"Me and Buster had these rats made out of the cardboard tubes from toilet paper rolls. Man, we used to give those rats a hard time, kicking them and stomping them and throwing them out the third floor window."

"Are you taking me to your apartment?"

He smiles and tells her it was in the Police Force that he

first found human companionship. He could see himself
reflected in the faces of the other cadets. Sometimes members of his class at the Police Academy would let him go
with them when they went out at night. It was just like
having friends, and the happiness he felt spilled into the
enthusiasm he had for his work. Eventually they turned
against him, evidently jealous of his rapid rise through the
grades.

"These locks here on my door are the finest steel, with
triple rollers and a six-inch deadbolt in each. You have to
open both at the same time or you can't get in. Don't worry,
though, you can learn it with a little practice. Here, now,
you can see all my things. These are my things here. You'll
notice how I've built shelves for them."

"These things? You mean souvenirs from police cases?"

"Oh, no. Most of these things I've been given, or have
bought for myself. And this is not all, not all at all. I have
a bedroom that's been converted into a storehouse built
with racks and bins and everything is waterproofed and
neatly labeled and, and everything."

"Things you've been given?"

"By friends, yes. Although not so much friends as people
I deal with. People who work in stores, where I shop."

He finds a chair and clears away the stuff on it for
Beatrice to sit down.

"How can you move around in here?"

"Well, there are still things that haven't been organized
yet. I need more shelves, bigger shelves, but see these? Do
you know how many of these glasses I have?"

"Those are just jelly glasses."

"Yes, grape jelly glasses. But do you know how many I
have here? And here, too?"

"In all of those boxes are jelly glasses?"

"And these are just this year, the ones I got this year. I have radios, hubcaps, goldfish bowls, electric blankets. I have shoes, shoe trees, shoe polish, shoe polishers, old newspapers. I have picture frames, toy planes, apple corers, paint sets, phone books . . ."

"Are you some kind of fence?"

"No, not at all. But I want you to know that all these things you see here are, are . . ."

"Are what?"

"Are mine. But you can use them."

"I'm not going to stay here," Beatrice tells him, trying to suppress a rush of elation. In his own apartment he's just another citizen. That means he's vulnerable, like everybody else.

"Let me show you some of the things I've got in the kitchen."

He leaves the room but comes back immediately when he realizes she's not going to follow him.

"I have my own place, you know," she says somewhat flirtatiously. "I get along pretty well by myself."

"An automatic drip coffee maker, a microwave oven, a sixteen-speed electric blender that can even crush ice, a broiler for toasting perfect English muffins every time. . . ."

"Listen, I'm sorry, but I decided a year ago that I wouldn't get involved in any serious relationships."

He holds one hand out in supplication toward the kitchen. "An electric can opener, a butter-up popcorn popper, a self-cleaning stove that ends all fuss forever. . . ."

"It couldn't work out. You'd hate my past. Every time you looked at me you'd see those hundreds and hundreds of guys who'd been there before you."

He sinks heavily to the arm of a sofa that is piled with boxes of laundry soap and plastic model airplane kits. Beatrice can't get the door unlocked and turns to ask him for help. He doesn't seem to hear her. His eyes are glazed and staring at the wall. She notices that the little automatic pistol has appeared in his hand. She doesn't know how long he's been holding it. It's just there, like some sort of ugly blue polyp.

"A shower massage," he whines, the pistol hanging loosely from his fingers. "Two hundred feet of extension cord on a spring-driven rewind drum."

"Let's be a little careful with that thing." Beatrice can tell by the layout of the apartment that there's no back door, and all of the windows seem to have iron grills over them.

"Golf clubs and hair dryers, a brand-new clarinet."

"Listen, why can't you leave me alone?" she says, backing away from him as he stands, the pistol coming up in front of him.

"An electric blanket with dual controls!"

"Please?"

Pop! A box of baking powder explodes behind her left ear. The pistol is shaking in his hand but is still pointing right at her. Tears are streaming down his cheeks and dripping off the welts her fingernails left on him the night before.

"An electric swizzle stick, a digital clock, a replica of the U.S.S. *Constitution* made entirely of toothpicks and dental floss."

The little pistol goes off again just as Beatrice ducks, diving for him. She wrestles him to the rug, knocking over boxes of junk and somehow putting a bullet through an aerosol can of shaving cream that rockets around the room leaving a foamy trail of thick rich mentholated lather. She gets the pistol away from him and struggles to her feet. She can't move because he's wrapped his arms around her ankles and won't let go.

"Where's Buster?" he whimpers.

"I'll get him for you."

"I want Buster."

She finally forces his hands open and locks herself in the bathroom. She can hear him sobbing on the other side of the door. She tries to flush the automatic down the toilet but it gets stuck.

"Buster?"

There's a Hotel de la Croix bath mat on the floor that looks old enough to qualify as a childhood pet so Beatrice opens the door to toss it out to the weeping Inspector, except he's sitting coolly on the couch, smoking a cigarette and slipping shells into an automatic shotgun, not a trace of any emotion left on his ugly mug.

Beatrice gets the bathroom door slammed in time to see a face-sized hole blown out of the top of it. She ducks behind the toilet and pries frantically at the little pistol but it won't budge. Another section of the door blasts past her shoulder and she's out the window without even stopping to wonder if she can survive the fall. She lands on a fire escape beneath the bathroom window. She clatters down the zig-zag stairs to the bottom level and drops the accordion ladder with a clank to the alley below. She's halfway down the ladder when the fire escape is washed with a hail of lead pellets, so she drops the rest of the way and comes up running. She has lost her shoes somewhere in the apartment, but that just helps her run faster. A few more pellets bounce past her but she's well out of range. The last thing she hears is him yelling how he knows where she lives, he can get a warrant any time he wants.

"Hold it, bud."

Harold stops. On his arm is a fat hand, not threatening yet, but heavy. There's a guy dressed like a uniformed cop standing behind him, crash helmet, black sunglasses, leather jacket, the whole costume.

Harold's cool. He's just doing a little casual reconnaissance down here in the Civic Center basement arcade. Another guy slides up behind him, same kind of outfit. "This punk giving you any trouble, officer?"

Harold watches the people walking by. They look like civil servants on their way home after working late. They're being very careful not to notice him, just bland faces moving by like so much raw bacon. He wonders if these two guys are real cops.

"What's your name?"

Harold still doesn't look at them directly. He's pretty sure he doesn't want any hassle down here.

"This a roust?" he says quietly.

"What's your name?" says the first one, and Harold starts backing up, trying to open out an angle on them in case he has to run for it. Another one comes up silently behind him and grabs him and shoves him back between the first two.

"Where do you think you're going, punk?"

Harold reaches up slowly and straightens his coat. He'd wanted to try to figure a couple of routes into the hospital before he started looking for Beatrice. These guys might just be enjoying some arbitrary harassment, at least he hopes that's what it is.

"You got some I.D., punk?" says one, and another says, "Shit! All the I.D. in the city won't get us off you!"

They move Harold up against the wall. People are still going past, pretending not to see anything. Harold's afraid they're going to frisk him.

"I don't know you guys," he says, trying to slide past them.

"Resisting arrest," says the first cop.

Another draws his service revolver. "You're resisting arrest, punk. You're going to need a lesson in how to act."

"There's a public lavatory past the escalators, let's take him there."

They start marching down the corridor, one cop out in front opening a path through the crowd and the other two each with one of Harold's arms locked in a come-along grip.

"You fucking punks think you can come down here and do whatever you want to, don't you? We're going to beat the shit out of you. We know who you are."

Groups of people are still moving by, frozen faces looking forward. Harold can tell something is not quite right. Things seem less and less accidental.

They get to the lavatory but it's full of guys. The cops are surprised by that and stand looking at each other, wondering what to do. Finally, one suggests they take him down to the boiler room. They move farther along the corridor, then stop in front of a low, unmarked door. The first cop has a set of skeleton keys and manages to get the door open after a lot of fumbling. There's no light beyond the door. Harold can't see anything but a narrow steel ladder. One cop holds him in a hammer lock while the other two start descending.

"It's slippery," says the first one. "Be careful."

Harold waits until the second cop is on the ladder then kicks him just under the chin. He grabs his partner as he falls past. It's silent for a moment, then there's a distant crunch as their bodies land in some sort of machinery.

Harold drops down and ducks off to one side. The cop behind him just about gets his revolver out before Harold kicks him a shot right in the nuts and the guy ends up groaning in a heap on the polished plastic floor.

Harold's hot-footing it down the middle of the corridor. He's almost made it to the up escalator when he gets shot. The slug tears through the fleshy part of his thigh and knocks him sprawling into a pile of people crouched in a doorway.

Damn, it hurts, the pain burning through him, blowing up flames crackling through his head like shattering ice. He gets his Colt out and rolls over onto his stomach, the whole corridor rotating over him like a wet red shell. The cop takes another shot and the bullet whangs against the hard floor a foot from his face. People are hollering and ducking down, jumping out of the line of fire. Harold can't find the cop and then he spots him, stumbling stupidly up the middle of the corridor, waddling like a duck he's so bent over with pain. Harold cocks the hammer back with his thumb and gives him a minute to get past a couple of old ladies stuck against the wall; then he drops him.

He starts working his way down the corridor, dragging his dead leg; he can't put any weight on it at all. He knows he's leaving a trail of blood so he stops and takes off his necktie and tries to form it into some kind of bandage. The corridor is lined with people pressing against the wall, their faces white and cautious, staring at him. He realizes he's still holding his Colt so he slips it back under his arm.

He rides the escalator up to street level, trying not to vomit. His leg hurts like a son of a bitch. He takes a step off the top of the escalator and collapses. He dozes off for a few minutes and dreams he's being washed and wakes up with his face in a pool of vomit. He rolls over trying to get away from the stench, his stomach wrenching with dry heaves, and fades out again, a cool gray water coming in from back beyond his mind.

"You all right, fella?"

Some nice lady's looking down at him.

"You sick?"

"I been shot."

He can feel the soft wetness pulling away, maybe he's not going to pass out again.

"I been shot in the leg," he says. "It hurts awful."

"Is that it in the left leg?"

Harold groans. "Help me, lady." People heading for the down escalator almost step on him and occasionally even stumble over his wounded leg.

"That *must* hurt."

"Please, lady."

"Is it bleeding much?"

Another lady stops by the first one. "What's the matter?"

"This man's been shot."

"That's terrible! Shouldn't someone call a policeman?"

"I suppose so," says the kind woman doubtfully.

Harold tries to move himself farther away. He can pull with his hands and push with his right leg, but dragging his bad leg hurts so much he almost passes out again.

"A cop's been shot!" shouts some guy coming up the escalator. "Hell, you ought to see him, lying down there deader than a side of beef!"

A ring of people looks down at Harold. Two old ladies are in the back muttering about how it's a disgrace all this violence and how something ought to be done about it, trying to sidle around so they can get a better view.

"This guy's the one who done it!" somebody suggests, prodding Harold's bloody thigh with the toe of his boot to see what that might make him do.

"A shoot-out! Like on television."

"Except not as dramatic."

The woman who was helping Harold is gone now, and he's got to try to force the pain down long enough to figure out how he can escape. He braces himself on one arm and holds up his .44. He's fighting hard to keep that gray water from washing through his brain again. His head's so heavy he can't see anything above feet and knees.

"Look out! He's got a gun!"

"The next motherfucker," Harold rasps, his throat burning from the vomit, "that touches my leg's going to get shot!"

People begin backing up, although reluctantly; they realize how badly he's wounded and so want to stick around to see what's going to happen next.

Blam! He fires a shot into the ceiling and that starts clearing the foyer out right away. He pulls himself along the railing next to the escalator and waits, his whole body throbbing. Pretty soon a guy comes up, not knowing what's going on. Harold sticks his pistol in his face and tells him to carry him on his back.

"What?"

"Come on! Piggy-back into the rear of the building."

"Listen, mister, I got a wife and kids and and . . ."

Harold leaves the guy tied up in a janitor's closet. He

makes a bandage out of his shirt and some black electrician's tape he's found. He takes the guy's pants too, although he leaves him his wallet. His thigh is getting stiff, but he's learning how he can move with the aid of a cane he's made by breaking off a mop handle. Just about the time he's starting to feel cocky about how well he's doing, he hears some more cops coming so he has to scram, heading deeper into the building.

It's nice back here now; he hasn't heard anybody for fifteen or twenty minutes, and his thigh's almost completely numb. This part of the Civic Center has never been used, nothing but row after row of empty new offices covered with a layer of dust. Some of the rooms even have piles of metal office furniture in them, hunched under tubes of light like the stillborn fetuses of huge machines.

It would be nice to stay in here, to make a hide-out in one of the empty rooms and live like a stone festering in the bowels of the government. He could launch short raids against the enemy ligatures, chopping apart electric cables and filling hydraulic valves with tar. It would be pleasant to bore holes through the outside walls and let in actual air, then sit back and watch the climate control system stutter itself into a paroxysm of binomial rage, circuits ripping at their own innards with the ons and offs of exploding electrical teeth.

Then Harold looks behind him, thinks: fool. Drawn in the dust down the middle of the corridor is a trail his dead leg's scraping, so obvious even a cop could follow it. He's got to get out of here fast; they must know right where he is. Probably they're trying to surround him, that's why they're giving him so much room. He tries to speed up, dragging his leg behind him, but that hurts too much and he's worried about opening up the wound again. He comes to where his corridor intersects with a larger one and stops. There are dozens of footprints, all going in the same direction. They must have him cut off. He limps into the larger corridor, mixing his trail with theirs, then returns the way he came, trying to stay in the tracks he's already made. He gets back to where there's a door marked *emergency exit* and forces it open. It's nothing but a staircase going down and he wouldn't chance it except he hears the snuffling rasp of running boots a couple of corridors over and figures this is just about his last shot.

There's no light so he has to feel his way down the stairs, dragging his stiff leg then lowering it in front of him, bracing against the wall. There doesn't seem to be any bottom, nothing but the stairs going deeper and deeper into the ground.

There would be people playing cards back at the Rolling Ring, and drinking whiskey. Darlene would be teasing Moe, and Maude would still be whining about the breakdown in the Inner City. It would be going on right now, somebody playing the piano, the ladies coming down the stairs in low-cut gowns, smiling and saying, evening, evening, nice to see you. Harold smiles to himself. Too bad he can't be there.

The wall has become rougher, and the stairs are uneven as if they had been left half-finished. Harold is noticing moisture now, too. There must be an underground river seeping in. At one point the little door high above him opened and someone shone a flashlight down toward him. He was long since out of range of its weak beam, and it showed no more than a fleeting twist of light.

The angle of descent grows gradually shallower and up ahead Harold can see a faint glow reflected on the sloping floor of a tunnel. He rounds a bend and stops in front of a dozen children standing frozen in the silver light of a lantern, staring at him with huge pale blue eyes. They're armed with little picks and shovels and even have a couple of small wheelbarrows.

"What are you kids doing, playing coal miner?"

They drop their tools and run down the tunnel, leaving him the lantern.

"Hey! I'm just passing through."

He picks up the lantern and follows them, hoping they aren't setting up some sort of ambush. It seems to be getting slightly warmer in the tunnel. He notices that his leg is bleeding again and stops, trying to adjust the bandage, but it's soaked through. His thigh is starting to throb again, too. He liked it better when it was numb. He tries to remember what he heard about gangrene. Tissues die because of loss of blood, but he can't remember if a throbbing pain is a good sign or a bad one.

He's never been shot before, never really even been seriously injured. You don't realize what it's like until it happens to you, he tells himself. All the movies and TV shows in the world don't do you a damn bit of good when it's you that's getting hit, when it's your turn to get up on stage.

He wonders if he might really die and tries to make himself think about Beatrice instead. It doesn't work. He keeps visualizing himself dead, wondering what that would be like.

Roy didn't know. He didn't look surprised about it. He just looked dead. The place you can see it is in the photographs of men taken just before they're executed, when they're lined up waiting, maybe even being helpful because they realize there is absolutely no escape, cocking their heads a little sideways to unhook the noose that's caught on an ear. Damn. You can see it in how slumped they look, how they sag like bags of water, how dead they look even though they still have a few minutes. You can always tell. The minute some guy knows it's going to happen to him, the weight comes into his face.

Roy looked real dead, no mistake. Poor old Roy.

His whole pant leg is soaked through, clear down to the ankle. He's losing too much blood. He tries to rearrange the bandage again, but the tape won't hold, it keeps slipping off. He looks up and notices a wind blowing in toward him. He pushes into it for about fifty feet and is suddenly outside, under the stars. Spread out in front of him is the wasteland, and beyond that the low flickering lights of the Inner City, five miles away.

He knows he could never make it.

Harold's waiting at the edge of the firelight, but nobody seems to be interested in him. He was walking along the edge of the desert when he first noticed the smoke coming up from behind one of the middens. He had to cross five hundred feet of open space, an easy target for anyone watching for him.

He's in some kind of hobo jungle. He doesn't know how many guys are here, voices curl out of the darkness without any bodies attached. Three men are tending the fire, cooking something in a big stew pot.

"I'm hurt," he says. "Can you help me?"

A man wearing a derby hat sticks his finger in the pot and tastes it, squinting to savor it better. "Another carrot!" he says and Henry answers, "Right, carrot," reaching down the front of his baggy pants, and feeling around until he can come up with one.

Derby Hat eyes it suspiciously. "This fresh?"

"Found it Tuesday."

"What's today?"

"Thursday."

"That's good enough," he says and unfolds his pocket-knife to cut slices into the pot.

An old lady wearing half a dozen layers of skirts and coats comes up and peers in. "Nice-looking soup," she says, "What's in it?"

"Mostly carrot," admits Henry, squatting back on his heels.

"Carrot soup!" cracks the old lady, and claps her hands together. "My favorite!"

"Listen," says Harold, "I been hurt, I need some help."

They stop and look at him.

"Who's that?"

"I never seen him before."

"Get a little food going and every goddamn deadbeat crawls in to get some."

"Now Tom," says Derby Hat. They go back to working on the soup, tearing up old catalogs and feeding them into the fire.

"One turnip," says Derby Hat, "just one, and a good soup would become a great soup."

"Yeah," Henry says, "and some salt; we haven't put any salt in it for a week. You can tell it needs it."

"I'm bleeding, my leg."

"Salt?" says the old lady. "You want some salt? I know where some salt is." She turns away from the fire and disappears into the darkness.

"Keep an eye on her, Tom."

"I need some bandages, or at least some tape."

"Tape?" says Derby Hat, and Tom starts muttering about how they're turning into a damn Salvation Army out here.

The old lady comes back dragging a rusty bucket full of some kind of stinking mud.

"You can't eat that," says Derby Hat. "It'd likely kill you."

"It's salty."

"Damn well might be; nevertheless, we got to obey basic nutritional and sanitational precepts. No eating found stuff that nothing else has been eating on. We don't want to try eating anything that nothing else wants to eat."

"What a bunch of bullshit," says Tom, shaking his head and going over to sit on the other side of the fire.

Harold sits down, his bad leg sticking out straight in front of him.

"What do you want tape for?"

Harold shows him his leg.

"It's bloody," says Henry.

"Yeah. Maybe you ought to rest with us for a spell, keep your weight off it. Get him a cup of soup, Henry."

Derby Hat cuts Harold's pant leg off at the crotch, then splits it down the seam.

"I used to be a doctor," he says, trying to unpeel the cloth. "But I quit. We'll have to boil some water. And get that mud the hell out of here, won't you, Henry?"

"You really a doctor?"

"Sort of, on TV, on *daytime* TV. That's why I quit, couldn't stand it anymore."

He rips the bloody pant leg off and Harold yells.

"I bet that hurt, all right," says Derby Hat. "But you don't have to worry, I was a damn good TV doctor."

Henry comes back with a pan of water and some blankets. Harold notices that people are starting to gather around him. They're dressed in ragged clothes, and their faces have been burned by the wind and sun, although none of them looks really mean. Henry folds a blanket under his head for a pillow. "You need anything else?"

Derby Hat shakes his head. "This is going to hurt," he says. "Somebody get him a drink of some runoff."

A guy hands Harold a flask of colorless liquid that reminds him vaguely of antifreeze. "You're best to swallow it down without breathing," he says, "makes it easier not to taste it."

Harold sucks on the bottle while Derby Hat washes around the wound. Whatever it is he's drinking, it acts pretty fast because by the time the work on his leg gets really painful, he's distracted by trying to remember the second stanza of the "Battle Hymn of the Republic."

Harold wakes up just before dawn, his leg throbbing. Everybody else is still asleep, spread around the various nooks and crannies of the huge midden. The fire has died down to warm coals and Derby Hat and Henry are wrapped in blankets across from him.

Lying with his head on his arm, he can see along the flat cool sands all the way to the Inner City. It's blurred into a line of low gray smears at the bottom of the morning sky, like a backdrop behind the black mounds of rubble. It's as if he can see to the rim of the world, beyond the bullshit and the hustle, all the way to where there's nothing but sterile sand glittering with little bits of broken glass and twisted stalks of wire. He squints, trying to focus on a particular building, but it doesn't work. He can't make out borders. He can't see anything but patches of color, and it's hard to tell where one ends and another begins.

Hell, he thinks, another hundred million years or so and the sun'll burn out. Not actually all that long to wait.

The sky's a lighter blue now and the only star left is Venus, clinging low on the horizon against the coming day. It's going to get hot later, but it's still cool in this silent morning, clean and lovely at the end of the rainy season. His leg aches. His friends are dead, his lady gone, maybe in trouble, and he's probably got only about one more day of living. Not actually all that long at all.

"Pretty, ain't it," says Derby Hat. Harold didn't know he was awake.

"Yeah."

"How's the leg?"

"It hurts."

"I don't doubt it. Who shot you?"

"I got hurt in an industrial accident."

Derby Hat rolls over. "I guess I'll go back to sleep," he says, "try again later. I could have sworn you said you got hurt in an industrial accident. That TV show I was on was a crime drama. I know a gunshot wound when I see one."

Harold feels like a piece of shit but Derby Hat's got his back to him. He closes his eyes and tries to think of Beatrice, but she won't come up, just the shape of her, like the shadow of her body or the echo of her laugh.

He dozes off again, then wakes up to find Derby Hat standing next to him holding a spear made out of a heavy knife blade wired to a long wooden handle.

"Fresh meat," he says, dropping the bloody carcass.

"Found him skulking around the edge of the next midden. And I always thought poodles were supposed to be smart."

He squats down next to Harold and begins to roll a cigarette. "I never did like this kind of damn little yappy dog, all wiggle, and piddle, and pink ribbons."

Harold notices that Henry's got a fire going and somebody else is starting to assemble a crude spit.

"I got shot by a cop."

Derby Hat's stropping his pocketknife, getting ready to skin the little dog. He's got his cigarette stuck in the corner of his mouth, the curling smoke causing him to squint.

"I killed the guy that shot me. He may not have been a real cop."

"It's hard to tell these days all right," says Derby Hat, "what with so many special cops and private cops and guys who just like wearing cop suits running around."

He starts skinning the little dog, working carefully so as not to damage the grain of the meat. "Tastes about like you'd think," he says. "Stringy weak flesh, an hour later and you're hungry again."

He stops and gestures toward Harold with his bloody pocketknife. "Your basset hound, your corgi, your dachshund, those wide low dogs, now they make a meal." He peels the pelt away and spreads it neatly over the gutted shell of a washing machine.

"Can't find them much anymore," he sighs. "I guess we already ate them all. Should've been more ecologically minded, I suppose, but what can you do when you're living with hungry hoboes and loonies? Everybody's gobble, gobble, gobble, as fast as possible. No thought for tomorrow."

He cuts off the head. "Henry, you want to wash this out for me? We'll use it for soup stock. And tell crazy Gloria

I'm going to make her a nice fur collar out of the skin."

He slits open the belly to scoop out the guts and spills them in a slippery pile by the fire.

"Who did you say?" says Harold. "Gloria?"

"Big crazy Indian woman that's living with us. Been here right from the beginning. You know, it's too bad about these intestines. We tried to make sausages but they'd always go bad right away."

He reaches back inside the thorax and pulls out the other inner organs, carefully placing the ones that can be eaten on an old hubcap.

"Look at the ulcerations on that stomach. You won't find that much in bigger, calmer dogs."

"I been looking for a woman named Gloria Cloudfinger, an Indian."

"Likely you've found her then. You're welcome to her, too. I'm sure Tom'd be happy to get her off his hands."

"Her brother's also looking for her. He killed my friend, and some cops."

Derby Hat sighs. "That happens," he says, "that happens. Come to think of it, there really isn't much of a tomorrow, is there? Not for us at least. You know, the cops could come out here and use us for target practice. Nobody'd ever be the wiser, and even if they were, who'd care? Malcontents, that's what we are, nothing but a bunch of bums and crazies. Better off without them, that's what they'd say downtown. No sir." He smiles. "Not much of a future at all, might as well eat up the fattest dogs first."

Harold stands up and tries his leg. It's weak, but he can walk on it.

"You did a fine job."

"You going somewhere?"

"I got business."

"You're a damn fool."

"I know. I noticed."

"You want to get shot full of holes?"

Harold shrugs. "That Indian's pretty wild," he says. "He's out here. Looking for me, looking for his sister, looking for anything that'll replace whatever he seems to be missing. I'd be a little careful if I were you."

"Hell," says Derby Hat. "We been around a long time. We're nothing but tough."

Harold starts walking toward the tunnel opening, his leg stiff but not too painful. He stops and looks back.

"What happened to her, anyway? How come she went nuts?"

Derby Hat's helping Henry slide the skinned carcass onto the spit. Raggedy hoboes are beginning to wake up, clambering down off the side of the midden, stretching and yawning and scratching themselves, still sleepy.

"Just happened, just an accident. She don't want to talk about it. Happens a lot, in fact. A better question might be why the rest of us *haven't* gone crazy."

Harold starts walking again but after a few minutes he stops.

"I'd have liked to stay," he yells. "It's nice out here. There're things I got to do. I don't have any choice."

A couple of hoboes heading out to take a piss stare at him as they trudge past.

"Yeah?" shouts Derby Hat. "That's because you're a goddamn fool."

"I'm sorry about Roy."

"Yeah, I know."

"No, I mean I really am."

Abandoned crates of electrical fuses have been left stacked in the alley. Harold kicks his foot against the nearest one and the rotted cardboard ruptures, spilling a bright cascade of the little glass devices down over his toes.

"It's okay, Bea."

"When it happens, it happens awfully fast, doesn't it?"

"Are you sure your apartment is being watched?"

"I'm not sure about anything. But I don't want him to catch me again. He could do anything."

"He might not be a cop."

"I don't care what he is. A guy that wants to be one but can't is worse than the real thing."

"Too much television."

"I don't care. He's out there, and he's looking for me. I can feel it."

"In your bones?"

"You bastard!" she laughs. "You still remember that? I was only a kid then, and when it's hard like that, it seems like it has a bone in it."

"Gullible Beatrice, believing the big kids' lessons on sex."

"Harold, why did you come?"

He picks up a couple of fuses and holds them against the sun. "Pretty, aren't they. Why are they just left out here?"

"Some sort of screw-up. It happens all the time. Nobody pays any attention to what they're doing. Invoices are misread, deliveries are made to the wrong address, that kind of thing."

"What are you going to do?"

"Just hide out. Just keep moving and try to lay as much space as possible between me and that psycho."

"What about your job?"

"Fuck the job. It was a phony. Some asshole I never met claimed to have rehabilitated me. He was getting government money and had to show some results."

"Which was you."

"Results. That's what I was. A documented case history for them to lick their chops over."

They stand quietly for a moment. Beatrice spots some children dragging a lot of videotape gear down the alley and gets panicky. The top ten floors of the building behind them have never been occupied, so Harold follows her up there.

"A little paranoid, aren't you, Bea?"

"Just another name for protective coloration."

She crosses to the far wall and rips open the dusty plastic drapes, allowing the morning sunlight to stream in around her, illuminating the tiny golden hairs on her arms and throat. She looks down across the city.

"You can see all the way to the Inner City from here. I didn't realize this building was so tall."

"I can help you escape, but I got to get into that hospital first and hit that guy."

"The river's lovely from here," she says. "It's glittering in the sunlight. You can just see the far edge. It looks like a silver road leading back through the hills up into the mountains. Except the mountains don't look real, they look more like cardboard cutouts."

"Beatrice?"

She turns around and looks at him, her arms folded across her breasts and her face dark against the bright glass.

"You really would ask me to do that?"

"I don't want to."

"You don't have to kill that guy."

"I don't have any choice."

"You don't want any choice."

"That's not true, Bea."

"Don't you understand that I've got to get out of here? I told you a year ago I didn't want to be there when it happens. I thought I'd see it in some stupid newspaper: Harold Baine, alias Laughing Harold, son of deceased mobster chieftain Big Jim Baine, died today. . . ."

Harold pulls the plastic dust cloth off one of the couches clumped up in the middle of the room and sits down. The office they're in occupies the entire northeast corner of the top floor. It has been completely equipped with office furniture, but nothing's arranged yet. The pieces are spread randomly around the room, each shrouded in gray layers of plastic skin dulled by the year's accumulation of dust. The only flash of color is Beatrice's bright lime-green blouse that appears briefly beyond the angular shapes as she prowls around the room. Without her, it'd be like living through a black-and-white TV set that's getting poor reception.

Harold puts his hat beside him, gingerly touches his bandaged leg. He thinks of the ghosts of all the unborn bureaucrats cocked like solitary kernels in the heart of each empty desk, yearning to blossom into bland white puffs of commerce, and laughs. His wound is still closed, the bandage holding. Derby Hat did a fine job.

Beatrice is standing at the far end of the room in front of the window, unwinding coils of hair that fall down her back in smooth brown sunlit flames.

He watches her undress but she's too far away for him to see clearly. She's no more than a white shape in motion, moving toward him through the ceremental wings of shadows.

"I can't take off my shoe, or pants, my leg's too numb."

"I'll do it."

She bends in front of him, her breasts swaying down heavily, the nipples stiff.

"Will that bandage be all right?"

"I think so."

She kneels between his knees and takes his penis in her hands, rolling it lightly between her palms.

"Did you think you'd see me again?" She smiles.

"I always thought I'd see you again."

She pulls on it, still watching him, and fits her lips around it, tickling with her tongue against the tip, then stops again.

"Yes, I always did too."

Harold lies on his back and wishes he had a cold beer. For some reason the overhead light fixtures are gone, or more likely were never attached. The ceiling is quartered by the amputated wrists of insulated wires protruding from cracked rubber sockets. Beatrice has discovered that there is no water, but continues to stand beside the dry fountain, holding a wad of invoice triplicates up against her while she's draining.

He has a growing sense of a governmental inability to finish things, an unwillingness to complete projects. Perhaps the minds behind the Civic Center hope that as long as everything is under construction, there is no reason to have to confront the fact that all they're forming is another version of the same old failure.

Except that isn't it, because they're as likely to be afraid of arriving at perfection as anything else. It may not be as simple as it seemed. Perhaps the Police Captain really does want him to join them because they realize a dose of anarchy might keep the system from stagnating. Maybe he's not just being set up. In all their efficiency, there is always a tendril of ineptitude growing in between two plates of the machine.

He has a strange intuition that he may be able to get away with it. He may be able to walk boldly into the hospital and blast the guy.

In which case he might be doing what they want, so wouldn't he be better off not doing it? Although if he is paranoid and they are sincere, then whose side should he be on?

Are there even sides?

Or maybe this is what they want him to think and he's stupidly falling into their trap, freezing himself into indecision.

There's only one way to find out. And that's to do it.

"I always thought I'd see you again, too."

"I thought so."

"I wasn't sure I wanted to."

"I like Eva, but it's not the same."

"She's awfully young."

"Yes. I think she's going to be okay."

"That's nice. I worried about her."

"She doesn't concern herself much with alternatives. Things happen to her and she watches them without much more attention than you'd apply to television. It's her world, such as it is."

"Such as it is."

"She has a dog now."

"That's nice."

"Named Duane."

"Funny name."

"Yes."

"I remember your father's funeral, all those shiny black cars lined up in the middle of the cemetery, each one with the motor running and a driver in the front seat and a sawed-off shotgun tucked under the dash in case of trouble. It was a lovely funeral. You were only four but I was older, I remember. A mound of dead flowers piled on the coffin. My mother wept all afternoon, she wouldn't eat. The next day the same, crying for him."

"Beatrice . . ."

"It doesn't mean shit! She's dead too. What does it matter? Every single person from that time is dead."

"There's one who isn't."

Beatrice looks at him, the coils of smoke from her cigarette blue against the lime-green blouse. She taps the ashes off against the edge of a wastebasket.

"Then go kill him! You've had your good-bye fuck. Now go kill him! You want the excitement."

She paces in front of the window, her arms folded over her breasts and the cigarette held delicately between the tips of her long fingers.

"All those long black cars, it was like a celebration. Everybody came, including the press. It was a ritual, and it was spring too, very symbolic. I don't suppose you know what a vegetation god is?"

Harold shakes his head. "Not exactly."

"Something more than a complicated carrot, but it doesn't matter, not your style, right? Besides, it was more like summer than spring. A hot sunny day, hot even in the morning, there was a lot of sweating going on, must've been the black suits, right? Or maybe the weight of bulletproof vests, or maybe the uncertainty of not knowing who was scheduled to get hit next? Just why do you suppose there was so much sweating that day of the funeral?"

"Bea . . ."

She stops in front of him and stubs the cigarette out against the inside of the wastebasket.

"I never wanted to have babies. I never wanted them. I couldn't have stood holding them here," she says, cupping one breast in both hands. "It would have been like suckling a corpse."

"Stop it!"

"Do you remember the iris garden? All the different kinds of iris lined along the walks, how they would sway in the wind. You said we'd get a house and plant a garden, buy bulbs at the nursery and choose all different kinds. We'd buy fancy show iris if we had enough money but I said even the regular blue would be okay, anything would be okay, remember?"

He nods his head. "Yes, I do."

"Well, so much for that. So much for that, such as it is, or rather, as it was. And I'm going to be all right. Once I get past the goons out there, I'll be in the clear. You won't hear about me decorating my wrists with razor blades the way some of the people around here seem to feel obliged to do. Or face down across the bed with a belly full of pills and a dead white hand six inches from a dead white telephone, how pathetic, and the phone counting, beep-beep-beep!

"You're not laughing, Harold, don't you think it's funny?"

"I think I'll be able to pull it off. I know a way out of the Civic Center."

"Why don't you just go away now? Remember what we used to say? How we'd escape into the mountains and live. Build a house on the edge of a meadow and farm and fish and hunt. It was a lovely vision, the season was always mid summer, full of wild flowers and tame deer and gentle breezes."

She stops in front of him, lights another cigarette.

"How would you have costumed me? In rabbit pelts? Deer-hide bikinis sewn with colored beads? Or would you have preferred me nude, wearing nothing but crude boots and lots of clunky peasant jewelry, little silver bells tied to my wrists and ankles so you'd always know where I was flitting.

"I'd get a lovely golden tan all over and never get any older. My breasts would never sag and my thighs would never loose their firmness and my stomach would always stay perfectly flat. I'd drink nothing but the pearls of dew that collect in the cups of flowers in the morning and eat only the nectar tucked in the little velvet sacks under the petals of violets."

"It's not my fault."

She stops again and looks at him. "It's nobody's fault. It just isn't worth a damn anymore."

"Maybe I'll get away."

She smiles at him. "It's nice to think so."

"You'll help me?"

"Why didn't you come ask me a year ago when there was still a chance to try something?"

"I don't know. I guess I was ashamed."

"Of what?"

"Of that you'd left me."

"You're a fool. I never left you."

They sit looking at each other in silence. Then she tells him she can get him into the hospital. There are ways in and out that won't be guarded, even if they are watching for him. Once he's in the hospital itself, he's on his own, she can't stick around waiting for him.

"What are you going to do?"

"Just get in motion and stay that way," she says. "I've got some money and I'm going to travel very inconspicuously. I'm on the road right after I see you into that hospital."

"Don't cry, Bea."

"It stops here, Harold, it really does."

Harold knows the guy's dying in here somewhere, but he doesn't know which ward. He'd like to ask a nurse. He approaches one, but there's something about the stiff white dress and sensible shoes that holds him up.

He stops beside a sick guy sitting parked in his wheelchair. The patient's upper torso is held in place by two white canvas straps lashing him to the frame. Harold figures it might not be a bad idea to look like he's involved.

"Say, pop, you want a push?"

The old man looks up at him blindly, two streams of drool sliding down his jaw to his chest. Harold starts him rolling and is just getting some speed up when he notices he's being followed by two guys dressed like orderlies. He turns right, then right again, and they stay with him so he knows it's a bust. He slips into an elevator and pushes the up button for every floor above him. He rides up one floor, gets off and into the next open elevator and does the same thing again, figuring it'll take those two thugs the rest of the afternoon to figure out where he got off.

"You like it along here?"

They're strolling down a wide bright corridor, one wall of which is glass. They pause to look through the window. Inside is nothing but shelves full of premature babies, row after row of them ticking in their cases like little pink flowers linked together by the stems of their yellow plastic drain tubes. A couple of nurses are working the far end of the line with a mobile feeding nozzle.

"Look at that, pop, they're getting lunch."

The old man seems to be making an effort to focus, but Harold doesn't know if he can see anything or not.

"You don't look like no orderly."

Harold turns around. There's a guy behind him dressed in a long white doctor's coat with a stethoscope hooked around his neck. Harold notices he's wearing shiny black combat boots, never a good sign.

"I'm just starting," says Harold. "I don't know my way around yet. I'm just getting Mr. Brown here some exercise."

"That guy's name isn't Brown, and I never saw an orderly dressed like you."

The guy moves to the side, trying to trap Harold against the glass. Harold starts backing up and keeps his patient between them.

"I haven't had time to pick up my white suit yet. In fact, that's just where I'm going now, thanks for reminding me."

"You better come with me."

A group of ladies slides up next to them. "There's Melvin!" one of them squeals, pointing at baby number 476. "Doesn't he look just like his father? Particularly with his mouth hanging open."

Harold slams his patient into the guy in the doctor coat, the steel footrests of the wheelchair cracking him sharply on the shins. He gets a nice jump on him but his leg starts hurting again after the first few steps and he's afraid he's going to open up his wound. He glances back once and the guy's moving even more slowly than he is. That chair must've given him a nice clean bite. Good thing he's not packing a gat, Harold wouldn't be real hard to hit.

He's about half running and half limping now, but the guy doesn't seem to be gaining on him, and he's thankful but also a little bit worried. People in the corridors give him room, stop and watch as he runs by; not too much excitement here, running in hospital corridors having been popularized by television.

But what's bothering him is that the guy chasing him doesn't seem to be trying as hard as he could. It doesn't feel so much like hot pursuit as it does like getting herded by a clever sheep dog.

He cuts down into a narrower corridor where there aren't so many people. His leg is really starting to drag on him now. Maybe he ought to try to get somebody to look at it; this is a hospital, after all. The corridor is a dead end so he takes another right, turning into a low passageway just wide enough for him to move, except it's another cul-de-sac, lined with doors.

He goes through one and finds himself at the end of a long, wide hall. A lot of fancy machines have been shoved against the near wall, some even piled on each other as if they wanted to open up a section of the floor. As far as Harold can see down the length of the room, there are groups of doctors and nurses, some dressed in pale green surgical robes and others just wearing their regular white doctor suits.

A woman pulls on his arm until he bends down so she can whisper into his ear. "I'm an anesthesiologist," she giggles.

"That's fine," says Harold, trying to back away.

"My name's Barbara, but everybody calls me Barbie."

"Hi, Barbie."

"What are you?"

"Self-employed," Harold says, moving deeper into the room.

"I mean what do you do?"

"Some dog work, some people work, nothing fancy." Harold's having a hard time walking backwards, he keeps bumping into things.

"That's lovely. You help take care of people?"

"In a sense."

"That's why you're here?"

"More or less. I'm not a doctor though."

"No. But everybody can't be doctors."

"No. You got to have sick people too, or there wouldn't be any point to it. You wouldn't have anybody to slice steaks off of but each other!"

"I don't understand?"

"Not funny," says Harold soberly. He's managed to back right into the middle of a group of young doctors who seem to be on some sort of break. One of them offers him a beer.

"You got booze here?"

A sign over their section says UROLOGY. The guy opens a small steel door in the side of a cabinet. It's a refrigerator; the top shelf is full of urine-sample bottles, each with a neat little label on it, but the bottom is beer. There's some sort of tough-minded medical irony going on here, but Harold doesn't bother to figure it out. The guy hands him a beer and gives one to Barbie.

Everybody's looking at Harold. He figures they must be waiting for him to propose a toast.

"Well," he says raising his can, "here's to health!"

Nobody moves, they're still smiling at him.

"Down the hatch? Mud in your eye?"

"Who is this guy, Barbie?"

"A guest, some sort of paramedic, I suppose."

"Figures. Tourists! You aren't a urogenital man are you?"

"Well, not exactly, but . . ."

The guy raises his can. "Here's to vulvovaginitis," he says, "our meat and potatoes!"

"Vulvovaginitis!" they chorus, and knock back their beers.

Barbie's hanging on his arm again, rubbing herself against him, saying how ever since she was a little girl all she ever wanted to do was be an anesthesiologist. For as long as she can remember she's been intrigued by anesthesiology. As a medical student she used to dream about the day when she would be the one to bear the sweet freedom of relief from pain.

"That so?" says Harold.

"I make them be very quiet," she says, "where they can't be hurt anymore. Consciousness is such a burden, don't you think?" she asks, then excuses herself to go to the ladies' room.

"Bladder with the capacity of a lima bean," a guy whispers to Harold, watching Barbie walk away. "I've seen whole wards with the same condition. Sometimes we induce vomiting just to take the pressure off the faucet."

"That so? You've examined Barbie?"

"Everybody's examined Barbie," some guy snickers. "She's an anesthesiologist."

Harold is drinking his beer, trying to appear as affable as possible.

"You guys must like being doctors, huh?"

"A very challenging life," says one, "a very rewarding life, a very rich life."

"That's fine," says Harold. "That's just fine."

He moves deeper into the room. There's not as much traffic back here, so he can relax a little and try to figure out what's going on and how he can use it. At one point he thought he heard the sound of a heart-lung machine, or some other form of life-support system, *tick-plock, tick-plock, tick-plock*. He knows the guy he's looking for is hooked up to that kind of device so he headed over to take a look but it was only a ping-pong game in progress, and not very aggressive ping-pong at that, the point seeming to be to keep the ball in play as long as possible.

He sits down to rest and a cute little blonde with a name tag saying Sonja pinned to her left breast sits beside him.

"My friends call me Sunny."

He nods.

"I've been looking all over for you."

"That so?"

"You're my kind of guy."

"Oh yeah?" Harold says, feeling a little uncomfortable as she mentions right away that she's an anesthesiologist. He's wondering what it is about him that keeps attracting the same medical speciality. Nobody wants to think of himself as the kind of guy that turns on anesthesiologists.

"You look very gentle," she says. "I'm sure you'll be kind."

He's following her obediently even though his leg is throbbing again. There is almost no light and sometimes they stumble into pieces of heavy equipment. The floor seems to be slightly sloping downhill, and the ceiling and far wall are lost in darkness.

"You sure you know where you're going, Sunny?"

She's leading him by the hand now. They're blocked by what seems to be a huge bank of dials. Harold's fingers can feel their round glass faces and grooved plastic reset knobs. Occasionally, one is illuminated with a tiny electric gem, but neither the calibrations nor the units they're measured in means anything to him. He gets to the point where he's looking forward to the little chips of light simply as demonstrations of the fact that he hasn't gone blind.

"We're right under the main operating theater. We used to have problems with the ceiling leaking. You can still see the stains, but it's okay now."

"Oh."

"You aren't afraid of the dark, are you?"

"Well, not exactly afraid, no, but uncomfortable."

Once they get past the bank of dials, Harold realizes they're still in the same room, but that it's L-shaped, and this section of the L is immense. Huge high-intensity lamps hang extinguished from the ceiling, a few with jagged holes smashed in their parabolic mirror reflectors. The only light comes from the red and green glowing jewels of EXIT and NO SMOKING signs lined down the flanks of the far wall.

Sunny skips into the elbow of the vast room. A dusty cluster of empty beer bottles is suspended from one of the overhead lamps by lengths of surgical tubing and Harold laughs about how those urogenital boys really seem to get around, but Sunny doesn't understand the joke. The bottles clink softly against each other like wind chimes as she dances past them.

"I haven't been down here in years," she says. "When we were medical students, we used to come down here to get away from the grind."

She stops in front of a display cabinet labeled: THE DISEASES OF THE HAND. Inside are enlarged photographs of hands collapsed and frozen by paralysis, hands folded into impossible knots by outrageously advanced cases of arthritis, or covered with the pulpy crusts of leprosy. Below the diagrams of surgical techniques are jars of severed hands preserved in a thick silver liquid. Some of the hands have too many fingers, some are webbed. A small one in front glows faintly phosphorescent, suspended like the lingering pearl of a lost child, perfectly cupping death in its delicate bones.

"You wanted to go to Terminal Intensive, but this is as far as I've been."

Harold looks at her, and she gestures vaguely toward the shadows at the far end of the room.

He's on his way now, moving deeper into the bowels of the building. It isn't actually a problem of location anymore. The room has opened up so much wider that there doesn't seem to be any place other than where he is, and all he has to do to keep from walking in circles is to memorize one of the constellations of electric jewels glowing in the distance and then use that to realign himself whenever he becomes disoriented in the maze of abandoned machinery.

He wonders if there shouldn't have been some sort of sign, some form of demarcation that would have at least announced the existence of the Terminal Intensive ward if it didn't point out where it actually was. He keeps telling himself what he's doing here, but the explanations don't sound like much more than the words they're floated in, unhooked and meaninglessly detached into the clouds of dust that are continually descending.

Many sections of the room are lost in shadows and he pushes through these as long as he can stand the darkness, then stops to listen to the sound of his own panting, to strike a match and hold its bright shifting blades against the blank disregard of the silenced medical instruments heaped in sagging bins. He locates an occasional oasis of light where there still seems to be a residue of life, a thin scum coating the lens of a dead dial, or lichens plumed with their symbiotic lips pressed against the naked throat of an insulated cable. And those machines which haven't been vandalized appear to be merely asleep, humming to the steady glow of the blind ruby eye that must mean some circuits are still capable of functioning, some dreams are to be prolonged in the collapsing haze.

The immense corridor gradually resolves itself into a series of life-support facilities, the main ones ringed by steeply pitched loges for the use of medical students. From the top row of seats Harold can see out over large sections of the floor. Fogs are forming in the canyons between banks of machines and there are even pale white clouds unfolding slowly from under where the ceiling must be. Harold wonders if this means it's raining again outside, if that weather influences this in here, but suspects that the distances are too great, the climate control system too complex.

Far down the length of the room, he can make out a pattern of high-intensity overhead lamps, burning in their wire baskets and arranged like ranks of heatless suns. It's too far to see clearly, but that would seem to imply the presence of human activity.

He's gotten about halfway there when he sees somebody standing on the edge of the shadows waiting for him.

"Maybe you could use some help, young fellow?"

Harold stops just out of reach. It's a tiny old man so caved in with age the skin over his face has shrunken to no more than a layer of leather stretched tightly over the skull.

"You don't know me," he says, "but I'm a friend of Floyd's, a friend of the Indian's. He's down here somewhere too, looking for you, as a matter of fact."

"That so?"

"He seems to think you've done something to his sister."

"Tell that Indian his sister's living out in the Urban Renewal wasteland."

"You'll probably be able to tell him yourself."

Harold whips out his pistol. "Stick 'em up!"

"Don't be silly. I'm too old."

Harold frisks the guy but he's obviously not packing any iron. His body is so frail he probably couldn't support the weight of a pistol anyway.

"Okay, now what's going on? Where's that Indian?"

"You don't understand at all. I'm just an innocent bystander, interested in what happens to you young fellows."

Harold looks at him for a minute. "You stay out of my way if you don't want to get hurt."

"No problem. I'm just watching."

Harold moves to within about a hundred feet of the Terminal Intensive theater. The grandstands beyond the banks of instruments are dark and seem to be empty although he almost thinks he can see tiny chips of orange light, like the glowing tips of cigarettes. Except you aren't supposed to smoke down here, he wonders, but if there are people waiting in the darkened loges, would they necessarily obey the rules?

He hides behind a set of thick plastic tubes that are pulsing slightly, almost as if they're alive. He can see a couple of white-robed technicians working on the bank of instruments beyond the central altar, taking readings and adjusting dials. They don't appear to be much interested in what they're doing and at one point one of them seems to make a mistake and they both laugh. Harold leans against the nearest tube and it's warm—body temperature. He pinches its skin and can feel it twitch, as if it was startled by the bruise he gave it.

About a half dozen men are working in this section. Their machines and computers are arranged in a horseshoe pattern with the open end being dominated by the black plastic terminal platform with its high altarlike table. The top of the table is about ten feet from the floor, linked to the surrounding machines by a variety of pipes and wires all radiating into the white bundle perched in the middle of the altar, sitting up frozen in a fetal position.

"It was easy to find him, wasn't it?"

Harold ducks down, hisses at the old man to be quiet.

"They don't care. They'll be glad to get rid of him."

"What the hell's going on?"

"Look at the way they work. They don't have any feeling for their jobs. It's nothing but a series of interlocking processes they've been trained to perform. Watch this," the old man says, and awkwardly tosses a chunk of broken machinery in the general direction of the technicians. Nobody bothers to look around, even though Harold is sure they must've heard it. He watches while three of them try to connect two electronic devices with a cable. They insert the plug into a socket without grounding it first and blow out a bank of dials in a quick whoosh of electricity. A little plume of blue smoke rises from the dead instruments. Two of them collapse in laughter, but the third gets mad and cracks the nearest one over the head with his clipboard. They get out a tool box and start disassembling the front panel of the console, still chuckling about the explosion.

"They're selected for this kind of job," the old man says. "They're able to deal with an unending series of errors without succumbing to despair. The secret is in the imagination."

"Huh?"

"They don't have any. Every disaster comes as a complete surprise."

"That so?"

"It's the secret of the success of science," he says, one rubbery eyelid slipping out of control and sinking lizard-like over its eye. "Men like to be dependent on their fistful of tools. The grace of calmer creatures such as the pig is beyond us, no doubt because we designed their slaughter-houses in our own image, recognizing how nicely they would work. We do what we're told, but at bottom, either end of the butchery is acceptable."

"So what?" says Harold, and climbs the small ladder that leads up the back side of the altar, hoping none of the technicians will accidentally look around. He drags his leg up onto the top, fits himself between a couple of pipes, and sits down facing his enemy.

The body is completely wrapped in shiny white plastic bandages. There's a kind of gray sweat oozing continually from cracks between the bandages keeping the altar as musty as the inside of a turtle.

"Well, well, well," says Harold, "so you're the man that ordered the contract on Big Jim. Long time, no see."

He pries apart a couple of the bandages over the face, exposing a grainy beach of dead skin the color of dirty bath water. It doesn't look much like what he remembers lying in the alley, but it has been years. He uncovers the eyes. They're open but focused on infinity. They blink closed once every minute to keep the surface of the cornea moistened. Harold opens the awl blade on his penknife and pokes it into the eye, pressing until the point of the blade scrapes against the back of the eye socket. Nothing happens. The eyes continue to moisten themselves. He slides the blade out and the eye collapses, the fluid seeping down into the bandages over the cheeks.

"You were old then, you must be about a hundred by now. How many years have you been up here like this? Since that day in the alley?"

He cuts away the bandages over the knees. The skin has grown together where they're crossed, they've been immobile for so long.

"I guess they just don't change these bandages for you, do they? These are just to help you retain some liquids, I suppose, keep your skin from fissuring."

He peels back some more bandages to see if the arms have grown together too. He can't figure out what keeps the body upright until he notices that one of the pipes leading directly into the skull is steel rather than plastic and functions as a spine. Harold feels for the body's original backbone, but it's gone, nothing left but soft rubbery nuggets suspended in jello.

Harold pulls out his Colt, cracks open the cylinder, and

slips a bullet into the chamber he usually keeps empty.

"You realize of course that I'm going to blow your head off."

He taps the barrel of his pistol against the guy's nose but it's metal touching metal. He reaches out with his other hand. The nose is a dummy, some kind of compact pump system with a tiny electric motor and a series of flow-by valves. Harold fits the can-opener blade of his pocketknife in one nostril and pries. The nose comes off with a tearing sound and the little motor snarls in his hand for a moment then goes silent. Immediately a warning buzzer sounds in one of the consoles below him. He ducks down behind the edge of the altar and peers over. Nobody's looking up toward the body, but a couple of guys are standing with their hands on their hips watching one of the instrument panels. They try various things without any success until one of them haphazardly gets another section of the console functioning. Harold pulls back and notices that the body is shaking a little, quivering with the impact of some alterations in its systems. Then the chest shudders as if shocked, and one of the gray plastic pipes attached into it begins to breathe, collapsing and expanding with the pressure variations, and the body is calm again.

Harold looks into the face. "Almost killed you, huh? Simple thing like a nose. You're real fragile."

A dark brown fluid is seeping out of the raw hole where the nose was, leaking in two rivulets down the front of the face. Harold slams the blade of his knife deep into the nose hole and twists, trying to gouge out any flesh or nerves that are left, but the body doesn't respond and all he tears out are layers of fine metallic mesh sandwiched between sheets of soft plastic.

"You aren't helping me, you know?"

He rips the bandages down from the rest of the face, cutting them off until the whole head is exposed. He pinches one lip and tugs it away from the teeth. It seems to be real, although the guy's actual skin isn't quite as healthy as the layers of plastic and rubber blended into it. The teeth are clenched shut, the jaws fastened by a stainless steel plate that fills the mouth, connecting the palate and chin with small screws that the skin has grown over. The back-up respiratory pipe is fastened directly into the throat. Harold notices how the gray skin has grown out from between the bandages to cover the jointure for an inch or so onto the pipe. He puts one hand on the pipe and feels it breathing, the warmth of it making him a little sick.

He cocks back the hammer on his .44 and points it right into the middle of the face.

"This is for what you did to Big Jim!" he says self-consciously, and pulls the trigger, splattering bits of brain and plastic and that oily brown fluid all over the nearest console. Two or three alarms go off simultaneously and some guy yells, "Ninety-seven percent brain collapse!" then checks a couple more dials. Another technician saunters over to where the first one is and they stand together fumbling with some of the knobs. They confer for a minute, then shrug and start closing down the console, passing its functions on to another set of instruments.

Harold turns back to the body. There are some stains splattered down the front, but it's still sitting upright and still seems to be breathing about as well as it was before.

"This isn't exactly what I had in mind."

The shock of his shot broke the top of the brace bolting the mouth closed, and now the lower jaw's moving as if it were trying to say something, the steel mouth plate scraping against the teeth. Laughing Harold sits and stares at it. A lot of the forehead is entirely gone, but it doesn't seem any deader than it did when he first got up there. He considers shooting it a couple more times, but all that would do would be to simplify the support systems. He could keep cracking away at it until there was nothing left but a few flakes of skin floating in a saline bottle with an electric current passing through it, but why bother? He's cleared; what's left is not his problem.

Then Harold sees the sweaty red globe of the Indian's face rising like an angry moon above the lighted banks of dials.

"Don't do it!" Harold shouts. The nearest technicians jump around and look up at him surprised. The Indian is crouched on top of the console, ready to spring across the open gorge between them. One of his arms hangs down stiff and useless from where Harold shot him.

"Excuse me, sir," says one of the technicians, "but you aren't supposed to be here."

"It's a mistake!" Harold yells, pointing his gun at Floyd. "It's all over! Your sister's okay."

Floyd pulls out his tomahawk and swings forward, gathering the momentum to leap.

"Sir?" says the technician.

The Indian lets out a yell and Harold shoots the console beneath him. There's a terrific explosion, the whole top of the machine bank blowing out in the red and yellow flames of a gigantic flower. The concussion almost knocks Harold off the altar. His legs and feet are lacerated by bits of flying metal, but he's partially protected by the body of his enemy, which took the main impact of the explosion. He looks over the edge and is choked by the acrid smoke billowing from the bottom of the console he shot. Two of the technicians are lying motionless on the floor, but the Indian's gone, nowhere in sight.

"Hey," he yells, his voice a croak. "You, Cloudfinger, it's a mistake! Don't do it!"

He can't find the Indian anywhere. Alarm bells are sounding and technicians are at their stations trying to contain the damage. Harold senses movement in the darkened bleachers beyond the far bank of consoles but he can't see anybody. Sooner or later, all this smoke and noise is bound to attract a lot of attention. He turns back to check the other side of the altar, and stops. The body of his enemy is shredded, hanging in burning tatters of skin and smoldering plastic from the steel crucifix of its artificial spine. The whole front of the body has broken open into layers of black rags, each edged by the stinking little yellow teeth of flames.

Harold starts to slide off the altar away from it when the console directly behind him explodes and the hot shrapnel blows him to the floor. Both legs buckle under him and seem to be broken. He can't stand but pulls himself upright with the narrow ladder.

A technician in a white coat rushes up with a fire extinguisher and starts spraying the burning console.

"You're not supposed to be in this section," he shouts, but Harold ignores him, still looking for the Indian. A gray wave washes through him and he holds himself still, fights it down, struggling to retain consciousness. He pulls himself around to the other side of the altar and sees a man working on one of the consoles. He must have been wounded by shrapnel because the back of his coat is soaked with blood. Harold watches as he carefully adjusts a couple of knobs, still stupidly trying to get two needles lined up on a big dial.

A siren sounds and a bundle of burning wires blows rolling out from the other side of the altar. Harold feels the soft gray wash rising through him again and leans back to support himself but he misjudges the distance and falls to one side. He cocks the hammer of his Colt and points it in the general direction of the wounded technician and his console. Just as he starts to fade, he pulls the trigger. The machine goes off in a shower of sparks, catches itself for a minute, then explodes deep inside and begins to emit a stinking white smoke. The technician sinks back slowly. He covers his face with his hands and curls down under his console. Then the machine next to him explodes too, shooting a geyser of sparks so high toward the ceiling that Harold can almost make out the vault with its crisscrossing girders.

"Cloudfinger . . . ?"

Harold thinks he saw the Indian burning, but he can't be sure. The whole place is blazing now, devices exploding one after the other. He thinks he saw him still standing, flaming like a torch, the tomahawk burned out of his raised fist and his dead face howling with the winds of the fire storm as it burns down the row of consoles.

Harold drags himself toward the ring of darkened loges, still unable to see if there are any people there. The gray water is washing through him steadily as he pushes himself toward the darkness, trying to fight it long enough to find out if there's an audience.

Then he's on his back seeing the turbulent clouds of white smoke rolling against the ceiling, forming themselves into the immense bodies of naked women, holding against

the distant ceiling like destroyed angels, faceless and ob-
scure. Harold strains to shape the clouds into Beatrice, but
it's too late, the water has him, he slides into it, floating
away into effortlessness.

Derby Hat raises his hand and says stop, so they stop.
The children don't come any closer either.

"You want something?" he says in a loud voice, and
whispers to Henry to fan out slowly to the left in case they
attack. One of the loonies behind him starts blubbering and
he tells Tom to see what's the matter, but Beatrice says
she'll do it.

"We're just passing through," he shouts at the children.
"We don't want any trouble with you."

The one in front has some sort of bundle wrapped up
in an old rag. He places it carefully on the broken base of
an overturned toilet bowl, then the group of them silently
moves back around to the other side of the midden.

"You still see them, Henry?"

"They seem to be going."

"Who are they?" says Beatrice.

"Children," Derby Hat says. "Awful children. They've
been out here for a few years, but nobody knows anything
about them. They won't talk."

"What happened to them?"

"I don't know. There are groups of them out here, but
they don't seem to do much."

"They're going," says Henry.

Derby Hat unwraps the bundle. It's a pistol, an old
Colt .44.

"It's been burned," Henry says.

"What's the writing on the barrel?"

"Names, women's names. Lots of them."

"On the other side there's only one."

Derby Hat puts the pistol back on the broken toilet and looks at Beatrice.

"You said you thought you might be pregnant. I don't suppose you'd want anything like this?"

"Why should I?"

"Well, I don't know." He smiles and hitches up his trousers. "I thought it might have some sentimental associations for you."

"I don't know what you're talking about."

"Yeah," says Derby Hat, "that happens."